"Well, goodbye," BJ said and automatically stuck her hand out to shake. When he took it, she felt silly.

Shaking a man's hand at the end of a date signaled that there would be nothing more that night. But this had not been a date.

When Joshua took her hand into both of his, she knew that he'd guessed her intention. It made her feel gauche.

"Would you like to come in?" she asked, and then wished she hadn't. He didn't answer and seemed undecided—but then staring directly into her eyes, she felt somehow as if he was reading her mind.

"I'll walk you to the door."

At the door, BJ fumbled with her keys, managing to drop them on the ground at their feet. Why did the man make her so nervous, she wondered.

"I'll get it." Instead of giving them back to her, he unlocked the door and stood back for her to go in. Unexpectedly she wanted him to come in more than she would have believed.

"Thanks for having lunch with me," he said.

"Thanks for asking me." She doubted they'd ever see each other again. Why should they? As for the shirt, he could simply mail the ticket.

"Have you ever seen the Afrikan Poetry Society?" Joshua asked as if on impulse.

"No," she said, praying the grin that spread across her face wasn't as eager as it felt. He smiled back at her and raised his eyebrows.

"If I can get tickets, would you like to try it some evening?"

"Sure."

They laughed, and BJ suddenly felt on top of the world.

TIMELESS LOVE

Look for these historical romances in the Arabesque line:

BLACK PEARL by Francine Craft (0236-0, $4.99)

CLARA'S PROMISE by Shirley Hailstock (0147-X, $4.99)

MIDNIGHT MOON by Mildred Riley (0200-X; $4.99)

SUNSHINE AND SHADOWS by Roberta Gayle (0136-4, $4.99)

SOMETHING SO RIGHT

Layle Giusto

Pinnacle Books
Kensington Publishing Corp.
http://www.pinnaclebooks.com

PINNACLE BOOKS are published by

Kensington Publishing Corp.
850 Third Avenue
New York, NY 10022

Pinnacle, the P logo, and Arabesque are Reg. U.S. Pat. & TM Off.

First Printing: March, 1997
10 9 8 7 6 5 4 3 2 1

Printed in the United States of America

Chapter One

"What's wrong with being single? I love it," Barbara Jean Jones, BJ to intimates, insisted to her best friend, Darlene.

"Shhh," Darlene hissed. "I simply said this year you should make a resolution to find a husband."

"I'm not going to tell you my New Year's resolutions, no matter how much you wheedle," BJ said.

"It isn't as if you're blowing out your birthday candles. And if it were, the cake would fall down with your thirty-five candles," Darlene insisted. "All I'm asking is a promise that you'll really look for a husband this year. Is that asking too much?"

"Then of course, you'd want me to spend all my time and energy chasing men," BJ hissed.

"Not chasing, never chasing. Maybe snaring. With a body like yours, you don't need to chase," Darlene said.

BJ's interest in Darlene's conversation waned. Lately the topic of her finding a husband was the only thing BJ's family and friends ever wanted to discuss. And truthfully

she was sick of hearing it. She had her own ideas, and it **was**n't something she was ready to discuss with the entire **world**. She glanced around the room.

It was an office party, given by BJ's godmother's, Lucy McPhearson's, office. Most of the people there worked for the New York City government and a few minor politicians. Lucy's position as chairwoman of the Community Board, plus the spiked punch, assured there would be a good attendance.

"What you need to do is get rid of these dumb tank dresses," Darlene continued, pulling BJ's loose jumper and white blouse from the back.

"Tent dress," BJ corrected, smoothing the dress away from Darlene's fingers as she continued watching the people around her.

"Whatever." Darlene waved a negligent hand. "But they're not in style anyway. You need to keep up with what's happening. When's the last time you even read the newspaper?"

That caught BJ's wandering attention, and she squirmed at Darlene's too accurate assessment. BJ tried to ignore her friend's jibe and hoped Darlene didn't know how close to the truth her remark had been.

"There's nothing but bad news in the papers," BJ answered.

"How would you know? All you do is work and read those novels."

That was true also. BJ actually had a novel tucked into her purse at *that* moment and was dying to get home and read it. BJ had sort of gotten out of touch because she was tired of all the negative things that were happening. Sometimes she yearned to move back to Columbia, Maryland, where she had grown up. There life was softer and slower.

"Speaking of reading materials reminds me," Darlene said as she started rummaging in her purse. "I have . . ."

"What?" BJ asked.

"Something for you." Darlene shoved a gaily wrapped package at BJ. "Your Christmas present."

"I hope you remembered not to open yours until Christmas?" BJ held Darlene's package to her ear and shook it.

"It doesn't rattle," Darlene said. "Look at it later. I didn't say that dress didn't look good on you, because it does," Darlene went on, not seemingly hampered by BJ's failure to respond.

"What?" BJ queried. Darlene's quick switch of subject confused her.

"The tank dress, BJ. Are you listening to me?" Darlene sighed and shook her head. "Everything looks good on your five-foot-ten figure. It's such a waste to hide that glorious body. Here you are with skin like burnished ebony, a body to kill for—and those glorious boobs. A D cup!" Darlene stared enviously at BJ's bosom.

"C cup," Barbara Jean corrected and uncomfortably crossed both arms over her breasts.

"C-D, who cares?" Darlene waved her hand impatiently. "I'd give my eyeteeth to have them."

"No, you wouldn't," BJ said. "They're not in style anymore. Besides, you'd learn to hate it when every man you meet talks to your chest. When you're my height, half the men in the world are on eye level with your breasts."

"Hmm, sounds like fun to me," Darlene murmured. Then something over BJ's shoulder caught Darlene's eye. "Would you take a look at that hunk!" BJ turned to see who she was talking about, but Darlene grabbed her. "Don't turn around. He's looking over here." Darlene gave the man a "come hither" smile.

Darlene was right, BJ thought, when she caught a glimpse of the man standing some distance behind her. He *was* a hunk. Although her glance had been brief, BJ thought he was the most incredibly handsome man she'd ever laid eyes on. Later, when she was able to look further, she saw that he was tall—at least six-three. Height, however, was only the beginning of what made this man beautiful. Aside from his height, he had rich caramel-colored skin and a body that made her heart accelerate.

He was also better dressed than any other man in the room. The outfit was supposed to look very laid back. It did. It also looked terribly expensive. He looked as if he just stepped off a magazine cover. He wore a fine Italian-cut wool suit that fit him to perfection with a muted gold silk shirt.

He was looking across the room at her and smiled when her gaze reached his eyes. Suddenly she could barely breathe and felt light-headed. She smiled back, totally forgetting the gorgeous blond woman that was hanging on to his arm. Of course he was taken, just as you'd expect. She turned away.

He'd probably make beautiful babies. Oops, where did that thought come from? Her face grew warm, and she glanced around guiltily, almost feeling as if someone eavesdropped on her thoughts.

Joshua Hendricks stood with a glass in his hand, thinking he was bored out of his skull. He wished he was home despite the fact his apartment was empty—that is, no furniture and no special person. At least his dog, Hannibal, was there. And there was no denying, Hannibal beat most of this crowd as company. He was getting tired of this part of his business, this need to socialize with politicians.

Linda Collins, his administrative assistant, was at the party with him. She held on to his arm, and he was tempted to move away. Linda had recently taken to touching him or talking to him as if they were better acquainted than they were. Although their friendship went back many years, they'd never been particularly close. She was a good-looking woman but somehow not for him. He wondered what he was doing here with her, too. He never became involved with employees, and Linda, despite their history, was still an employee.

Instead he'd been watching two women across the room. One was a dreamy-looking, tall, gorgeous milk-chocolate beauty, while the other was short and tan. It was the tall, dark one who'd caught his eye. She was like a goddess who had gotten lost among lesser people.

He found himself cataloging her assets. Her body language telegraphed that she wasn't totally comfortable. Underneath a loose nondescript outfit, he saw snatches of a temptingly beautiful body. She was high breasted and had long slim curvy legs. It was a body that she should have been proud of. Instead she had crossed her arms over her breasts defensively several times. It made him curious.

At first he thought he knew her. There was something vaguely familiar. He looked even closer.

With all the small-time political hopefuls who should have been concerned for their public images, the party was still progressively turning into a drunken bash. Watching the tall beauty gave him something to focus on.

Suddenly she turned, and as their gazes locked, he'd felt as if he were on the brink of some discovery. There was something marvelously sensual about her, which seemed strange, considering he'd thought her repressed. Whoa, he'd wanted to say out loud. *She was a mighty fine sister.*

She actually smiled, but it was brief. Although tentative, her smile was potent. It gave him ideas, and his body responded immediately—but that didn't surprise him, not even a little. However, there was more. He found himself yearning for something, remembering something. What? Home? A place of roots? What a joke. That strange thought brought him up short, and he raised his drink to take a sip. What had brought that on, he wondered.

It wasn't that she was flirting, that wouldn't have surprised him much. He was used to women coming on to him. But rather it was as if she had telegraphed some irresistible message. Unfortunately the visual connection was short-lived, and her friend caught her attention again. Joshua found himself feeling strangely disappointed.

"Now, now"—Darlene poked BJ in the rib with a rounded elbow—"it's not cool to moon over a man from across the room."

BJ's attention momentarily swerved to Darlene. "I wasn't mooning," she said, coming to herself with a start. "I simply wondered if I knew him from somewhere."

"Hah! Tell that to the marines."

"Does Carlos, your husband," BJ emphasized that, "know you're still checking out the men in city government?"

"Neither marriage nor motherhood has made me blind," Darlene answered. "Anyway, I wasn't thinking of him as someone for me, I was thinking he'd be perfect for you. Look"—Darlene grabbed BJ's arm—"your godmother's talking to him. Let's ask her to introduce us." Darlene tugged BJ's arm, trying to pull the taller woman toward the group.

"No." BJ pulled back.

"What's wrong with getting an introduction through Lucy? That's not chasing."

"Forget it." BJ started to walk the other away.

Darlene had to move her short legs quickly to keep up with BJ's long-legged stride.

"Your biological clock is ticking the same as mine was. You need a husband so you can have babies."

"I'm so sick of hearing that. Can't you talk about anything else?" BJ said.

"Like what?" Darlene asked as she daintily lifted, with some subterfuge, an hors d'oeuvre from the buffet table they were passing. BJ glanced at her watch, wishing she could leave. She hated to admit that lately she *was* feeling that her biological clock was running out. It wasn't that she was ancient. She still had plenty of time to have children. Women could reproduce up into their forties and even later. But no one could deny that some things were best done when you were young. "You know what my doctor called me?" Darlene cut into BJ's thoughts. "An elderly primigravida."

"You *are* an elderly prima donna," BJ answered absently.

Darlene's usual chatter simply wasn't holding her attention. For one thing, she had another conversation going on in her own head, not to mention that she was trying surreptitiously to look at the handsome man who was still talking to Lucy.

"Not prima donna—primigravida. It means the first pregnancy," Darlene's voice droned somewhere in the background. "Honey, it near killed my poor over-the-hill body. Speaking of husband material, look over there. It's Norman. I used to work with him."

Despite herself, BJ looked and then swung around, peeved that she'd given in to the desire. "Don't point!" BJ pulled Darlene's arm down. "And how do you know he's single?"

"I always know these things. It's a habit," Darlene explained easily. "You should be glad that I still have all the old instincts, especially when I can use them to find a husband for you now."

"Darlene, for the one millionth time, I am not looking for a husband," BJ reiterated. But I wouldn't mind if one came along, she amended.

"What's wrong with him?"

"I don't know, he's too self-absorbed," BJ said.

"How can you tell from just one look?" Darlene sounded peeved.

"It's a given with most of those guys."

"You can't afford to be picky. As long as he's a man and

successful." When BJ moved again, Darlene worked hard
to keep up with BJ's quick escape.

"I don't feel that way. If I never find a man, I'll be all
right," BJ said. "Besides, if you remember, I've already
dated Norman once before."

"Maybe you could start with twins," Darlene said, obviously not listening.

"Twins! Would you stop? If I want a baby, I'll just have
one. I don't have to have a husband."

"Yes, you do. You're too traditional to do it any other
way."

"Anyway, I've already decided how to handle it. . . ." BJ
hesitated before moving on.

"How's that?" Darlene demanded suspiciously.

"When I'm ready, I'll go home to Columbia. The men
there aren't like these."

"And you'd be bored to tears," Lucy McPherson, a tiny
fifty-nine-year-old woman said over the two women's shoulders.

Both BJ and Darlene were startled by the sudden intru-
sion. Both BJ and Darlene were slightly intimidated by the
tiny, energetic older woman. BJ always marveled that Lucy's
small size often mislead people to believe that she was a
sweet pushover. While she may have been sweet, she was
also tough. Lucy had a tendency to attack first, a practice
which kept people off balance.

"Darlene," Lucy said, "looks to me like half that weight
you gained during your pregnancy wasn't baby. How much
did you gain?"

"Oh, I like to think positive about these things. What's
a few extra pounds?" Darlene answered airily.

"Humph, looks like you kept about twenty *positive*
pounds to me." Lucy turned and grabbed BJ's arm, pulling
her along. "BJ, you're slouching again." BJ immediately
pushed her shoulders back. "I'll never understand why a

big girl like you is always trying to fit herself into a small package. Be proud of your height."

Usually BJ was proud of her size, except whenever Lucy was around. Lucy, who looked younger than her years, always made BJ feel big and gawky. Her godmother was a small bird of a woman who rushed energetically everywhere she went.

"I have someone I want you to meet," Lucy said. The older woman shot a quick, calculating glance at Darlene and said, "You can come, too, Darlene."

"Oh, thank you, Chairwoman McPhearson," Darlene said, sounding flattered by the invitation.

Lucy didn't respond to Darlene but turned to BJ and said, "Still no special man? I hope you're not still pining over that Basil?"

BJ groaned, saying, "I have no interest in any man at this moment, and I barely ever think of Basil until you bring him up."

"Don't get persnickety," Lucy said.

"I am not persnickety. When the time is right—" BJ started.

"Ms. McPhearson," Darlene cut in, "I've been telling her the same thing. This should be the year she finds a husband." With this, Darlene was in her element and began to really pontificate. "Every step we take in life starts with a commitment to an idea."

Lucy stopped short, turning to stare at Darlene. BJ, caught unprepared, almost tripped over Lucy's little feet.

As BJ sought to right herself, Lucy stood with arms crossed over her breasts and looking exasperated.

"Really, BJ, you must do something about your tendency to fall on your face." Lucy tapped one foot in exasperation.

"That never happens to me until you're around," BJ said, annoyed. However, Lucy had already turned to talk with Darlene.

"You know something, Darlene"—Lucy looked at the

plump woman with her head tilted and a calculating expression on her face—"for once you've got a point. Let's do lunch some afternoon."

Darlene's face beamed with pleasure. Lucy's habit of keeping people on the defensive served her well. On the moments that the older woman was kind, people usually felt as if they'd won a great honor.

"I'd just love that, Ms. McPhearson," Darlene said, sounding effervescent and falling right into Lucy's trap.

"Don't you two gang up on me," BJ spluttered. "And don't start on your blind dates, either. I have no intention of ever going out with any man that either of you chooses."

BJ was so busy talking that she didn't see where Lucy was leading. Suddenly Lucy leaned sideways and gave BJ a hearty slap on the back. BJ barely kept from shrieking.

"Straighten up. Push out your chest," Lucy hissed.

Used to obeying Lucy from habits learned as a child, BJ straightened to her full height and was suddenly looking into the most incredibly sexy eyes of the gorgeous man that she'd been staring at earlier.

Standing this close, she could see that his eyes were a bright honey brown that seemed to call across time to her. He smiled down at her.

"Hello," he said, just before his eyes drifted down to rest briefly upon her breasts. His gaze reminded her that she was standing there with her breasts poked out at Lucy's insistence.

BJ would have gladly fallen through the floor. She wanted to stomp her foot. There she stood, ramrod straight, with her boobs pointing straight at the same man she'd been ogling across the room. Why, she wondered, did she let Lucy manipulate her? She slouched slightly, trying to stand more naturally without being obvious.

BJ could barely draw a breath. Her heart tripped in like a jackhammer. Then she became aware there was a blond woman hanging on to the man's arm. The woman scrutinized BJ and appeared quite piqued. Ah, well, BJ thought, wouldn't you know it. Seems all the great-looking men already have someone.

Lucy, still holding on to BJ with an iron grip, stepped in such a way as to edge the blonde out of the picture.

"Barbara Jean, this is Joshua Hendricks and Linda Collins, his administrative assistant." Linda's name seemed almost an afterthought. "Josh is one of New York's finest builders, and Joshua, Barbara Jean is just the woman you need to speak with. She's a social worker at Three Ashley Place." Turning back to BJ, Lucy added, "Joshua and I were talking about that old ramshackle place and how that block brings down property values in the rest of the neighborhood."

"All it needs is a little sprucing up," BJ said, peeved with Lucy for denigrating the street.

"Hah, that old horror needs Saint Peter to pass it through the pearly gates. Not even the garden you planted really did much help."

Just as BJ would have further defended Ashley Place, Joshua Hendricks cut in, and all her attention became riveted upon him.

"Barbara Jean," he acknowledged, and her name suddenly sounded lyrical and wonderful.

As she reached to shake his hand, he enfolded hers within both of his. Lucy looked quickly from one to the other and grinned triumphantly.

BJ glanced back to where Darlene stood with Linda Collins. Ms. Collins looked even more annoyed now.

"Oh, Darlene," Lucy said, "why don't you show Linda around the office and explain some of the things we do here."

BJ's face burned in embarrassment. Now she prayed that if the floor did open up and swallow her, it would take Lucy, too. BJ only hoped that for Lucy's sake, she was more subtle in her political dealings.

It took a moment for Darlene to catch on before she jumped right in to assist Lucy's contrivances. "Oh, yes," Darlene said, latching on to Linda and launching into a spate of distracting chatter.

Linda Collins looked increasingly put out. BJ, feeling like a fool, swore she'd never attend another of Lucy's soirees.

BJ didn't hear much of what Darlene said as Lucy had a death grip upon hers and Joshua Hendricks's arms as she pulled them both away. One glance at Joshua's face and BJ knew he was only too aware of Lucy's intentions.

Then as fate would have it—the mayor of New York City walked in, causing quite a stir.

"Oh, shoot," Lucy said and looked from BJ to Joshua. "Wouldn't you know he'd come today when he never did before? I'll be right back. You two just wait right here and get to know each other."

BJ watched helplessly as Lucy proceeded to bustle away toward the mayor, leaving her standing with Joshua Hendricks.

"Well, Barbara Jean, it seems we're all alone. Why don't you tell me what you want?" he drawled.

Chapter Two

What the hell is wrong with this woman? Joshua thought. *Maybe I came off a bit too flirtatious, but surely she doesn't think I'm going to attack her in a room full of people?* Besides, he would have sworn she'd been flirting in her own rather repressed way. *Talk about double messages.*

At what he had considered a harmless remark, she had actually looked panicky for a second. Her hand had flown to her throat, and the eyes that she'd turned to meet his had been frightened.

"Are you all right?" he said, reaching out to touch her, and knew instantly that that was another mistake. She went stiff and jerked away, now looking as if she wanted to jump ten feet.

"Yes, I'm fine," she responded a bit tartly. But she took a deep breath and seemed to calm down. She put one slim lovely hand up to her forehead. "I have a slight headache, I guess."

"Is there something I can do?" he asked and realized he actually did want desperately to help.

"No, it will pass.'

She put her hand down, looked at him, and smiled. It wasn't a true smile but rather one that was supposed to cover all awkward social situations. Still he felt captivated and couldn't help grinning back. He also felt the oddest urge to protect her from whatever had caused her fright.

Joshua prided himself on reading people, and so after her curious response he decided to be more circumspect. He'd been referring to Lucy's McPhearson's transparent efforts but sensed that somehow his remark had gone awry. He took another gambit at conversation, suspecting that any minute she'd find a reason to be gone.

"Barbara Jean," he said, "nice name."

Her eyes flew to him again and he wanted to hug her.

"Thank you." She cleared her throat, then her eyes fell away as she added, "Please call me BJ."

"BJ it is," he answered.

She looked horribly embarrassed and seemed to be psyching herself up to say something. She took a deep breath and barely met his eyes before she spoke.

"I'm really sorry about Lucy. She's always trying to play matchmaker." Her voice came out in a breathless whisper. "But if we hurry, you can slip back to your friend, and Lucy will simply have to give up. She has too many other guests, and besides, now that our illustrious mayor has arrived, she won't have time for her little schemes."

She looked so serious that he had to chuckle. If Ms. Jones thought that chatting with her was a hardship, she was very wrong. After a quick startled glance, she shrugged and joined him with a little smile of her own. The tension between them lifted slightly.

"Does it bother you?" he asked. When she looked puzzled, he added, "The matchmaking schemes."

"No," BJ said and then seemed to think about it. "Sometimes it does."

"Matchmaking is as old as the human race. But if it bothers you, then you should put a stop to it."

"Hah, if you knew Lucy, you'd know how difficult that would be. Once Lucy has an idea, she pushes forward at full steam and is about as easily stopped as a locomotive. She usually manages to get her own way."

"I do know your aunt."

"Not my aunt, she's my godmother," BJ corrected.

"Aha! Like in 'Cinderella'?"

He watched her to see if she would recoil again at his levity.

BJ shrugged. "Not likely. How do you know Lucy?"

"She's the lady holding up a building permit that I need." Then changing the subject, he said, "So, BJ, tell me about yourself."

"There isn't much to tell," she said after a pause.

"Sure there is," he coaxed. But he realized that by not talking about her work, she understood what he wanted. "Start at the beginning. Where were you born? And don't I detect the hint of a southern accent?"

Exactly what his motives were for trying to hold her there eluded him. There was something vulnerable about her that called to him. She reminded him of someone or something, but he couldn't quite remember who.

Although his questions were simple, she took a little longer than he expected.

"I'm from Maryland, Columbia," she answered, and her voice sounded a little stronger. "Where are you from?"

Ah, he thought. She's decided to stay and try to be sociable. *Why do I care?*

"I'm a New York boy, nothing interesting there." He brushed that off with a quick return to questions about her. "What was Columbia like to a little girl who wanted to be called BJ?" She tilted her head with a puzzled smile. "Good guess?" He moved slightly closer. He stopped when she looked disconcerted. "Well?" he prompted, "weren't you the one who chose BJ as your name?"

"Yes," she admitted. "I wanted to stop my family from giving me other nicknames."

"Such as?"

"Oh, I can't remember what they were now," she said, and her laugh sounded forced.

She looked around as if searching for her friend, and he took her elbow, gently guiding her to the buffet table. She followed, though she didn't look quite comfortable. She glanced down at his hand on her arm.

"Sure you do," he said.

"What?" Her gaze shifted from his hand to his face.

"The nicknames. Don't tell me you're still bothered by them."

There was no doubt in his mind that this woman was uncomfortable with the small talk between men and women but determined not to show it. It was refreshing and even charming. It allowed him to become the pursuer, something which he missed lately.

"Baby-girl," she said, sounding a little reluctant. "They used to call me baby-girl until I insisted on the name BJ."

He laughed aloud, and she looked miffed, although he suspected she wanted to hide it.

"Were you the youngest girl?"

"I was the only child."

This time she laughed with him. It was the first time he sensed she was really loosening up. He handed her a cup of punch, which she took with a genuine smile this time.

"Thanks." She took a small sip of her drink.

The room was becoming more clogged with people who were increasingly more inebriated. One of their nearby neighbors bumped into her, and she knocked against him. He hated to admit it, but he enjoyed the feel of her. He touched her arm momentarily to steady her and was loath to release her.

"You're a big girl, aren't you?"

She looked disconcerted for a moment, then answered tartly, "Yes, I am. It was a big help when I played basketball in school."

"Yes, I bet you did," he remarked.

"You're pretty tall yourself. What did you play?" she challenged.

"Play?" He was taken by surprise.

"Sports," BJ explained.

"As little as I could," he said.

"You didn't play sports?" She looked surprised.

"A little," he admitted. "But I guess I was too busy for anything like that. I worked in construction during holidays."

"You started your company in college?"

"Not the company I have now. That came later. But I did a lot of scut work whenever I could during school."

"You were a construction worker?" She glanced quickly at his clothes, and he realized that now she was the one asking the questions.

"Yes. During the later years, before I graduated, I had a small rubbish removal company. I also had to keep my marks up for my scholarship."

He couldn't help himself, he was trying to impress her. He wanted her to admire him. Instinctively he knew it was a mistake.

"You went on a grant?"

"An academic scholarship," he corrected, hoping she didn't catch on that he was bragging a bit.

"I should have guessed," BJ said.

She sounded a bit sarcastic, and he was slightly miffed himself now. *What's wrong with an academic scholarship?*

"Do you still play basketball?" he asked to take them back to a safer topic.

"Rarely. There aren't many women's amateur teams."

"Too bad. You sound as if you miss it."

"I do other things now like aerobics and stuff like that. What about you?"

"Sometimes," he said, not particularly interested in talking about himself. He was in serious danger of showing off to her. "I get in a little racquetball, but that's not too often. Don't have the time."

"You should try." She sounded prim and not a little self-righteous. "It's a great way to relieve stress. It would help you loosen up, play a few hoops or something."

He certainly didn't like the way this conversation was shaping up. Did he need loosening up, he wondered. He'd been under the impression she was the uptight one.

"I don't have time for things like that." He regretted his answer as soon as it was out.

"Maybe you should find time. It would help you stay in shape."

Now that irked him. He was in damn good shape and wanted her to notice. His pride was definitely tweaked; he was sorely tempted to flex biceps. Besides, he knew he didn't look like a man who needed more exercise. She was getting back for his pressuring her.

"Maybe," he answered before moving on. "You don't sound too enthusiastic about our mayor."

"Huh, you should see what he tried to do to some of my clients' budgets," BJ answered. Then as if she had said too much, she hurried on. "Are you one of his party?"

That made him smile again. "No, you're safe."

In a more conciliatory voice she added, "He's all right, I guess. Anyway, it's politic for him to be here and Lucy is nothing if she's not politic."

"And you're not?"

"Not particularly," she answered.

"Your godmother is quite a woman."

"Darlene swears Lucy is the female equivalent of a Mafia godfather."

"Well, she's certainly a no-nonsense woman. We've been

seeing quite a bit of each other, what with her having so much influence over the permits and me being a builder.''

''Will this be your first project in New York?''

''My first in Queens. You know the Humphrey Building in Manhattan?'' and when she nodded, he continued, ''That's one of ours.''

''Ours?'' she queried.

''Hendricks Development Corporation.''

Finally all his bragging was having some effect. She looked impressed. He was pleased to note that the longer they talked, the more relaxed she appeared.

''Oh, I really admire your work. Didn't you also do the Clinghauser Building?''

He was surprised that she knew that. ''Yes,'' he answered with a smile. ''That was quite a while ago, though. It was a landmark that needed only refurbishing.''

''It's wonderful. Every time I see it, it reminds me of the early twentieth century. I love old architectural sites. Are you planning something like that for Ashley Place?''

He hesitated, before shrugging slightly and saying ruefully, ''Perhaps.'' Then because he didn't really want her to think he only refurbished, he said, ''We also did the Hudson River site.''

''Oh, yes, that's where you tore down all those buildings.''

''They were abandoned and an eyesore,'' he reminded her.

''Yes, I guess so, but I prefer it when you can reclaim rather than tear things down.''

''Each site has to go on its own merits. But I thought you were going to tell me about yourself.''

For a minute, Joshua thought she was going to balk.

''I'm a social worker for the VanderWeil Foundation,'' she said.

''I've heard about them. Don't they give those big charity balls?''

"I don't see much of that end of the Foundation. Have you attended them?"

"Yes, they're a great tax write-off."

"I guess so."

"But that's not your forte?"

"No, I work with elderly clients who often live on small Social Security payments or pensions."

"Sounds like a much needed service."

"I'm so glad," she said in a rush, "that yours is the company offering to do the refurbishing. It's such a wonderful area." Joshua swallowed down the wrong pipe and began coughing. "Are you all right?" she asked, looking terribly concerned.

"Yes," he said, and now that she was showing some real interest in their conversation, he had to admit that he was tempted to milk her for a little sympathy. That usually worked very well with women. *Don't be a cad,* he admonished himself and restrained from the impulse.

He was a little uncomfortable because, although she was friendlier now, she was totally mistaken regarding what he planned to do for Ashley Place. He started to correct her, then decided to let it ride. That could easily put them right back to the beginning of their talk. He decided on another gambit.

"Thinking of Lucy arranging dates for you seems quite amusing," he said.

"Oh?" she said.

"Well, for one thing, it doesn't sound like the Chairwoman Lucy McPhearson that I've been dealing with. And for another, you don't look like a woman who needs that sort of help."

Unfortunately, he thought, glancing over BJ's shoulder and catching sight of Linda bearing down on them with Darlene in tow—all good things must end. Curiously enough, before these two women reached them, Lucy McPhearson was back.

"Oh," Lucy trilled. "I see you two are getting along famously." This seemed to make the older woman quite pleased for she clasped her hands to her bosom.

One glance at BJ and he realized how embarrassed the tall beauty was. BJ looked helplessly at him. By that time, Linda and Darlene had arrived as well.

"Yes, BJ was telling me about her work at Ashley Place."

"Oh, wonderful," Lucy responded. "Isn't that wonderful, Darlene?" Lucy gushed to the other woman.

Councilwoman McPhearson proceeded to actually pat BJ lovingly as if the beautiful tall woman was still a child. In order to do this, Lucy had to reach upward, which almost made Josh laugh out loud. BJ looked increasingly more trapped.

"How nice," Linda put in. "We'll have to meet one day at the site after we've gotten the permit, of course." Linda glanced meaningful at Lucy.

"That's a wonderful idea, Joshua," Lucy said to him, completely ignoring Linda and the fact that the suggestion had come from the blond woman and not him. "We'll have to make an appointment for you to meet BJ at the site. And BJ and I would simply love to have you up to dinner. Right BJ?"

"Well . . ." BJ looked flabbergasted at Lucy's brashness.

"Yes, BJ can cook," Lucy rushed on. "She's an excellent hostess, you know—"

"Lucy," BJ said, "It's quite possible that . . ." Joshua watched BJ try to stop the older woman.

Joshua had no idea what it was BJ intended to say for the other women turned suddenly to her, and somehow BJ's elbow was jostled, and before he realized what was happening, the lovely woman was stumbling toward him again. Instinctively he reached to catch her, and though he managed to stop BJ's fall, this time he wasn't so successful with her drink.

The contents of her glass splashed toward him and made

icy cold contact with the front of his shirt and then rolled down toward his pants. Somehow his pants never got a speck on them, but his shirt was a sodden discolored mess.

All of them stood stark still for a few moments before the women all began to cluck around him with various feminine handkerchiefs or crumpled up tissues. He hadn't a clue where most of them had come from and was quite surprised at how fast they'd been produced.

Joshua noticed that poor BJ looked as if she'd been turned to stone. He suddenly wanted to hug her again.

"Can't you be more careful," Lucy McPhearson admonished BJ.

"Yeah," Darlene agreed.

"For pete's sake!" Linda exclaimed.

With a sour glance at BJ, the blond woman elbowed the tall dark beauty aside and pushed everyone away to swipe at his shirt. Suddenly, Joshua realized, he was getting sick of Linda.

BJ looked guilty and rolled her eyes to the ceiling as if looking for divine help. The gesture made Josh feel as if he wanted to help her. At least he certainly hoped that was the reason for his jumping with both feet to her defense.

"Leave BJ alone! It was an accident, and there's no harm done." He took the handkerchief from Linda and motioned everyone away. His voice had come out both louder and sharper than he'd intended.

All four women turned to stare and he couldn't for the life of him remember when he'd felt like such a complete fool.

Joshua's rush to her aid had startled BJ. She stood staring at him for long moments before realizing that everyone else was gazing at him also.

She spoke to cover the sudden silence. "If you give me

your number, we can arrange to replace your shirt," she said.

She hoped she sounded more reasonable than she felt. The whole of the last twenty minutes or so had seemed to be a dream.

"Replace? Why don't we try to clean it first?" he suggested in a soft, kind voice.

"Anything you say," she blundered.

BJ was so rattled that she hadn't realized he was holding out his business card. When she took it, her nervous fingers fumbled, and she dropped it. As she watched it sail to the floor, she wanted to cry.

"Excuse me," she said.

Before she could pick it up, Joshua had hunched down and retrieved it himself. When he stood up and smiled down into her eyes, her pulse thumped.

"You'll be hearing from me," she said breathlessly.

"I look forward to it," he grinned, then added, "Why don't you give me your number, just in case?"

In her agitation, she scribbled something, which she hoped was legible and possibly was truly her address, on the back of the card he had handed her. She could barely meet his eyes, and when she did, Joshua's smile seemed to light up the room.

"So we'll be talking," he said.

"Yes," was all she could answer.

BJ watched Joshua Hendricks and Linda Collins leave. For a man who'd obviously spent a great deal of time and money on how he looked, she thought, he'd taken his ruined shirt well.

Linda Collins, however, wasn't as forgiving as Josh had been. Just before they both exited, the blonde turned and gave BJ another of her sour looks.

"BJ, how could you be so clumsy?" Lucy launched into her as soon as he was out of hearing.

"It was an accident. I'm sorry."

"Sorry?" traitorous Darlene squeaked. "That shirt cost a bundle. It will take months for you to pay for it on *your* salary."

"That ought to teach you to be more careful," Lucy said. Then the older woman tapped her lip with a finger. A speculative expression came over her. "Still, everything obviously isn't lost. Did you see the way he took BJ's side?" The older woman spoke this last to Darlene.

"Right," Darlene said, making the word long and drawn out. She tilted her head to the side. "Wonder what *that* was all about?"

Chapter Three

Neither Joshua nor Linda spoke as they went down in the elevator. Although he was vaguely aware of Linda fuming at his side, he wasn't particularly interested. Joshua was too busy trying to puzzle out what had prompted him to speak so hastily in BJ's defense.

The silence lasted until they were in his car and had pulled into the Queens traffic on the way to the Mid-Town Tunnel. It was Linda who spoke first.

"Can you believe what happened?" Linda said. He glanced over at her. "What a hayseed that Barbara James, or whatever her name, was."

"Barbara Jean, or BJ, is her name," he said. Linda gave him a strange look at his correction. He was curious about Linda's opinion. "Is that the way you saw her? As a hayseed?"

He was a bit puzzled. He hadn't seen that in the woman. Linda didn't appear to hear him.

"And Lucy McPhearson," his assistant rattled on, "is absolutely without a doubt trying to find her a husband."

Layle Giusto

Something about Linda's stiffened back made him feel she was gauging his reaction. But Joshua had to laugh at her remark about Lucy McPhearson. His laughter seemed to comfort Linda because she stopped fuming and laughed, too.

"You're right about our community chairperson," he said.

"Barbara James, or BJ," Linda acknowledged with a curious glance at him, "must be a country cousin or something. I guess with her being such a big clumsy klutz, you can't blame Lucy?"

Joshua thought a moment before answering. "Big—maybe—clumsy? Well, certainly at times, but not exactly a total klutz."

"That's not how I saw it. It's funny to hear you say that, too. Do you know that most people are intimidated by the great Joshua Hendricks, builder extraordinaire?"

He glanced at her briefly. Linda was a sharp woman, maybe a little more cynical than need be, but she didn't miss much.

"Where's this leading? he asked. "You got a point you want to make?"

"Just that it's not like you to be so kind to someone who just ruined a beautiful and very expensive shirt."

He looked down at his shirt ruefully. No matter what Linda said, he'd found the encounter charming—that is, until she spilled her drink on him.

"Maybe you're right," he answered. To himself he added, clumsy or not, BJ Jones certainly did have something.

"Sure, I'm right," Linda said smugly. "But I've got to say that I admire your style. It was smart of you to charm the social worker at Ashley Place. She may be useful."

Is that why I enjoyed BJ so much? Joshua wondered. *Was it because she could be useful?*

"And it can't hurt with Lucy McPhearson, either. Did

you see how ecstatic she was? Are you going to go for it?"
Linda asked, shifting to sit where she could face him better.
When he didn't answer, she added with a smirk, "I know
you. I've never seen a man more able to charm himself
into the money than you."

"What do you mean?" Joshua queried.

"The way you had Lucy McPhearson gushing over you
when you were nice to that hick was a stroke of pure genius.
Are you going to use it to get Lucy to act on those papers?"

"I hadn't thought of that."

"Hah, I know you think of everything. I have to give it
to you. You're still the best I ever met."

Then he remembered how he'd not corrected BJ's
impression that he was going to renovate Ashley Place.
Maybe he wasn't on Linda's wavelength, but he had his
own demons to wrestle.

He deliberately didn't answer, which was his usual
method. He was inclined to listen rather than talk, and it
always served him well. It always amused him that Linda
thought she was privy to his inner motives, but he rarely
bothered to correct her. Plus, if he was honest, he was still
more bewildered than he wanted to admit at the effect
Ms. Barbara Jean Jones had on him. Despite whatever
Linda said, BJ was a beautiful woman. Maybe it took a man
to know that, but that didn't explain why he'd jumped to
protect her.

However, Linda's assumption did make him wonder, as
he knew what he wanted to do with Ashley Place. BJ Jones
wasn't going to like his plans very much. But then she
was a big girl and looked quite able to handle a bit of
disappointment.

Who was going to defend her from him, he wondered.
Joshua fingered the card he'd put in his pocket with BJ's
name on it.

Linda didn't know he had allowed BJ to misunderstand
what his plans were with Ashley Place. The woman thought

he was going to renovate that rundown old shack of a
building, when he had every intention of tearing it down.

That girl—woman, he corrected—needed to be looked
after. *Maybe it was the punch that made me react as I did. It
must have been stronger than I thought.*

BJ banged into her apartment, slammed down her purse,
jerked off her coat and scarf, and flung them across the
couch. She sat down to stretch her legs and laid her head
back on the couch.

She decided to call her parents then and spent the next
half hour talking to them. It was her father who picked
up first, but the minute her mother realized who it was,
she was on the other extension. This was a common occurrence—for both parents to talk at the same time with her
on different extensions.

When she'd first come north, she'd been so lonely for
them that she'd bought a speakerphone. Then when she
called, it seemed almost as if they were in the same room.

What frequently happened when she talked with her
parents was they started to squabble with each other while
supposedly talking to her. BJ knew their tiff would continue
at long-distance rates while they argued over something
they could have easily discussed face-to-face.

She also knew their squabbles weren't serious. Their
marriage had been built on bedrock, and the small spats
meant nothing in the end.

After her parents hung up, BJ's thoughts returned to
the topic of Joshua Hendricks.

She could have gladly screamed.

What an incredibly horrible day. It had been bad enough
that she'd felt obligated to attend Lucy's little office party,
but she couldn't believe that she'd allowed herself to be
aggravated by both Lucy and Darlene as much as she had.
Both of them had managed to embarrass the hell out of

her with their attempt to throw her at Joshua Hendricks. Yet despite everything, she had to admit he'd been very good about it.

And would you believe in the end, she'd spilled her punch on him? The memory of his face as the liquid ran down his clothes came into her mind. There was a split second when he had seemed to be in shock. But then he'd recovered and came to her rescue when all the women had blamed her. She wasn't sure how she felt about that.

The really awful thing was that she was often awkward and bumbling when Lucy was around. There was something about bossy, short people—and were there any short people who weren't bossy?—that often made her feel as if she was doing pratfalls for the whole world to see. She hated that. When she was with other people, she never had any trouble, but would anyone ever believe that? Of course Josh Hendricks wasn't short, but he did make her nervous. For one thing, the man was so gorgeous that he shouldn't be allowed to walk around. He should be a statue or at the very least a Greek god or something like that.

How unfair could life be? Between his gorgeous face and unbelievable beautiful body that he admitted he rarely exercised—he had to be brilliant, too.

"I had to keep my marks up for my academic scholarship," she said, throwing her voice in an attempt to imitate Josh's baritone.

A real Mister Perfect. He's probably the scion of some upper-middle-class black family, born with a silver spoon in his mouth.

Wonder what he saw in me? She looked in the mirror. Well, I've got good skin, she thought. Thank heaven for that. Her glance traveled downward over the dress Darlene had complained about. There was no joking about it, the dress had been a mistake. It was one of those things she'd bought that she should have returned immediately.

With a sigh, she picked up her coat and scarf to hang in

the closet, then went into the kitchen. After fixing herself a snack, she sat in the living room and finally pulled out the novel that she had in her tote bag. Only now, she couldn't focus on it.

In the meantime, she saw the gift-wrapped package that Darlene had given her and looked at it again. BJ was pretty certain that she knew what it was—a book, and probably something about how to get your man. BJ put it under her small Christmas tree.

Poor Darlene. They'd been friends all through school, and now that the other woman had married and had a child, she was working very hard to get BJ in the same situation. Although BJ did very much want a baby, lately she was beginning to feel that what she didn't want was a husband.

She couldn't keep her thoughts from straying to Joshua Hendricks. She suspected he was probably the result of prep schools. The man was too perfect not to have been born to the manor. Besides, you could see that he was conceited and full of himself, thinking that he was all that.

Funny how he'd kept her talking about herself, she thought. And wouldn't you know it, she'd blabbed like a kid on a date with a movie star. Ah, well, she'd never win any awards for being scintillating. The world would have to accept her as she was. Still she did wish she had shut up and gotten him to talk about himself more.

Despite his obviously being a water walker, he'd been very nice, and she had to admit that she'd been gauche. At times she had even been rude. She put her head in her hands. It was just that he'd unnerved her.

BJ had to admit that he was a charmer. Instead of getting antsy and looking for the woman that he'd come with, he appeared totally relaxed, as if he didn't have a thing in the world that he wanted to do other than talk to her. He directed so much intensity to her that she had felt as if she was the most important person in the world.

She remembered when he'd touched her, only placing a hand under her elbow to lead her toward the punch table. The sudden physical contact had made her feel disoriented, and she had to work not to show how affected she was.

Joshua Hendricks probably had some pretty impressive chromosomes, and that was something that needed serious consideration. She turned her book facedown and stared off pensively into space.

Three weeks later, on a Sunday morning, halfway through a dreary, miserable January, Joshua Hendricks stood looking through the window of his high-rise condo. The view was of midtown Manhattan's west side. It overlooked Broadway and farther west, he could see parts of the icy Hudson River. The last few weeks had been busy tying up loose ends as he waited to start work on Ashley Place.

I need to get out, he thought.

He felt at odds—lonely. Loneliness wasn't a common feeling for him, but he wasn't unfamiliar with it, either. Then, too, the holidays always made him edgy, although the feelings rarely lasted this long.

He threw down the pencil and stood up from the desk where he'd been working. He stretched both arms high overhead before sticking his hands into his pants' pockets.

When he left the living room, his dog, Hannibal, stirred. The huge, shaggy Saint Bernard padded behind him; the nails on his large paws clicked on the marble floors. He followed Joshua into the kitchen.

Josh drew a cup of the dark strong liquid from the coffee maker. Hannibal nudged against his legs, and Joshua patted the dog absently. If he hadn't already walked the animal that morning, he would have gone out now.

Josh glanced around his home, slightly annoyed at the emptiness. It was a large apartment in a newly built high-

rise that towered over midtown Manhattan. It was almost
bare. The living room contained his desk, a huge monster
that served him well, and a futon, a piece of utilitarian
Japanese furniture that served as a couch. The only other
object in the room was a model of the apartment complex
that he intended to build once he had the go-ahead. It
consisted of a complex of two-story buildings with an inner
court.

His bedroom, though strictly utilitarian, was better fur-
nished. He had a huge platform bed with a batch of pillows.
A wrought iron butterfly chair sat in a corner.

He'd been there more than a year. It was way too long
to still be living in an unfurnished apartment. Actually all
he had to do was bring in a decorator, but something
made him wait.

He went to the wide window that covered one wall in
the living room and stared down at the Manhattan streets.
It had snowed during the week, and the streets had quickly
turned into gray-black slush. From this height, the yellow
taxies looked like scuttling beetles, and the people
appeared as even smaller, less significant bugs.

He looked upward at the heavy laden sky, wondering
why his thoughts were running to comparing people to
bugs. Maybe it was because his life seemed so empty lately.

He returned to his desk, picked up the pencil again,
and tried to concentrate on the plans there. Several minutes later, he knew it was no use. The dog nudged him
again, and Josh remembered he'd bought a pet toy for
the animal. He went to his jacket, rifling through his pockets for the toy. There he encountered a piece of paper.

He pulled it out and read the pink telephone message
note. Immediately he remembered the tall sleek woman
at one of the many Christmas parties that he'd attended.
BJ Jones, who had ended their conversation by pouring
punch on him. She'd called before, and he'd been too
busy to return the call. Of course the shirt had already

been taken to be cleaned, but he found himself reading the note again. He remembered how fresh and charmingly different she had been.

Joshua remembered something else, too. The image of her smiling at him. He never thought of himself as a conceited man, but he knew when a woman was interested. He hadn't missed her curious glances. And although she'd been distant and even tart later, there was something decidedly sexy about the glances she'd given him. It made him feel only a little smug.

She'd had a haunting sort of beauty. Something that she seemed to be trying to hide or at the very least was totally unaware of.

Without examining what he was doing, he picked up the telephone and dialed. After one fast glance at the building model, he swiveled so that he didn't have to look at it.

"Hello," she said. After they had reintroduced themselves, she went on, "I wasn't able to contact you before and wanted to find out if you'd had your shirt cleaned."

"Sorry I didn't get back to you," he said. "You were very prompt and conscientious, too."

"I try to be, but I'm not often successful." She sounded breathy, and he wondered what she'd been doing when he'd called. He had sudden visions of her doing something very physical, and it made his groin tighten.

"Not often conscientious?" he asked, although he understood what she meant.

Something made him want to tease a bit. Suddenly he put down the pencil that he'd been holding and got comfortable.

"Not very successful at being prompt, I mean."

"Yes," he said more seriously when she'd taken his statement at face value. "I understood."

"Oh." The conversation stopped exactly where it was. "I just wanted to remind you that I would reimburse you."

"We'll see," he said, deliberately stalling. Then on the spur of the moment asked, "How about we meet? I can give you the ticket, and you can tell me all about Ashley Place."

The thought occurred to him that he wasn't the least bit interested in talking about that beleaguered street but thought it sounded very plausible. He didn't think she was terribly interested in a cleaning ticket, either.

"Okay, ' she said after a slight pause. "When?"

"How about today?" He was still rushing along on impulse. This could be a very special day, he thought. Having lunch with a beautiful sister might cure what was wrong with him.

"Well, I don't know. I live on Long Island—Queens . . ." Her hesitation made him believe she was thrown by his request.

"I'll drive, it's no problem," he tried to reassure her.

"I guess it's all right," she agreed reluctantly. Finally he exhaled and realized he'd been holding his breath.

"How do I get there?" he asked, not wanting to give her a chance to change her mind.

"We could meet at Shu-Fly. It's a soul food diner on Linden Boulevard near here."

"Sounds good to me," he said.

"I'll see you there."

He was a little disappointed that he wasn't going to her place but knew that in today's world her request was a safe and prudent move. After she gave him directions, they settled on a time. "I'm looking forward to this," he said.

"Yes," she answered but sounded noncommittal.

After hanging up, it dawned on him that he'd just suckered himself into a long drive to Queens. What the heck, he'd asked for it. Fortunately it was a Sunday afternoon, so there wouldn't be as much traffic. That made him feel a little less like the chump he'd first thought himself to be.

Indeed, not only did he not feel as foolish as he should, he actually felt great as he rushed into the shower. The thought made him stop. Why was he feeling like a kid, just because a woman accepted a luncheon invitation? The truth was that in New York, men were in demand. Women rarely turned him down, and he'd have had to be deaf, dumb, and blind not to have noticed that. So why was this time so different?

When he couldn't come up with a feasible explanation, he shrugged. Who cares? he thought. He'd been so busy in the last few years that getting together with BJ Jones sounded like just what the doctor ordered.

Fifty-eight minutes later, Josh was driving around one block after another and had begun to wonder if he was going to be late, when he finally sighted the restaurant. BJ was standing on the corner a few feet away. She looked both ways, obviously searching for him. He liked the mental images that thought caused. One glance at her outfit, and he knew they had both dressed with different scenarios in mind about this luncheon. She was in jeans and a pea jacket with a woolly hat pulled down over her ears. He was more formal.

He watched as the wind blew tendrils of the hair that stuck out under the cap. Suddenly he wanted to hold her and shelter her from the wind.

Huh, he thought, *got to watch that imagination.* Been too long between women. Now I've just become the knight in shining armor for a woman that I met a few weeks ago. He remembered blundering in to defend her from her godmother. He could laugh about it now, though he'd been pretty shook up when it happened. It was funny because while he had thought himself in love at times, it wasn't in his nature to fall for anyone that fast. *I've just been working too hard.*

He tapped the horn, catching her attention, and she waved at him. She looked a little uncertain. He parked

and stepped out into the cold and the wind blew his coat-
tails around his legs. She was standing with hands in pockets and shoulders hunched up.

They stood there smiling at each other in the midst of
the flurry of swirling wind. He could see that she was even
lovelier than he'd remembered. Her eyes seemed brighter
than was possible until he realized they were probably
tearing in the freezing temperature. That brought him
back.

"Come on, let's get out of this weather." He took her
arm, guiding her into the restaurant. "I hope you weren't
waiting long?" he asked. She glanced at his hand on her
arm briefly.

"I just got here. Did you bring the ticket?"

He missed what she was saying because he couldn't help
watching her mouth. It was lush, more so than he'd noticed
the first time he'd seen her.

"Ticket? Oh, I forgot to bring it," he said, realizing that
he'd done just that. He'd been too excited to see her
again, wondering if she was the same as he'd remembered.
Looking at her slow beautiful smile spread across her face,
he knew she was better.

She suddenly looked shy and shrugged as she stamped
her feet to keep warm, "Okay?" she said with a bright
smile and shake of her head.

She was definitely more relaxed than she'd been at the
party, he thought, and laughed because suddenly he felt
lighthearted and full of anticipation. More curious was the
feeling that he'd just stepped into a magical land. He
wanted to wrap her up and keep her all to himself.

Josh was surprised at his desire. It wasn't like him. He'd
never been a man who thought of women as weak crea-
tures, needing protection. He'd never been interested in
women who expected deferential treatment. In truth, he'd
never had the time, and he never bothered with women
who didn't know the score. And now here he was acting

as if he was courting a very fragile flower that he planned
to marry.

That thought really threw him. It wasn't that marriage
wasn't on his life's schedule, but rather that it wasn't something he planned to do anytime in the near future. His
plan was to marry in about five or six years—by the time
he was forty-five. Surely that was soon enough.

BJ saw that the restaurant was set up with booths that
seemed to make each table a private space. There was a
hot table of incredible delicious smelling foods. As they
entered, women's heads turned, their eyes lingering on
the mismatched pair. Some seemed particularly enchanted
with Joshua.

The waiter assisted her with her coat and pulled out her
chair. The man's actions annoyed Joshua for a moment
before he caught himself. He realized that he'd wanted to
help her himself. He was definitely losing his cool over
this woman.

"You know—at Three Ashley Place," BJ said when Josh
looked slightly distracted.

"Yes," he said, "Ashley Place."

He sat and leaned toward her. It seemed as if he focused
his full attention on her. It was a bit disconcerting, but BJ
mentally shook herself before continuing.

"Most of them at Three Ashley Place are elderly theater
people. Some years back, when the St. Albans area became
a black neighborhood, many of the black theater people
moved there. Fats Waller lived there a long time ago, as
well as James Brown and others. You know LL Cool J, the
rapper?"

"The television star?" Joshua clarified.

"Yes," BJ said. "He grew up there, and so did Mark
Jackson, the basketball player. It's a beautiful town with
many lovely homes, although Ashley Place itself has sort

of fallen down." She stopped abruptly. He seemed to be watching her mouth for several seconds, and it threw her off. It was also causing her to feel strangely aroused.

"Yes, go on," Joshua prompted, his eyes rising from her mouth.

"Well, Adella, she's one of my clients, is in her eighties and still full of vinegar."

"That's a curious way to describe her," he laughed and leaning closer, put one hand under his chin. "A southern expression?"

"Yes." She lowered her eyes, blushing, and smiled enchantingly. "There are several other elderly people there who are doing as well. Adella's something of a busybody, but she's really fascinating. They were all in the old black theater and are a wonderful living part of black history."

BJ knew she was talking too fast, but she found him so attractive that it was the only way she could stop the thoughts and feelings that he brought out in her.

"Lucy was right when she said you were the one that I should speak with about the area," Joshua said.

"Actually I'm surprised she recommended me, as she accuses me of being too involved with my clients there."

"Are you?" he asked.

She smiled and shrugged. "I think I've maintained a professional relationship, but I do find them fascinating."

"I can see that." He grinned back and her heart sped up.

"It's curious that you don't specialize in one type of building but are willing to add renovations to your work also." She'd spoken on impulse. "Fortunately that whole area has so much history, and you have so many possibilities."

"Yes, I suppose so." He changed the subject. "Enough about business. Tell me about yourself. When you picked up the phone this morning, you sounded out of breath.

Do you live in a large house and have to run for the phone?"

"That's a joke. Some people have closets bigger than my apartment. I was working out."

"Working out?" His voice had dropped sexily.

"Aerobics," she'd answered, feeling slightly foolish.

"Right, you were into basketball."

At Joshua's instigation, BJ told him about her days as a basketball player. She spoke of how women's sports were the stepchildren of school sports. He was all ears, and flattered by his attentiveness, she talked too much.

The subdued lighting seemed to catch the iris of his eyes and made them gleam. Joshua's eyes were a curious deep honey brown color. They were brown but a clear bright color, neither light nor dark. She was suddenly entranced by them.

"Now, let's see," he spoke and effectively brought her back to planet earth. "Born in Columbia. Mother and father still there?"

And they were off on another topic. "Yes," she answered.

"How did you convince them to allow their baby-girl to come to New York?" he asked, using the nickname she'd given him that first day. She was surprised that he remembered.

"Not easily, I assure you," she said, taking a sip of tea. "But Lucy helped sway them. She was lonely and wanted me to be close."

"Aha, you mean the indomitable Lucy needs human companionship? I was under the impression the lady was made of steel."

"Oh, I'm not too sure she isn't made of steel myself. But she swore that I would have a fantastic career and everything else to go with it."

"And was she right?"

"Oh, I don't know. I like my job."

"But? You say it as if it wasn't enough for you."

BJ shrugged, realizing that she was on the verge of telling him more than was wise. "I guess I was full of fantasies," she evaded his question.

It was a strange sensation. He made her feel as if he found her fascinating, as if he had nothing else in the whole world that he wanted to do at that moment except listen to her. The whole of his concentration seemed to be on her. It was heady stuff.

Later he refused to allow her to pay for her food, and while she felt responsible for her own bill, he said, "I invited you, right?"

"Okay." She'd shrugged. No sense in making a scene about it, she thought.

"You'll have to give me directions to take you home."

"You don't need to do that. I drove here myself."

"Then I'll follow and make certain you get to your door."

"You don't have to do that, either. I'm perfectly safe on these streets."

"I'll feel better if I do."

He was so insistent that she acquiesced with a smile.

The only moment in which she felt a bit bothered was when they were outside and he waited for her to bring her car abreast so he could follow. Her car spluttered and died when she stopped beside his.

Oh, well, there was no way you wouldn't notice the differences in their two vehicles. Hers was a noisy economy-size model about six years out of date, while his was a current maroon Mercedes that purred. It wasn't that she couldn't afford a new model, but everyone knew that after seven years, a car began to pay for itself. Didn't they? She sighed when the ignition caught and moved in front when Joshua waved her on.

At her home, he came out and walked to open her car so that she could step out.

"Well, goodbye," she said and automatically stuck her hand out to shake. When he took it, she felt silly.

Shaking a man's hand at the end of a date was something which she'd developed back in the days when she'd dated more often. It was a way of signaling that there would be nothing more that night. But this had not been a date.

When he took her hand into both of his, she knew that he'd guessed at her intention. It made her feel gauche. He further disconcerted her when he smiled and pulled her collar up over her ears.

"Would you like to come in," she asked and then wished she hadn't. He didn't answer for a few moments as he looked at her front door. He seemed undecided, but then he stared intently into her eyes and somehow she felt as if he was reading her mind.

"I'll walk you to the door," he finally answered as if making a decision.

At the door, she fumbled with the keys, managing to drop them on the ground at their feet. It wasn't such a big thing, but it made her want to stomp her feet. Why did the man make her so nervous, she wondered.

"I'll get it," he said, hunching down to retrieve them.

Instead of giving them to her, he unlocked the door and stood back for her to go in. Unexpectedly, she wanted him to come in more than she would have believed.

"Thanks for having lunch with me," he said.

"Thanks for asking me."

"We'll have to do this again."

"Sure," she answered, but somehow she felt a little sad. She doubted they'd ever see each other again. Why should they? As for the shirt, he could simply mail the ticket.

"Have you ever been to the Afrikan Poetry Society?" he asked as if on impulse.

"No," she said, praying the grin that spread across her

face wasn't as eager as it felt. He smiled back at her and raised his eyebrows.

"If I can get tickets, would you like to try it some evening?"

"Sure."

They laughed, and BJ suddenly felt on top of the world.

Chapter Four

As Joshua drove back to Manhattan, he thought of the time spent with BJ. His conscience pricked him over his not correcting Barbara Jean's erroneous conclusions. She thought he was still in the business of renovations. But he didn't want to dash cold water on the woman's hopes—or so he told himself.

But more powerful than anything was that ever since she'd mentioned her working out, his mind had been feeding him delicious images of her sweating and being intently physical. His desire for her was making him feel like a teenager. He seemed in a state of permanent lust.

It was several hours after the impromptu brunch with Joshua that BJ finally came down from the euphoric mood she'd been in since his telephone call. She was ironing her clothes for the next week when it hit her. It was about the same time that she realized they didn't really have a firm date for the Afrikan Poetry Society but rather a vague maybe. Then she remembered their earlier conversation.

Good grief! I did it again. I let him persuade me to blab my head off. I told him all about my wonderful old basketball days— that was years ago! He must have been bored to death. No wonder I can't keep a man's interest, I talk too much. But curiously enough, she couldn't remember the same thing ever happening with Basil, her ex-boyfriend.

He'll probably never call, and that whole thing about getting tickets to the Afrikan Poetry Theater was just a polite way to say goodbye.

How many times had she gone out with a man only to have him never call again? She doubted this time would be any different. He probably woke up this morning, bored out of his mind, and simply remembered her from the Christmas party last month.

There were a lot of women out there, and this was definitely a very attractive man. She also remembered how all eyes had turned to him when they'd entered the restaurant. Most of those eyes had been women's, and they'd been admiring glances, too.

There had been something in Joshua's acceptance of those glances that made BJ know he'd often been the object of admiring women. He had been in his element. He was very aware of his effect on women, probably conceited, too.

Why would he choose her when he could have his pick of many? The question depressed her.

Although she was still flattered, she promised that next time she would get him to talk about himself. That brought her right down to reality. After all of this, was she still deluding herself that there would be a next time?

She remembered his absolutely gorgeous brown eyes. *I wonder if the gene for those eyes is a dominant characteristic?*

It was early Monday morning and Lucy McPhearson was awake. I must be getting old, she thought. Everyone knows that when you start sleeping less, it's because you're getting older. However, growing older definitely had its benefits. She liked that.

At this age, she was less willing to wait until something happened to her. She much preferred making things happen. Anyway, she laughed at herself, having all this extra time in the morning meant that she could be up and doing before the rest of the world started. *So you lose a few, and you gain a few.*

Lucy was the sort of woman who considered God as the Major Investor in her life. She rarely did anything without talking with Him first. Although even she would admit that she didn't always follow His advice.

She opened the bay windows of her bedroom and stood on the terrace. She was facing the rising sun on the second floor of her home. There was snow on the ground. The lawn was pristine white, but already it looked pitted on the sidewalks where a pathway had been dug. Although the world looked beautiful from the terrace, it was bitterly cold and not particularly inviting. She closed the windows, and without further ado, knelt to say her prayers. Her Bible readings were next, followed by her usual ritual of Tai Chi exercises.

While doing the exercises, she considered several pressing problems that were currently tantamount for the Community Board. Naturally the first one was the recent complaints about the mayor's doings. This was a "given." But somehow she couldn't keep her mind on this. She was distracted and uneasy over problems much closer to home—Barbara Jean.

She was still exercising when she got the first glimpse of an idea. Later, when she made herself a cup of chocolate, the idea took form.

Lucy hadn't been born in Saint Albans. Actually she had been born and raised in the District of Columbia and had attended university there also. She loved both areas, but it was the town of Saint Albans, New York, that she was committed to. This was her memorial to her beloved husband.

Ten years ago, Lucy had convinced Barbara Jean, her goddaughter and child of her best friend and cousin, to come north after the girl had finished school. At first, BJ had loved the place, but lately Lucy sensed rather than saw a restlessness in BJ. BJ was at an age when it was natural for her to marry and have a family. However, Lucy thought, her goddaughter had begun to show signs of becoming too comfortable in the single state.

BJ's a good girl, Lucy thought. She's patient, loyal, and loving. She also had spunk, which wasn't always apparent. But let something happen to any of her friends and she'd fight like a tiger. For herself, she was inclined to be retiring. Lucy sighed. With men now—BJ was a klutz. *There she has Joshua Hendricks all ready for the grabbing, and she's dragging her feet.*

Lucy remembered how BJ had spilled her drink on handsome Joshua Hendricks's shirt. She wondered what had happened to that. He'd be such a good catch for BJ.

That thought brought her to wondering about Joshua's plans, and Lucy sighed. But she was honest with herself and admitted that supporting him would be good for her, too. His plans to rebuild Ashley Place could be the beginning of something that she had been planning for the last several years.

She looked at the ceiling, feeling a bit sheepish. "What am I going to do with her?" she asked of her Major Investor. Suddenly the idea that had only been a niggling urge crystallized. But just in case, Lucy said a prayer first: "Lord, I know I promised BJ that I'd wouldn't do this anymore but surely just this one last time."

Before she could change her mind, Lucy grabbed her Rolodex and found Darlene Rivera's home telephone number.

* * *

Darlene Rivera was in the process of feeding her small daughter, Tiffany, when she heard the phone. It was Lucy McPhearson. She listened for several moments as the older woman spoke.

"Joshua Hendricks?" Darlene squeaked. "I don't know, Ms. McPhearson, BJ will be angry . . ."

"Call me Lucy, darling," Lucy said. Her voice sounded as if it were dipped in honey.

Darlene glanced at the telephone, not too sure it wouldn't bite. "Lucy," Darlene amended, her throat feeling as if it would close up and choke her to death on the name. "I don't think BJ's going to like it. She always hates it when I do something like that."

"Never you worry about that. This time she's going to love it."

"Well, if you say so," Darlene acquiesced.

"We're only looking out for the dear girl's best interests."

"I sure hope so," Darlene muttered as she returned the telephone to its rack and positioned Tiffany on one hip. She put a dish on the breakfast table for her husband, Carlos.

Carlos came out with hair rumpled. "Who was that?" he asked.

"Lucy McPhearson."

"Lucy McPhearson? I hope you didn't let her rope you into any of her usual machinations."

"Oh, nothing like that," Darlene lied.

"What in God's name did she want this early?"

"Oh, nothing," Darlene said.

Carlos muttered some dire prophecy as he moved toward the shower. It sounded as if he said, "Lucy McPhearson always wants something."

Darlene realized how much she agreed with her husband. But she didn't answer as she hurried past Carlos into their bedroom, where she deposited Tiffany on the floor and began to dress for work. As she finished getting ready, she thought of Lucy's suggestions, and it made her smile.

"Hello," BJ mumbled into the loudly ringing phone, which had woken her from a delicious dream that was already fading from memory.

"BJ? Lucy here. Did I wake you?"

"Lucy?" BJ said, confused, and rolled over to take a look at her bedside clock. "It's okay," BJ mumbled, trying to wake up.

"I know it's okay." Lucy sounded tart. "You're supposed to be up by now. I'll never understand how a girl who's supposed to be athletic is so slow to get up in the morning."

"It *was* time for her to get up, BJ had to admit. Just at that moment the alarm went off with a blast from the radio. It startled her, and she dropped the phone, which banged against the table and fell to the floor as she fumbled to turn off the loud noise.

She always remembered how she'd been late on her first week at the VanderWeil Foundation. One morning her boss had glared icily and suggested she buy an alarm clock.

"What in God's name is wrong at that apartment?" Lucy demanded.

"Nothing," BJ answered.

"Listen, I have an idea."

Oh, no, BJ thought. She didn't like the sound of this. Lucy wasn't exactly a flyweight, and whenever she got BJ up this early in the morning and sounded that enthusiastic, it bode no good.

"I want to appoint you and Josh Hendricks to a committee to look into Ashley Place and see what can be done."

"What can be done? Why is everyone picking on that block?"

"BJ, wake up. There's no way you can stop the hand of progress. Someone's going to do something to that area. The community has been complaining about it for years."

"I know that, but you need to be careful on these things," BJ said.

"There are a lot of unhappy voters looking out of their windows and right into that broken-down, old rattrap."

"It's not a rattrap," BJ defended.

"Even the mayor's heard about it."

"Who cares about him? Why doesn't he fix Manhattan, which is in a lot worse condition?"

"Don't be pettish. I'm appointing you and Josh to a committee to fact find."

"Lucy, you don't have the authority to make that kind of appointment. And if you did, it would be a conflict of interest to have me, your goddaughter, a social worker in the area, do the job."

"Oh. Well, maybe you're right, but you could still show him around." Without missing a beat, Lucy said, "Whatever happened to the poor man's shirt?"

Actually BJ had been on the verge of mentioning yesterday's lunch with Joshua, but she hesitated. She knew only too well what would happen. Lucy would want a full analysis and the truth was that nothing had happened. True, he'd suggested they see each other again, but she hadn't pinned any hopes on that.

The other reality, BJ admitted to herself, was that she didn't want to tell anyone. It wasn't any big thing, after all, it was only lunch. It wasn't as if they'd been on a date. She decided not to mention it.

"Nothing's happened about his shirt," she finally answered Lucy's question. "I haven't been able to contact him." It was true, she told herself.

"What's wrong with you? Lately all you do is crawl into that little apartment and read. Why don't you call him?"

"Lucy, I have to get up now. I'll talk to you later." BJ was hanging up when she heard Lucy's tinny voice through the phone. She stuck the receiver to her ear again, just in time to hear Lucy still rushing on.

"By the way, where were you yesterday? I called several times."

BJ gently hung up.

She lay there for long moments, trying to remember the dream that Lucy's call had interrupted. Giving up on that, BJ realized she felt great, and thoughts of Joshua Hendricks immediately drifted into her memory. Seeing him yesterday had been wonderful. She had the distinct impression that he'd been personally interested in her. Although he'd been circumspect, he had forgotten the shirt ticket, and he'd hesitated about coming up yesterday. The whole situation was like a dream.

That's exactly what the problem was. It *was* a dream. It had to be. It was definitely too good to be true. She rolled over on her stomach and put the pillow over her head. Joshua Hendricks was an absolute fantasy, better than anything she'd ever imagined. And she couldn't think of a reason in all kingdom-come for him to be seeking her out.

Later, in the middle of curling her hair, BJ remembered there had been an article in *Ebony* magazine on Josh only a few months ago. She quickly unplugged the curling iron and put it on a tripod. She went searching in her magazine stand and pulled out all the *Ebony*s. She sat on the floor, flipping through each one, trying to find the article.

"Darn!" she exclaimed when she found nothing.

She threw the last magazine across the room when she couldn't find the article. *Please don't tell me I threw the thing out. Where else would I have put it?* There was a box in the closet. She crawled across the floor and opened her eyesore closet and went rummaging through the junk for the box with magazines. A box that she'd promised to donate to the local thrift shop and was now glad she hadn't.

There it was! She read an article about his building in midtown Manhattan. She flicked through the article until she came to a picture of him and a gorgeous singer who was making quite a name for herself. BJ held the woman's photograph at different angles, perusing it carefully. She was tempted to throw this one across the room also. There was just no kidding about it, this was a beautiful woman also.

On second thought, BJ did throw the magazine across the floor and then put her head on her knees and sighed. She realized that none of it mattered a fig to her. For one thing, she wasn't dating Joshua and indeed had no intention of doing so. She was only trying to get the ticket to his shirt. Even to her, that sounded a bit strange but she decided not to examine it too closely.

He was like so many of the guys she'd met since coming to New York and most especially among the people whom she had met through Lucy. All you needed was one look at him, and you could read him like a book: upper-middle-class background and used to getting everything he wanted. True, as these guys went he was pretty nice, but that was all you could say.

He reminded her of Basil, except Joshua was definitely more lethal. She was inclined to admire him more than she had ever admired Basil.

"Well, that's it," she said, getting up from the floor and brushing the dust off her hands. She lugged the cardboard box back to the closet, then on second thought, pulled out the magazine with the article. "This I'm throwing out right now before I let my imagination convince me that one luncheon is an omen of a great love affair between me and the magnificent Joshua Hendricks."

She stood holding on to the magazine, musing how this was like a romance story in which she, as a suffering hero-

ine, would renounce romance with the hero for some
noble purpose. She had always loved those stories because
things usually worked out in favor of true love. Of course
her situation with Joshua wasn't about true love. Fortunately all she was going to renounce was her daydreaming
over a magazine article. Too bad, she sighed.

Actually she might have stood there longer enjoying
feeling sorry for herself as the dramatic tragic heroine,
except she happened to glance at the kitchen clock.

"Oh, no!" she yelped.

If she didn't get out of there, she was definitely going
to be late. But when it came time to prove her resolve and
chuck the magazine into the garbage, she found herself
laying it on the kitchen counter instead. Then with a quick
glance at the clock, she rushed to finish dressing for work.

Later that morning, she took her coffee break with Darlene.

"I'm supposed to meet Lucy for lunch today," Darlene
said, pulling out a popular dress catalog to peruse.

"I hope this is not about that crazy scene at the Christmas
party! You two better not be ganging up on me."

"Of course not—you take yourself entirely too seriously," Darlene said.

"Well, maybe so," BJ acquiesced. "But you'd better be
careful. You know that Lucy always has some ulterior
motive whenever she seems the most innocent."

"It's only for lunch, BJ," Darlene said airily. It sounded
a little strange as Darlene was usually quite intimidated by
Lucy. BJ couldn't imagine her best friend actually having
a social meeting with the older woman.

"But what could it be about? Didn't she even give you
a hint?" BJ asked.

"No, she didn't," Darlene said, but somehow BJ thought
her friend looked a little evasive. "Where were you yesterday?" Darlene asked, changing the subject. "I tried to
call you and only got that crazy answering machine. It

squawked like crazy and cut me off in the middle of my message.'' Darlene riffled through the latest fashion magazine and drank her coffee.

''Oh, I went out for a while,'' BJ said and took a sip of her herbal tea. Part of her was tempted to tell Darlene what had happened with Joshua yesterday, but she didn't. She had to keep herself from fantasizing, and telling Darlene the curious story wouldn't help. Her best friend's imagination would only add fuel to the fire.

''What did you say?'' Darlene asked as she turned a page of the catalog. ''Where did you say you went?''

''I decided to go out for lunch,'' BJ said, feeling that it wasn't a total lie.

''All alone?'' Darlene persisted, though she was back to looking at the catalog.

''Mmm.'' BJ took another sip and deliberately made her expression bland.

Her subterfuge seemed to work at first, for Darlene continued to be engrossed within the colorful pages of the book for a few moments.

''God, that sounds sad,'' Darlene exclaimed after several seconds of silence. Then she shook her head as she surfaced from the book to glance at BJ.

''Huh?'' BJ said, having been caught wondering why Josh had called her yesterday.

''I said that sounds pathetic. I can just see you sitting all alone at some restaurant, eating your sandwich or something else just as dull. You know what you need? A man.''

BJ could laugh today because she had her own secret. Although it wasn't as if she had a lover or anything. It gave her a sense of having a life that everyone wasn't privy to. She couldn't remember the last time she'd felt that way. But when Darlene stared off into space, BJ became a bit uneasy.

Darlene shook her head and went back to glancing at

the glossy pictures in the book, saying, "Lucy is right. That's exactly what you need, a man."

"What's Lucy got to do with this? You just said this lunch isn't about some matchmaking scheme that Lucy's cooked up, right?"

"Right," Darlene said. "You've already told me at length that you have absolutely no intention of ever going out on another blind date."

"See that you remember it."

Before they parted, Darlene mentioned she was planning to experiment by cooking a fancy dinner sometime in the next few weeks.

"You're really getting very domesticated lately," BJ said. "You aren't tired of all the cooking counting from Thanksgiving right up to New Year's and Kwanzaa?"

"No, I'm not. Actually it's been fun. I only wish I could have planned something for Martin Luther King Day this year. Anyway, this will be for Tiffany's birthday."

"A late night dinner for Tiffany's birthday? Shouldn't you be having something in the afternoon for the kiddies if it's for Tiffany?"

"Tiffany is going to be a gorgeous sophisticated woman, and I want to start teaching her early."

To that all BJ could do was laugh heartily. "Count me in. What day will it be?"

"Give me some time to figure that out."

"I thought you said it was for Tiffany's birthday?"

"It is, but Tiffany has a working mother, don't forget. These things take planning."

Tuesday evening, BJ worked overtime and came home exhausted. She ate a quick snack in front of the television. A news program came on, and she clicked the remote to turn it off, muttering, "No news but bad news."

Her voice seemed overly loud in the small apartment. She picked up a book—a mystery. Since everyone had been laughing at her love stories, she decided to try a mystery. But when, by page twenty, three people had died graphic violent deaths, she threw the paperback book across the room.

As a last resort, she picked up Darlene's Christmas present and tried to read it with little success. Another book on how to get your man made her feel absolutely sick. Besides, she'd feel the fool, acting the way the book advocated.

"Might as well get ready for bed," she said to the echoing apartment and stood up.

She looked into the bathroom mirror and decided to shampoo and condition her hair. Sunday's luncheon with Joshua had delayed her schedule.

The light was bad in her bathroom, making her appear sallow—ill. It only reminded her of how depressed she had been in the last few months. True, two days ago, after lunch with Joshua Hendricks, she'd felt on top of the world. But now she felt dragged out and listless.

What's wrong with me?

She remembered Darlene accusing her of not even reading the papers and again felt embarrassed for her malaise. It was true. She simply couldn't get up the interest. Look at how she avoided television news programs.

I'm college educated with a master's in social work. I have a decent job, which I enjoy. And while the VanderWeil Foundation might be a rich man's way of saving on taxes, it was still a worthy job. So why aren't I happy?

Okay, so my love life is dead as the proverbial doorknob. That never bothered me before. And don't the experts say that single women live longer happier lives? I bet that's a lie. True, my sex life has never sizzled but so what? My one major love affair—make that semimajor, she corrected, had been with Basil. There was certainly nothing sizzling about him. Basil may have been the sophisticated type, like Joshua, but she suspected their similarities ended there. Basil and she had spent two years boring the tears out of each other.

It was curious that both Basil and Joshua were men who'd approached her. They were men whom you'd expect would want more glamorous women. With Basil it had been sex. But what did Joshua want?

She wondered if Josh really enjoyed her company as it seemed, or if he thought she was influential with Lucy and building permits? She certainly hoped not, because with all Lucy's wheeling and dealing, she was an honest women. He'd get his permit on his own merits or he could forget it. She suddenly wanted to cross her fingers that he'd call again.

"I'm a glutton for punishment," she said aloud.

Well, if Joshua was like Basil, he'd probably call any minute now and cancel. But then she reminded herself there was nothing to cancel.

The type of man she really needed was someone more traditional, like my father, she thought. Thinking about her parents made her smile, and her spirits picked up a bit.

BJ's mother was always talking about her getting married and producing a few instant grandchildren. However, her father thought differently.

My father always told me that my prince would come, and I believed him. However, Dad never found anyone good enough for me, and here I am still waiting! I'm beginning to think this could go on forever.

Thinking of her parents lightened her mood. As a young emerging woman, she'd resented their tendency to be overprotective. Otherwise, her relationship with her parents had always been fine. Now there were times when she actually enjoyed their tendency to treat her like a kid.

"I must be losing my touch," she said aloud. The sound of her voice made her shiver. "And I've got to stop talking to myself, that's for sure."

Later, sitting under the dryer, BJ thought that much as she hated to admit it, Darlene was right. She was seriously concerned about her biological clock.

She had once believed herself over that but knew better now. Four years before, she had been obsessed with marrying and having a baby. This was why she'd put up with Basil for so long. They'd talked about marrying. Basil had claimed that he needed more time, and she'd spent two years waiting. In the end, he'd found someone new. After a few tears, she had to admit that he'd been no loss. Basil was like most of the men she met in New York, not interested in any commitment. He was educated, career oriented, and enjoyed being single. Of course not all the men were single—some only enjoyed pretending to be single— and went home to their wives later.

It was beginning to look as if Mr. Right would never come along. But did that mean she couldn't ever have a child?

Just as she wrapped a towel around her head, the phone rang. She stood staring at it for a few moments before picking it up. For a split second, she wanted it to be Joshua inviting her to the Afrikan Poetry Theater. It was Lucy.

"I just wanted to know if you'd called Joshua Hendricks yet?"

"Lucy, will you stop worrying about it? I know how to handle this."

"Well, it certainly doesn't seem so. That was an expensive shirt you messed up, and it's inexcusable for you to wait this long. It's got to be weeks by now."

"I know that," BJ said, feeling somewhat stricken, "and I did try to contact him."

"About that fact-finding mission . . ."

"Don't even think of it," BJ said, responding quickly. "You're definitely overstepping your authority. It's probably even illegal for all I know. I am not going to take Joshua Hendricks to Ashley Place no matter what you do. I am not interested in the man, and I won't be taking him anywhere. Who do you think you are? The mayor?"

For once, Lucy seemed speechless. It was such an unusual situation that BJ was slightly alarmed when she said, "Lucy? Are you still there?"

"Umm," Lucy said. "That's a good idea. I think I will ask the mayor."

Without another word, Lucy hung up, leaving BJ holding the phone and feeling puzzled. She had just placed the receiver on its hook when it rang again. BJ grabbed it up.

BJ assumed it was Lucy, calling back. "Lucy, you'd better watch out before both of us go to jail."

"Hi," Joshua's sexy voice seemed right there next to her.

It took a second or two to accept that it was him. Then her heart thudded against her chest wall like a tom-tom.

"While you're in jail, should I arrange for bail money?"

"Oh, ha-ha." She tried to sound relaxed. "Just a little joke."

Chapter Five

"About the Afrikan Poetry Society," he said, "Do you really want to go?"

Here it comes, she thought, the brush-off. "Oh, it's all right if you have to cancel," she said, feeling disappointed and thinking he was going to a lot of trouble to let her down gently.

"I was thinking about those women's basketball teams—"

"Oh, listen," she cut him off, "I'm really sorry about bending your ear that way."

"I like to hear you talk about yourself." This made her feel soft and happy.

"I didn't mean to hog the conversation. You never got a word in," she said.

He laughed. Then he said, "Now, about those teams—you think the school was only trying to protect the girls? Maybe that's why they didn't give you as much money as they gave the male teams?"

It was a strange gambit for a telephone call, but he'd rung her bell anyway.

"They did it because they were sexist about sports, and they still are," she said without hesitation.

"You sure the guys weren't better?"

"Hah. I can see you're looking for a fight. But I'll just say this. All the guys had was bulk. We women had finesse and smoothness."

"I don't know. Can you prove it? Can you put your money where your mouth is?"

"Prove it?" She was almost spluttering.

"How would you like to go to a basketball game instead of the Afrikan Poetry Society, which we can do another time?"

"Go with *you?*" That floored her.

"Who else? I'm the man with the tickets to a game at the Garden. Being as you're the expert on this, I think we should go. Then you can show me how all this stuff about the game really works."

"Tickets to Madison Square Garden? How did you do that?"

"I have my means," he drawled. "How about it?"

"I'd love to," she finally managed to say. "When?"

Having him invite her out was the last thing she'd expected, but to have him take her to a game was surely more surprising than anything.

"Tomorrow night too soon?"

"Never too soon," she reassured him. "I'd move heaven and earth to go."

He didn't speak for a long while, and then she heard him exhale before he said, "I wouldn't mind your saying something like that about me." It was so soft that she almost felt as if she'd imagined it. Now her heart accelerated in earnest. "Tomorrow evening it is," he said as if he'd never spoken before. "I'll pick you up. After all I never gave you the shirt ticket."

They both laughed.

Later she mused upon his words. It was the most flirta-

tious conversation they'd had, and she couldn't have cared
less about all her earlier promises. All her good intentions
that she'd sworn to her godmother went down the drain.
Eating lonely dinners in front of the television made a
woman do strange things, not to mention the thought of
those wonderful chromosomes.

On Wednesday night, BJ was dressed and waiting downstairs in front of the building when Josh pulled up.

Joshua jumped out of his beautiful car and walked
around to seat her, including snapping her seat belt. At
one time, years ago, she would have been annoyed at his
solicitousness, but no longer. Now she loved it. It reminded
her of stories told to her in grade school. You certainly
couldn't fault the man for his manners.

Probably trained by the family retainers, she thought.
Everything he did made her see him as the doted-on son
of a well-to-do family.

She had been absolutely sure that Joshua would be
dressed causally for a basketball game. BJ had started to
wear something really comfortable, but then remembering
that she'd never seen him casual, she opted for a pair of
slacks. Sure enough, glancing at Joshua, she realized that
while he was dressed down, he wore a dark jacket with
gold buttons over gray slacks; he was definitely not sporty.
She was glad that she'd gone with her hunches. They were
not as mismatched as they'd been for the Sunday lunch.

In the crowd, milling about, BJ was thrilled when they'd
bumped into one of New York's famous black filmmakers.
The man greeted Joshua as if they were long lost brothers.
They stopped to talk. Of course other people were so
fascinated by the celebrity that he was swamped by the
media, snapping pictures, and by people wanting his auto-
graph. The photographers had also gotten shots of Joshua
and her when they recognized him. Once again, she realized how wise it was that she'd followed her hunches about

what to wear. *Wonder what people would have said about my old faded jeans?*

Once when she caught Joshua watching her as she stood up to clap and yell, he said, "I can't remember when I've had so much fun with a . . ." He'd stopped before finishing the sentence.

She puzzled over what he'd intended to say, wondering if he was going to say so much fun with a woman. However, she knew that he was enjoying himself when he jumped up to roar with the crowd, too.

By the halfway point, she was hoarse from screaming. Josh's friend, the filmmaker, got up and did something that sent the crowd wild. Even Joshua laughed so much he had to sit down. She was disappointed she hadn't seen what the gesture was.

The player, a real gentleman, managed to restrain himself and turned his back on the filmmaker's gesture as well as the spectators' antics.

"What did he do?" she asked Joshua.

"I'll tell you later," he said as he continued to laugh with the audience.

"No, tell me now."

"It wasn't something for a woman's eyes."

"Oh, for pete's sake." She slapped him on the arm.

By the time they came out, they were both keyed up by the game.

"Did you see when he went under the basket and flipped the ball over the side? He left them all flat-footed. Now I'm not trying to sound like a sexist, but are you sure a woman can do something like that?" Josh asked. His expression was one of wide-eyed innocence, so she knew he was only ribbing her.

"That was strictly a routine move. We'd have done it better," she bragged.

"Aw, you're kidding." He waved her away.

"If we were on a court, I'd show you," she went even further.

"You're on," he challenged.

She was slightly taken aback and then reminded him smugly, "We're not on a court."

"There's a gym not too far from here that we could use."

"A gym?" she repeated.

"Sure, I'm a member."

"You said you never play anything."

"I do go to the gym once in a while. How about it? Are you game?"

She glanced at her watch. "It's too late."

"We'll stay for only a little while, and I'll have you home so fast you'll soon be in your bed, sleeping like a babe. You're the basketball expert. You owe it to me."

"But you don't play."

"Oh, try me. Surely I can keep up with a woman even if I'm not much of a player."

"That's it, you asked for it," she said.

They went to a twenty-four-hour private membership gym in a luxurious midtown apartment building.

He parked his Mercedes in the underground parking lot, then guided her through the back entrance. There was a security officer sitting at a desk, surrounded by various monitors. The man looked up and waved, saying, "Evening, Mr. Hendricks."

"You must come here a lot," BJ said.

"Actually I live here," he admitted.

"Oh," she said and was quiet for several moments after that.

"We're going to the gym, which is on the top floor, not to my apartment."

"Oh." Now she was relieved.

                              *   *   *

Joshua studied her as they rode the elevator to the top.
He'd known that his suggestion to play a little private
one-on-one had been done as a way to get her into his
apartment, which was one flight downstairs. But when
she'd appeared so put out on realizing that he lived here,
he seriously doubted long sleek BJ would be visiting him
tonight. Ah, well, he sighed, it's the luck of the draw.

They found the gym deserted except for the attendant,
who provided a colorful set of paper shorts and top, as
well as sneakers, for BJ. They both changed, and Joshua
gasped when she walked toward him. She was like a work
of art and even more beautiful than he'd imagined. She
had long sleek legs and high breasts. The sight of her was
riveting. He had to force his gaze away.

BJ waited while he went to pick up the towels. The
attendant was so busy staring at her that Josh had to speak
to the man to get his attention. It irked Josh more than
he'd expected. If BJ hadn't been within hearing distance,
he'd have said something sharp.

Lastly Joshua checked the basketballs. He test bounced
several before choosing one. He walked slowly toward her,
bouncing the ball.

She waited, smiling sweetly and standing with her toes
turned slightly inward. There was something incredibly
endearing about the stance. It made her appear totally
guileless. It almost made him feel like a cad because his
own mind was consumed by thoughts of getting her into
his bed.

He moved faster, dribbling toward her. She gave him
another big sweet smile, and just as his heart swelled, she
swerved and slapped the ball downward right out of his
hand. He was left there with his mouth open.

The little minx had stolen the ball!

She feinted one way and turned the other as he tried

to follow and laughed her head off. It was more than a bit sobering. Every move she made was fluid and perfect. He wondered if his challenge to play her had been such a wise idea.

She was good!

He made several attempts to get back into the game, all of which she foiled. They weren't playing by any rules, and she headed straight to one basket, where she landed two shots right in a row. If he thought she was going to give him a chance to run the ball, he was mistaken. He was trying hard to be a good sport about it.

Finally she lunged one way and then switched directions on him. He tripped right over her foot. That landed him facedown, kissing the floorboards. BJ's laughter, both raucous and feminine, washed over him. He hobbled onto his feet again, feeling really sheepish.

The truth was that not only was she really good, but there were disadvantages against him that he hadn't counted on. For one thing, her beautiful body that he'd been lusting after was not only gorgeous, it was also strong. The other problem was even worse. She was female, and he'd always played with men. Why hadn't he thought of that before?

Although she was a big girl, every time he got too close he'd freeze up, terrified he'd hit and hurt her. He must have been crazy to challenge this powerful woman. But if he were honest, the worst injury he was suffering that evening was to his male pride.

She was dribbling circles around him, and then it finally happened—his worst fear.

They banged hips and his larger mass and extra pounds sent her flying. She bounced off him and seemed to fly through his fingers as he tried to catch her. Landing on her bottom, she slid five feet across the highly polished floorboards. When she stopped, she drew up into a fetal ball and remained perfectly still for several heart-stopping moments. She was curled on her side with one arm thrown over her eyes. His heart jumped into his mouth. She looked so small and defenseless.

"BJ," he yelled, but it came out a horrified, croaked whisper.

He rushed to her and sank down to his knees. He was afraid to touch her. He tapped her as carefully as he could on her shoulder. She moaned feebly.

"Ouch," she groaned, louder this time, and massaged her bottom.

His hand followed hers to rub her bottom also before he caught himself. He certainly couldn't take the liberty of touching her *there*. Could he?

"Are you okay?" he demanded.

She peeked from under the arm covering her eyes and then turned over onto her back. She broke out into laughter. She was so amused that she drummed both heels on the floor.

"You look so funny," she gasped between the laughs.

"Am I to take it that you're not hurt?" he said through clenched teeth.

She sat up, still laughing. "You should have seen your face." She seemed barely able to contain her mirth as she shook her head, indicating she was all right.

"What's so funny? I almost had a heart attack. I thought I killed you!" Lord, how he'd love to shake her until her teeth rattled.

"You turned gray," the irrepressible BJ said.

She set the basketball close by her on the floor as if to keep it near enough to grab if needed. However, it slowly rolled across the floor. That's when he realized that the minx had held on to the damn ball through the whole incident, including the punishing slide across the floor. With no further ado, he stood up.

"That's it," he said. "No more Mr. Nice Guy."

* * *

BJ had been thoroughly enjoying herself until Joshua
stood. He walked around to her back and unceremoniously
hauled her upward to her feet. One glance at his expression, and she sensed things were about to change.

Joshua's face was a study in male determination as he
went to retrieve the ball. He bounced it hard toward her.

"Oh, what's wrong with you?" BJ demanded, catching
the ball. "Can't you take a joke?"

With both hands on hips and glaring down at her, he
snarled, "Your ball. And be warned, I intend to whip your
butt."

"You and what army?" she challenged.

She knew immediately that it had been a mistake. Joshua
thumped the ball out of her hand, bumped her when she
tried to recapture it, and with a triumphant male laugh
pivoted and dribbled toward the basket. She couldn't keep
up with his longer legs in the mad dash down the court.
She also couldn't do a thing when he went up and dumped
it right through the net. He slam dunked the ball a second
time, leaving her totally ineffective. It was a good thing
they weren't being sticklers about the score. Now he
wouldn't let her get next to the ball.

"That had no finesse," she accused, "only male bulk."

She tried to steal again, but this time he was waiting for
her and moved out of her range. His arms were longer,
and he stopped her from getting close with a hand in her
face. Now she was peeved.

"Sore loser," he taunted.

Their pacing increased. They both banged into each
other constantly. Worse yet, she suspected that he was still
restraining himself, although not nearly as much as she'd
thought he was doing before.

With the two of them stomping, jumping, and yelling

their heads off, the sound bounced off the tile walls of the deserted gym.

Joshua seemed determined to give her a real race. Despite her spirit, she weighed a lot less than him. In a short time, it was as serious as a duel, and they both worked up a sweat, grunting and snarling. She knew she was no pushover, and he hadn't expected her to be so good. They weren't as badly matched as they could have been.

In the end, he tied the score despite her fighting like a she-cat. He roared with laughter, and she tripped him. As he was going down, he deliberately dropped the ball and grabbed her. Although she tried to evade him, they both sprawled down together as the ball slowly bounced the other way.

They both laughed, but old habits die hard, she thought as she watched the ball roll to a stop. When she realized that Josh was looking at her, she said, "Those girl teams were tougher than you thought, right?"

She lay back on the floor, breathing hard with her knees drawn up.

When she sat up to dry herself, he took the towel to wipe her back.

"I thought you said you couldn't play," she accused.

"Now and again," he answered.

"You've played more than now and again," she said.

He laughed. "I used to be on the team in high school."

"Did you go out for the team in college?" she asked as she closed her eyes to enjoy his rubbing the towel across her neck.

"No, my priorities changed, and I guess I had to make a few choices," he said after a moment of pause.

"I thought you said you *hardly ever* play. At least that's what you implied."

"Thought you had a patsy—right?"

He smiled at her, and suddenly basketball was the farthest thing from her mind. His pupils had expanded, changing his bright, shining brown eyes into darkened pools of smoke. She was so mesmerized by this that she never moved a muscle as he loomed closer. He cupped the back of her head and slowly, ever so slowly, his lips came down on hers. His mouth was sweet to taste, and she angled her head to mold closer. Even the light musky scent that emanated from his body intoxicated her.

His hands came to her shoulders, and he drew her to sit between his legs, deepening their kiss. Her head spun, and her arms went around his neck.

Waves of desire uncoiled within her, and she was weak with a need that arose to confuse her. When he moved away to watch her, she wanted to pull him back. He caressed her cheek tenderly with one hand.

"Open your mouth," he said, and she obeyed without thinking.

She thought he smiled in triumph and swept down to kiss her again. This time the kiss had intensified. When she moaned with pleasure, he pressed her so that she was lying across his leg. She'd never remembered wanting a man as much as she wanted Josh at that moment. Her very bones seemed to melt under the powerful erotic onslaught of him. She loved everything about him.

He released her mouth and turned to her ear. "We could go downstairs," he whispered. His warm breath sent shivers down her spine.

"Downstairs?" she murmured.

"My apartment," he answered, nipping her ear.

She sat up. She'd never wanted anything more than to follow him into his apartment. Her body craved it. She wanted nothing more than to have Joshua possess and be possessed by her. But somehow she couldn't.

"I think I'd better go home," she said.

He went still, although he was still holding her. "Are you sure that's what you want?"

"I don't do this sort of thing," she said. Even to her

ears that sounded more prim than she wanted. "I'm sorry," she added.

It wasn't that she didn't do this, it was quite simply a case that she knew when she made love with Joshua it was going to be very serious. One of the most serious things she'd ever done in her life, and she had to think about it before she allowed herself that experience. Now was the perfect time, she knew, but her heart knew there was more than just herself involved here.

Besides, she thought, why had she said she was sorry? It made her sound as if she was a kid. She didn't have to be sorry for not sleeping with a man she'd met only a few weeks ago.

He released her slowly and shifted away. She could see the frustrated lust in his body language, but his face was expressionless.

"Come on," he said softly. "Let's get you home."

Chapter Six

Ten days later, BJ picked up the phone to find her godmother there.

"BJ, I've made arrangements for you to squire Joshua Hendricks on a tour of Ashley Place today," Lucy said.

"Lucy, I told you that was out of the question. I happen to like my job, even if you don't give a hoot about yours."

"It's too late, he'll arrive there any minute now," Lucy's voice came over the phone.

"I'm not doing it," BJ insisted. "You can't just arbitrarily assign fact-finding tours whenever you want. The whole thing sounds like a conflict of interest."

"Nonsense," Lucy said. "And it's not an official fact-finding tour, which all I'd have to do is ask the mayor and I could do that also. I simply want you to show Joshua around Three Ashley Place."

BJ could have screamed. The one thing she desperately wanted to do was see Joshua again but certainly not as Lucy's representative. She hadn't heard from him in ten days, not since their private session of hoops.

"Why should I do that? He can see that building without me."

BJ looked around at her office space area and wanted to sigh. Her desk was hidden under a mountain of papers and folders because she simply didn't have enough space to file her caseload. She wondered if she could straighten up before Joshua arrived. She knew it was an impossibility. And how was she going to squeeze in the time when she really needed to tackle some of her paperwork?

"Well, you can introduce him to the residents."

At that moment, BJ looked up—and sure enough, Joshua Hendricks walked through the door, looking as if he owned New York or at the very least all of Jamaica. Every eye in the place settled on him.

The suit looked like pure Seville Row with a white shirt and red silk tie. He managed to appear completely comfortable in a roomful of gaping women and few men, most of whom were dressed in jeans. Even the few "home boys" in their baggy pants and oversized shirts looked impressed.

"Never mind, he's here already," BJ said. "Lucy, if this is any of your usual manipulations, I will totally wash my hands of it."

"Now, BJ, how could you even think anything like that of me? I'm trying to keep you informed on what's happening at Ashley Place. By the way, I've already spoken to Cody VanderWeil . . ."

"Cody! My boss? Are you trying to get me fired?"

"Nonsense. He was tickled pink to be of help. He thinks you'll like him better."

"Oh, puleeze."

"You know it's true. Cody's always had a crush on you. But if you're going to act like this about Joshua Hendricks, I can always find someone else to do the job."

That was not what BJ wanted to hear Lucy say. Much as she hated her godmother's interference, she'd hate it even more if Lucy took to setting Joshua up with other women.

BJ sighed. Look what happens when you go out with a man twice, you think you have dibbs on him.

"This is for your own good. You're too out of touch with what's happening in the city. A big girl like you shouldn't always be trying to fit yourself into small spaces. You used to be so well informed, and now all you do is retire into your own little cave. The only things you care about are those nuisance clients at Ashley Place. Someday you'll thank me for keeping you abreast of—"

"I'll speak with you later," BJ said.

". . . and whatever you do, don't forget that we'll be having dinner at your place a week from next Saturday."

"Why my house?" BJ asked. "Yours is much larger."

"I never have time to cook. You know that."

"And I *do* have time?"

"Now, baby-girl, don't be persnickety. You need to do more—"

"Stop calling me that, and I have to go now," BJ cut in and hung up, gently severing the line to her godmother.

She glanced up in time to see her boss, a long lanky man with thinning light brown hair, come out to greet Joshua. As BJ watched, the two men introduced themselves and shook hands. The handshake seemed to go on longer than needed, and when they broke apart, BJ had the distinct impression that Cody wanted to rub his. What fools men could sometimes be, she thought. All eyes were turned on them.

They were still some distance away, so she couldn't hear what was being said, but Cody pointed toward her as they approached, still talking. Her pulse speeded up, and she tried to wait patiently. The noncommittal smile that she'd pasted on her face felt as if it would crack.

It had been two weeks since they'd gone to the basketball game. All she could think of was the kiss they'd shared and how he'd moved in on her. She'd wanted nothing more than to go to his apartment and finish what he'd started. She took a deep breath—well, she could dream couldn't she?

She'd been annoyed that Josh hadn't called her after his efforts to seduce her had failed. It had disappointed her as well as stuck in her craw. Such were New York men. If she'd been in Columbia, it would have been different.

When she looked into Joshua Hendricks's bright brown eyes, all intelligent thought fled. She stared at him and totally forgot that she had been peeved with him. She felt as if she was turning to mush. His smile seemed to enmesh her whole body.

Part of her longed for him to kiss her again, and she was disappointed, knowing that even if he had wanted to do so, they were in an office. Wouldn't you know the first man that she'd be so attracted to would be a man like Josh? But it was just a waste of time. He'd probably pursue her until he got what he wanted, and then he'd move on to other fields to ply his wiles. Any man who could date celebrities was only having a little fun with someone like her. He'd soon be back to the women he preferred.

BJ pulled herself together and realized that Cody seemed puzzled for a moment as he glanced from one to the other. Then he said, "It's really been a pleasure meeting you, Mr. Hendricks."

"Hello," Josh said, after Cody had gone. He held out something in a paper bag toward her.

"What's this?" BJ asked when she finally came out of her trance.

"Coffee," he answered.

"Thanks."

She took it from his hands before she realized how hot the cup was. She held the cup gingerly, trying to save her fingers from the heat. It tilted precariously.

"Wait a minute. Don't hold it like that!" Joshua jumped aside.

"Sorry." BJ adjusted the cup just in time. It had come

terribly close to spilling on his shirt for the second time, she realized.

Josh took it out of her hand and carefully wrapped a paper napkin around the cup, insulating it so that she could hold it. It made her feel inept and slightly annoyed. It also didn't work. As she reached for the cup again, she dropped the pencil she'd been holding, and both of them went down to pick it up. Joshua bumped her hand, and sure enough, the cup slipped to an angle that ensured she'd spill the contents right onto Joshua.

He ducked, an act of pure male grace. The women who'd been observing every move they'd made, squeaked. That unnerved BJ, and the coffee slipped farther.

Sure enough, Joshua managed to dodge the first wave but got caught on the second. The two of them stood stark still and waited for the inevitable. Everything seemed to occur in slow motion. When it hit, Joshua looked like a small boy for a few seconds. In the end, the coffee splashed down his shirtfront, creating a real mess.

Joshua's quick thinking made him pull the shirt away from his body, which saved him from getting burned. He simply stared at the mess.

''I'm so sorry,'' she babbled, fearing that she was going to break out in tears, despite knowing that this time it wasn't totally her fault.

She felt such a fool. She was absolutely a menace around the man. She hadn't even cleaned the first shirt, and here she'd messed up another one.

Rubbing at the stain was a waste of time. It actually seemed to spread. Joshua took the tissue with which she had tried mop his shirtfront.

''I hope this isn't your revenge for my kissing you,'' he said softly. When she looked around panicky, he added, ''It's okay. I guess this is not my day.''

''Is this all you have?'' BJ asked and watched as he tried to wipe himself off.

She knew it was a silly question. Why would he travel with a change of clothes just to visit her?

"Yes," he answered as if everything she said was perfectly reasonable.

From the corner of her eye, she saw that the incident had galvanized the other workers, who'd been watching their every move.

Despite her momentary self-pity, she couldn't help noticing how quickly a veritable crowd of females surrounded them and all for a little spilled coffee. Joshua in distress brought women like honey brings flies or a magnet did to pins.

"Everything's fine," he reassured them as they fawned over him.

"Oh, you poor man," one grandmotherly type said, giving BJ a sour look. She brushed at him lingeringly. "What that stain needs is some talcum powder."

"No, cold water removes stains," another woman said.

"Not for coffee," another of the female workers contradicted. "For that you need hot water."

"Let's try all of them," the grandmother suggested.

One of the younger women clumped along in combat boots and mini-skirt to find her face powder when no one had any talc.

The woman then proceeded to dump the face powder on Josh's shirtfront. If he didn't look a mess before, he sure did after that.

Another woman went to get hot water, and it seemed to take a long time as the women worked to get the stain out. He obviously enjoyed every moment of the attention, making jokes that kept them in simpering female titters. There was no doubt he wallowed in all the attention and the women's ministrations.

Even her boss, Cody, had the nerve to look askance. "I only hope he doesn't sue," Cody said. "That's a designer shirt. Don't expect the VanderWeil Foundation to pay for your mistakes.''

BJ wanted to kick him in the shins. Actually she wouldn't have minded kicking a couple of the women's shins, either.

Finally, when she had had enough of the scene, BJ grabbed her coat and purse and was off, waiting for Josh by the front door. He had no choice but to follow.

Of course once he was away from his female audience, he didn't have to strut like a rooster any longer, BJ thought. He stopped mopping and simply stood, staring in horror at the spot.

He sounded resigned when he spoke. "I guess it's hopeless. I'll have to postpone our trip."

"How could that be?" she said and could hear the snippiness in her own voice. "With all that rubbing, certainly there's no more stain." To herself, she muttered, "A hole maybe, couldn't be any more stain."

Immediately she was contrite. She knew she was simply jealous and that the emotion was quite insane. She had no claim on Joshua. Besides, considering that the second ruined shirt was partly her fault, maybe she should show a little more charm. The problem was that despite all her denials to Lucy, she was disappointed.

At her tart remarks, Josh's expression went from woebegone to triumph. A smug smile spread across his mouth. He's probably remembering all the attention from those women, she thought.

"Your co-workers were very helpful," he said, examining his shirt.

She balled up her fists at her sides. What conceit, she thought, but she had resented his paying so much attention to that batch of sharks in her office. Even the married ones had come over to simper. She definitely missed his asking her to talk about herself.

"I have an appointment at City Hall that I'd scheduled for later. I'll have to go home and change." He stared intently into her eyes. "I was looking forward to this day with you."

Suddenly she heard herself say, "I could go with you while you change. Then we could go to Ashley Place for the tour."

It wasn't that she regretted her suggestion, but she wondered why she'd offered. The last time she'd turned him down when he'd suggested she go to his apartment. She wondered if her offer sounded as if she was trying to get a second chance. It wouldn't have done any harm for them to postpone. Also hadn't she just sworn to Lucy she wasn't going? Now here she was almost begging for the opportunity.

Joshua glanced at her with an unreadable expression as he appeared to consider her suggestion. "You're willing to travel all the way to midtown Manhattan? It wouldn't take up too much of your time?"

"It's all right. Cody knows I'm showing you around." To herself she thought, Cody will probably fire me.

Her mentioning her boss's name seemed to distract Josh completely from worrying about his shirt. "Cody's your supervisor?" he asked.

"Yes. His family started the foundation, and we were both hired at the same time. Cody is sort of doing his philanthropist thing, I guess."

"Sounds like you two get along well," Joshua remarked.

How he'd caught that, she had no idea. Or was it the handshake that had alerted him?

"We do," she answered. "We used to be partners when we both came here to work. But now of course, he's moved up."

"Partners?" Now he looked suspicious.

A sudden improbable idea occurred to her. Was Joshua as jealous as she'd been when the women had mobbed him? That thought made her feel a lot better.

"You can give me the shirt ticket when we go to your

apartment." She glanced wryly at his shirt and added, "I'll pay for this one, too."

He laughed. "Isn't this where we started? I think I like it when a woman offers to clean my clothes." Then after a pause, he said, "Let's go."

They spoke on inconsequential topics while driving to Manhattan, and she found herself studying him. He called Linda Collins on his cellular phone while they were in the car, telling the woman that he would be late getting to Ashley Place.

Aside from his obviously large male ego, she couldn't find anything wrong with him. Curiously enough, he didn't refer to having invited her to his apartment the last time they'd been together. It was almost as if the incident never occurred. She remembered their private game of hoops and realized as strange as it was, that game had been seductive. They'd fought not like two people playing a game but almost as if they were lovers.

She almost reneged when they entered his building from the parking lot and she realized that she would soon be alone with him in his apartment.

The same security man she'd seen before waved at them. He smiled, obviously remembering her.

She smiled briefly at the man and felt foolish, wondering if he thought she and Josh were lovers. She followed Joshua to the bank of elevators at the back.

"What floor do you live on?" she asked. "Maybe I should wait here."

Joshua's glance made her know that he knew her thoughts. "Don't worry, you're safe."

For some reason, that didn't make her feel good at all. Was she safe because she wasn't his type, she wondered.

"On second thought, I'll go with you."

He never blinked an eye at her sudden indecisiveness. All he said was, "No problem."

At his apartment, he hesitated before opening the door.

"You'll have to excuse everything. I've been working pretty hard, and it's still undecorated."

As he opened the door and they stepped inside, he said, "Be careful of the dog. Don't touch him, he's been trained especially as a watch dog—"

Joshua had barely spoken when a huge St. Bernard raced toward them, eluding Josh to pounce on her with his two front paws placed on her shoulder.

The dog had almost knocked her down before Joshua rescued her. Within a few moments, BJ realized from the wagging tail and the whimpering sounds that issued from the dog's mouth that he wasn't vicious but only lonely from being shut up in the apartment all day.

"Wait," she said when Josh pulled him away by the collar around the dog's neck. "It's all right. He only wants to play."

"No!" Josh yelled, "don't touch him," when her hand came out and rested on the dog's nose.

"That's a nice puppy," BJ cooed to the huge dog, and the animal rewarded her by licking her hand. "See? What did I tell you? He wants to be friends."

Josh loosened his hold on the dog's collar and sounded bewildered when he said, "But he's been especially trained as a guard dog. He's never friendly."

"Nonsense," BJ said. "He's just a lovable puppy. Who told you he was a guard dog?" She hunched down to hug the Saint Bernard, and he rolled over and presented his underbelly to be rubbed.

"The crook who sold him to me," Joshua muttered, looking askance with both arms akimbo.

"What's his name?"

"I don't remember, but as soon as I find out, I'll sue him."

"You don't remember the dog's name?"

"No, it's the crook who sold me the dog whose name

has escaped me." He scowled at her. "The dog's name is Hannibal."

"Hannibal?"

She wanted to laugh, but Joshua looked so annoyed that she didn't want to aggravate him any more than he already was.

Josh had the grace to shrug, and his beautiful mouth turned up with a rueful smile. "Well," he said, shaking his head at Hannibal, "Obviously the dog has excellent taste in women."

She allowed herself a small smile at that little sally.

He took her coat and hung it in a large closet. All of this had happened in a foyer that could hold almost her entire apartment. They stepped into a huge room with high ceilings and wide windows that took up an entire wall. Sunshine poured through the blinds, which were the only thing covering the windows.

Joshua pointed to the wooden frame with a futon that served as a couch. It was accented with large pillows. "Wait here and I'll change."

She sat on the low couch and glanced around.

He went into another room, leaving her with the Saint Bernard. BJ gazed around the apartment. Except for it being a luxury condo, it looked like the type of place where students on limited budgets lived. She assumed he had been there for a short time. Undecorated, she thought, was an understatement. However, it was large and roomy and would be charming once it was fixed.

Aside from the low couch, there was a desk with all the accoutrements, including computer. Off to the side was a work area with a table topped by a dust cover. She couldn't resist a little peek under the covering. Underneath was an extensive model of a multiple-apartment complex that was quite attractive and caught her eye. She walked around the display, examining it carefully. She was surprised at the detail. It was a work of art.

Her nosiness didn't stop there but carried her into the kitchen, which she found empty. Hannibal followed her every step, pushing his cold wet nose into her hand whenever he could. She quietly opened the fridge. It was bare, except for a piece of cheese that looked suspiciously aged and a box of stale crackers. Obviously Josh ate out a lot, probably with gorgeous singers or maybe with Linda.

"Tsk." She sucked her teeth disgustedly. "He'd better beware of ptomaine poisoning," she muttered under her breath.

"You say something?" Josh's voice was very close.

She jumped, not realizing that he'd come in so quietly and caught her going through his kitchen cabinets. Thank God, she thought, there's so little to nose around in here or I'd have been really embarrassed.

"Oh, no. I was just . . ." she said.

"Looking around," he finished and glanced around himself. "Place needs a lot of help, right?"

"It's a great apartment. Though you're right, it could use a little work."

He shrugged. "I'm afraid it's got low priority now. No telling how long before I can furnish it."

"How long have you been here?"

"Over a year," he said, shaking his head.

His admission surprised her. She found the apartment cold and uninviting and wondered how he managed to live there with things as they were. No wonder he ate out so much.

She glanced at his clothes, which appeared even more elegant than the first outfit. Lord, this man sure paid a lot of attention, not to mention money, on what he wore.

"Everything all right?" Josh asked, catching her in the act of checking him out.

"Oh, sure. Everything's fine." She quickly looked away from his sartorial splendor. "I couldn't help admire that model." She pointed toward the table. "It must have taken a long time to finish, and it's so detailed."

Joshua appeared as if he wanted to speak but then thought better of it and said, "Thank you."

"I don't recognize it though. Is it something you've done out of town?"

"No, it's a plan for something I'd like to build in the future."

"Really nice," she said.

"Glad you like it." He glanced at his watch. "We'd better get started."

He held her coat, and she turned to put her arms into the sleeves. She'd stepped back too far and bumped into him. Lord, she thought, am I ever going to stop doing pratfalls when this man is near? His hands came out to catch her. He turned her to face him, and his mouth loomed close.

His lips touched hers lightly, then suddenly he deepened the contact. She had no question of what he wanted. An instant inner heat sprang up in response to his touch.

It wasn't as if they'd never kissed, plus hadn't that been all she'd been thinking of all morning? But she knew this time was different. She found herself wondering if his sparse furniture included a bed. And surprisingly she wasn't thinking of his DNA.

When he drew her near to him, she went willingly. They were fully clothed, and it shouldn't have mattered that they were standing so close, but it did.

He moved back and watched her. His eyes had become molten smoky pools again. They beckoned to her with an invitation she desperately wanted to accept. A hunger flared up from deep within her.

"You're a very potent lady," he said in a slightly roughened voice.

It brought her to her senses. Knowing she had to stop this before she was totally captured, she reluctantly stepped back. Maybe she should have run, but it was the best she could manage.

"I guess we'd better go," she said.

Joshua stepped back and held up her coat. She suspected by his stance that he was annoyed and suffering some male frustration.

She couldn't blame him. Her own frustration levels were sky high. Plus she was sure that she was sending out double messages. One said how much she wanted him, while the other message said wait, not now. She had to be sure.

She couldn't allow her own physical desire to cloud her vision. There was more involved than a momentary sexual thrill.

Although she couldn't keep herself from wanting Josh, she tried to put her thoughts together. She wanted to do the right thing and not take a serious step on her emotions only. By the time they had reached the building's underground parking lot, she had managed to still her anxieties.

"Is there something wrong with what I'm wearing?" Josh said, catching her checking out his outfit again.

"No, you look very nice. You certainly do like to be well dressed, don't you?"

"A man's appearance is important." A short time later, glimpsing her staring again, he said, "Out with it.

"I told you there was nothing wrong."

"Then why are you staring?"

"It's just that you're very dressed up."

"You said that already. And—?" he encouraged.

"Well, I guess I expected a hard hat."

"Hard hat? I'm not going to work on the site today. And if Lucy doesn't agree with my proposal, I may never work on-site. Today you're going to show me around and maybe introduce me to some of the neighbors, right?"

"Yes," she agreed but thought: I bet he'd look absolutely gorgeous in jeans and a hard hat.

"You like hard hats?" he asked, and she jumped, feeling as if he'd read her mind.

"Yeah," she tried to sound disinterested. "I guess so."

After that she caught him glancing at himself in the mirror. She wanted to smile at the signs of piqued male vanity. But more than that, she wished he'd kiss her again.

Manhattan's traffic en route to the Triboro Bridge was heavier than it had been when they'd come over from the Queens side. Soon they were completely tangled in the snarled mess of vehicles with blaring horns.

They came to a complete stall on the bridge, and while they waited they were accosted several times by people panhandling. Joshua became increasingly more impatient with the delay. It was quite noticeable as usually Josh seemed fairly good natured.

"We probably should have taken the bus or subway," she said to distract him.

"I never take public transportation if I can avoid it."

Excuse me, she thought. She was still basking in the glow of his kiss, while he obviously had moved on. She gazed out the passenger window.

One young freckled-faced man whose red, running nose looked terribly painful tried to convince Joshua to buy a single rose. Joshua waved him away abruptly.

Another man came to her side and tapped on the window. He was quite dirty and disheveled. In one hand he held a small squeegee and gestured as if he wanted to wash the window. The sudden tapping startled her. He had his hand out, looking for money.

Once she'd realized what he wanted, she pressed the button, rolling down the window. She patted her pockets for change. Finding nothing, she opened her purse to search for coins. Suddenly Joshua reached across her.

"Get out of here!" Joshua shouted at the man.

It was almost as if he wanted to push the man away. She suspected that if he hadn't been hampered by his seat belt, he'd have done just that. Josh's behavior caught her totally unprepared. She'd only known him for such a short time, but somehow she'd thought him mild and tolerant. This angry, surly man was someone she didn't recognize.

BJ stopped him. "Please. I'd rather give him the change, if you don't mind."

"I do mind," Joshua said in tight-lipped fury. "He probably makes more than you do."

"Maybe he does, but . . ." BJ admitted as she clutched a few coins close to her chest.

She stared in shock at Joshua. Instinctively she had drawn away from him as had the beggar. Josh's smooth caramel coloring had turned red across his nose and cheeks. Those beautiful brilliant brown eyes that were so mesmerizing now blazed with a rage that seemed palpable.

Joshua glanced down at where she clutched the money to her breast, and he turned to put his hands back on the steering wheel.

"Go on if you insist!" he said.

She turned and pushed the money at the beggar. She gave the man more than she wanted because she felt rushed by Joshua's displeasure. As soon as her hand was free of the window, Josh closed the window, using the button on his side.

"Thank ye, sister," the man said, bobbing his head as the window swooshed upward. With a glance at Joshua, who sat glaring straight ahead, the man was quickly off.

"Would you do the same thing if you were alone on the street? Leave yourself completely vulnerable? What if he should attack you?" His anger flared higher as if it fed upon itself. His whole demeanor had changed. "It's not a smart move to stop and open your purse for beggars."

She actually agreed with him but hated to admit it. "I feel that if something should ever happen to me, I could be in the same position. I try to be as generous as I can," she said.

"That doesn't help them. Most of them have substance abuse problems to begin with, and I seriously doubt he's going to buy any food with your money."

"I'm aware of that," she said, feeling guilty somehow for an effort that she had meant to be kind. It soured her mood incredibly. The dreamy haze that his kiss caused had evaporated quickly.

"So you're enabling him. Is that what you wanted to do?"

"He looked hungry," she snapped in defense. She was fed up with people who didn't understand about the homeless. "And at least he offered to work for the money."

"What, by messing up my windshield? You could donate to a charity that deals with this sort of thing. Giving him money only encourages him to bother people in the street."

It wasn't that BJ didn't agree with him, it was the intensity of Josh's anger that frightened her.

Somehow Josh seemed to work at controlling his anger. The red flush faded, leaving the beautiful caramel color. He took a deep breath. He evidently now simmered at a lower heat. When the car ahead of them moved, he changed gears and followed.

"Do you do this sort of thing regularly?" Joshua asked in a calmer voice.

"I guess I believe in the dignity of the human spirit." She was miffed and didn't try to hide it.

"You saw something dignified about him panhandling you? It's a dangerous practice. How can you be sure he wouldn't grab your purse?"

"I can't. But I can't help feeling sorry for him. Maybe you can't understand, but this is a harsh city for the poor and homeless. In the winter, it turns deadly."

"And you think you understand better than me? Make no mistake, wherever he lived, he'd be expected to support himself."

"Don't you have any sympathy at all?" BJ asked.

"Why should I? They're idle and dangerous. I feel sorry for the women and children but not for an able-bodied man who needs to get a job."

BJ actually thought she could hear his teeth grinding. This was very definitely another facet of Joshua Hendricks.

Chapter Seven

They were both silent after that. The air was so tense, she wondered why it didn't crackle. Thirty minutes later, BJ was glad when the car stopped in front of Three Ashley Place. She quickly unbuckled, planning a hasty retreat from this new Joshua Hendricks—a man capable of raw fury.

Before she could get away completely, he'd captured her hand, effectively halting her escape.

"I'm sorry about what happened back there," he said.

Somehow she didn't think he was truly sorry but rather that he regretted her witnessing his anger. She nodded and got out.

Although the apology made her feel better toward him, nothing could change the fact that she'd learned something about Joshua Hendricks that day. She'd made a big mistake before in her estimation of him. She'd been fooled by his soft eyes, good-natured smiles, but mostly by his willingness to listen patiently to her stories. He had seemed such a pussycat.

He was anything but.

She'd forgotten that he was a successful businessman and nobody's pushover. She had judged him as a gorgeous flirt and something of a clotheshorse, but he was also a brilliant man—and dangerous.

Outside the car they both stood together for a few moments, looking at Ashley Place. The site was an old dilapidated area that had seen better days. It was one block tucked into a neighborhood that had been carefully manicured and maintained since the early part of the century. And although there were parts of the area that had not been continuously kept up, most of that had been gentrified during the last decade. But when the winds of change came, Ashley Place had been passed over.

Three Ashley Place, which stood near the corner, was an old rambling building built in a mock Tudor style. Paint peeled in some spots. You could see it had been a grand dwelling once but no longer. Neglect was responsible for most of the damage. The building had been divided into a multi-dwelling at some point in history. BJ had always wondered how the owner had gotten the zoning board to agree to this.

She glanced surreptitiously at Josh's face, wondering what he thought of the place. He stared at the old building with narrowed eyes. He looked distanced, perhaps even condemning.

An unwelcome thought crept into her mind. Suppose Joshua's response to the old crumbling house was the same rejection he'd shown to the beggar. It made a shiver go up her spine. She felt a traitor for bringing him here. She wanted to delay their visit inside. She took his arm to lead him away from the old building.

"Why don't we do the nearby towns first?" she said. It came out sounding hasty and garbled. "That way we can come back here and see it in comparison with its neighbors."

He stared down at where she clutched his arm and then up to her face.

"If you like," he answered coolly.

They did a tour of the territory, including looking at a development some blocks away, which had been built some years ago. BJ didn't think much of it. The builders had pulled down several older houses and replaced them with a moderate-sized apartment complex.

"I never liked these houses. They're too bland and without character."

"But the plumbing works, right?" He sounded slightly sarcastic.

She didn't say anything more but decided to talk about the history of the area, which she had learned by research.

"A lot of famous people have lived in this area."

"I remember your telling me before," he answered.

"Yes. Well, I suppose you do know all about that."

His lack of enthusiasm made her wonder why he was doing this. Several times, she'd been tempted to ask. But she comforted herself by remembering the work he'd done at other parts of the city where he'd carefully restored lovely old architectural marvels.

At the last, she even took him to a really rundown area in South Jamaica, hoping he'd see Ashley Place in a better light by comparison.

However, stall as she might, there was no way she could keep him away forever, and the time came when they were once again on the site.

Joshua parked at the other end of the street this time, and they got out to walk and look at the housing there. In the middle of the block, they passed a vacant lot. There were the remains of the garden that she had helped plant. She stopped to look.

Although the neighbors might have given up on the street, the tenants of Three Ashley Place had not. BJ remembered how, last spring, she had loved helping them

with the flowers. Much of the heavy work had been done
by BJ or one of the tenants' grandson. She had volunteered
several weekends, but it had been well worth it when the
area was a wealth of magnificent color. It looked bedrag-
gled in the winter, with residues of snow covering the
ground. The trees stood with stark, eerily twisted black
branches under a gray laden sky. Dry brown leaves littered
the lawns. The flowers were dead, their twisted stalks lying
flat on the ground. Josh stood at her side.

"Ah, this is the garden you helped plant last spring?"

BJ glanced at him before turning back to gaze at the
plot for a few moments. She'd almost forgotten telling
him. "You should have seen it in full bloom—before the
winter started. It was beautiful. It looks so scraggly now."

"Maybe its time has come."

That was not what she wanted to hear. She looked
around at the block, wondering if the time had come for
the whole street.

Three Ashley Place was a site where BJ had several clients.
Most of the tenants were elderly retired theater people
who'd made it their home many years before. She had
become quite fond of them, and perhaps Lucy was right.
Perhaps she had grown so close that she couldn't see them
clearly anymore.

The old building had seen better days and was more
neglected than ever in the last year or so. It seemed to
have been abandoned by its absentee landlord.

As well as this building there were five smaller houses
that all seemed to be in the same sad state. It was as if the
dwellings on that one street had been blighted with the
same economic slide into disrepair. You only had to look
across the street to see other houses that looked stable and
prosperous.

BJ knew the surrounding residents looked askance at
the block, and you couldn't really blame them. The tract
had to bring property values down.

Not only the opposite street looked better, but the whole neighborhood was in appreciably better shape than Ashley Place was. The vicinity had a variety of large, gracious, one-family homes that had been beautifully maintained. Houses that during the real-estate boom sold for hundreds of thousands. Ashley Place was the stepchild of the region.

BJ was still worried about Joshua's opinion and glanced nervously at him. She was relieved to see that he was no longer as tight-lipped as he'd been about the beggar.

She wanted this renovation project to work, and she tried to imagine what obstacles could stand in the way. There had been talk years ago of tearing down the whole street. She feared the hardship that would cause her elderly clients. Renovating was the perfect answer.

Joshua would be a great person to do this, she reminded herself, remembering his previous work. And as for his reaction to the beggar, that didn't have anything to do with Ashley Place. Her fearing that there could be a connection was just her imagination.

After all, just looking at Josh, you could see he came from a privileged background. Chances were he'd had very little contact with street people.

"All the buildings need on the outside is a little paint," she began. "A facelift."

"More like a few tons of siding," he corrected.

"Well, maybe the painting would work inside."

"After a mountain of dry wall," he said quietly.

Her prolonged spiel about all the wonderful things she could envision for the block was apparently not impressing him. For everything she said, Josh seemed   have a contradiction. But instead of his statements stopping the verbal rambling that she'd started, she talked even faster. She was afraid of what he was going to say next.

As they neared the corner, they both spied Linda Collins, his assistant. She was talking with two men. One of the men had begun to set up what appeared to be surveying equipment, while the other waited. Josh's longer legs sped up. The three turned as he approached.

"Why are you doing this today?" Josh asked the men. BJ sensed his displeasure.

The men looked at each other and then at Linda, who smiled and moved to speak. "I thought you wanted all of us to be here."

Josh's voice was cool, but BJ sensed undercurrents when he said, "No, I asked *you* to meet me here, not the crew. No one is to be here until all the paperwork is finished."

"But we're losing so much time. Spring is almost here, and we need to move on this."

"Let me worry about that," Josh said. BJ was becoming more curious the longer they talked. Josh soon put an end to the conversation by saying to BJ, "You know Linda, and these men are a part of Hendricks Development Corporation."

BJ smiled at Linda but felt a certain coolness in the other woman's reception. Josh then excused himself, going to speak with the two men where they worked to pack up their equipment.

It left BJ and Linda standing alone. Linda turned to look down at Josh's pants, reminding BJ that Josh had changed. BJ was suddenly rattled, wondering what implication Linda would assume. Although BJ knew there was no reason for her to be uncomfortable, she found herself wishing none of it had happened.

When Linda's blue eyes turned back to BJ, they were sharp and her mouth had tightened.

"No wonder it took so long for you two to get here. You made a little stop."

"Josh stopped to change after he got coffee spilled on his clothes."

"Another spill? Really?" Linda said with raised eyebrows. The woman's mouth now tightened to a hard thin line.

BJ chafed under Linda's attitude but worked not to show it. She had nothing to be embarrassed about.

"Joshua and I go back a long way," Linda said. "We went to school together. And, of course, we've always worked well together. That's because we understand each other perfectly."

Now it was BJ's turn to say, "Really?"

But her mind churned. Exactly what was Linda saying? Did the phrase "understand each other" mean they had an understanding? The terms had different connotations. Was there something besides a working relationship and friendship between Josh and his assistant?

She remembered the scene in the gym the night they'd played basketball. He's been quite definitely in the mood for intimacy. Right from the first, she'd known he was flirting with her. Surely Linda Collins had noticed, too. Why hadn't the woman said something at the beginning? But BJ also knew that just because Josh wanted to take her to bed didn't mean he wasn't involved with someone else.

BJ had always disliked men who flirted when their girl-friends could see it. It was so crass. Somehow it didn't seem like something the very smooth Joshua would do. But who knew?

"When we were in school, we used to sleep in the same dorm and spent so much time together." Linda's voice implied that they slept together.

None of this made sense, BJ thought. If he and Linda were together, why was he pursuing me? Did he have an ulterior motive here? The next time Linda spoke, BJ almost felt as if the woman was psychic, so perfectly did she appear to read BJ's mind.

"Sometimes I think Joshua will do anything to get some-thing he wants—like a building permit." BJ stared at Lin-da's smirk as the woman's soft voice, like a dagger, went straight to her brain.

Linda's words started BJ to wonder. Was he trying to

use her to get to Lucy? What other reason could there be for his calling her? She knew that Joshua found her physically attractive, but he could have other reasons, too.

She certainly didn't believe it was about his ruined shirt. He seemed to forget about that most of the time. And now there was a second shirt, when she'd never paid for the first one.

Suddenly BJ wanted nothing more than to escape from Linda's presence. The woman made her uncomfortable.

When Joshua returned, BJ had ambivalent thoughts. She was glad to have him interrupt the talk with Linda, but she found herself watching him with new questions in her mind. She didn't have a chance to ask him anything because Saint Albans was nothing if it wasn't also like a collection of small towns. Each block functioned like an insulated cell of the town.

Despite the cold weather, a small curious group of residents had formed. The people had seen the men with the surveying equipment. A group of two older men and several younger women were approaching. Both the older men and one of the young women were her clients and greeted her before launching questions at Joshua.

"Hello, there," Mr. Green, an older man who was a tenant of Three Ashley, said. After he shook hands, he addressed Joshua. "We see you're checking out this old street. Glad to see someone's finally going to fix it up."

One of the women spoke. "This block is such an eyesore. No one will miss it, that's for sure."

"I read about it in the *Law Registry,*" the older elderly man said. "That's a Long Island paper. You don't see it much in Queens."

That surprised BJ, as she hadn't heard anything until Lucy's party. How long had this been going on, she wondered. It just went to show, she was definitely getting out of touch with things.

"Gee," Linda cut in. "It must be nice to have so much

time on your hands that you can indulge in reading such periodicals."

Linda's mildly condescending remark caused a short pause in the talk. It wasn't such an important thing, but it sort of implied the people didn't work. A fact Linda couldn't know for sure. Besides, Linda obviously hadn't really paid much attention to the group.

The men looked to be past the retirement age, while the women looked like young housewives. It was even possible that they were night workers. Still, no one responded to Linda's words, and the talk continued.

It was too cold to remain still for any length of time. When BJ began to hunch up and move from one foot to the other, Josh stopped the talk, saying, "Before anything will be done to your street, there will be a meeting with the community."

Then to BJ, he said, "Let's get you out of the cold."

They went inside. There was no light in the small hallway. Coming in out of the bright sunshine, she was suddenly blinded in the darkened area. Josh, the consummate builder, took a flashlight out of one pocket of his dark wool overcoat.

"How many vacant apartments are there?" he asked.

"Two, I think," she replied, watching him check the door frames of the apartments on the first floor. He turned both knobs, finding them locked but rickety.

"Both on the first floor?"

She realized he knew more than she'd thought, and if he knew so much, she wondered, why was he asking her? When he'd finished, BJ started for the stairs, but he stopped her.

"I want to look at the basement."

"Oh." She thought briefly of mice.

She wasn't exactly dying to see that area of the house. Reluctantly she went with him down the rickety stairs.

He looked upward, turning his flashlight on the ceiling

and then started slowly walking around the cold, damp concrete walls. She followed behind him as he walked and he began to check various things such as the wiring in the ceiling. She checked everything along with him and felt foolish because she had no idea how to remedy most of the old building's problems.

Once or twice he shook his head ruefully at some particularly shabby section. She was annoyed at his implied disapproval. BJ had quickly become fond of the people of Three Ashley Place and resented any criticism of them, no matter how small. Finally she had to speak.

"It's hard living on fixed incomes. . . ." She stopped lamely when he turned to watch her.

"Yes?" he encouraged.

"Well, they do the best they can."

At that moment, Linda's voice came from the top of the stairs. "Josh, can you come up to look at this invoice? And don't forget the time," Linda reminded with a sour glance in BJ's direction. "You also have that appointment."

Time! BJ glanced at her watch and realized she'd spent the whole day schmoozing up with Joshua in something that really wasn't her business. And although Cody had agreed to her taking Josh on a tour, he hadn't given her a holiday. She carried a heavy caseload and certainly couldn't spare the whole day away from her work!

They returned to the first floor, where Linda waited. Linda took a folder from the briefcase she carried and handed it toward Josh. However, Josh was still in his builder's mode. He knocked at a wall, and BJ heard what sounded like plaster rattle loose and fall behind the wall.

While Josh's back was turned to the two women, Linda watched BJ with hardened eyes. The look the other woman gave her made BJ think of the old saying: "If looks could kill . . ."

BJ almost squirmed under the other woman's cold stare.

Besides, she had already witnessed as much as she could tolerate of the old building's falling apart.

"I'm going up to apartment four," BJ said in a rush.

At her words, Josh turned and appeared puzzled by her haste. She fled up the steps.

Going up the stairs, BJ thought about what had happened that morning. The day had been a disappointment. She was sorry that she'd let Lucy convince her to do this. There were huge differences between her philosophy and Josh's. He'd actually referred to her as an enabler. And look at the way he dressed. Walking down the street with him, she wondered if people thought she was his maid or something. She glanced down at herself—*well, maybe his secretary. At least I don't have on my sweats today.*

Look at how differently they'd reacted to the beggar. True, she shouldn't have let the man panhandle her like that, but she knew he'd needed help. Josh's first thoughts were that the man should get a job.

She stopped at apartment four and tapped lightly.

And then Linda—BJ's thoughts continued as she waited for a response—was Josh involved with Linda? Linda had certainly implied that he was. But for some crazy reason, she didn't believe it.

There was an aura about Linda that left BJ particularly unsettled. Something seemed false, as if the woman were hiding something.

True, there was the fact that BJ felt slightly snubbed on the two times that she'd met Linda, but it was more than that. BJ believed herself a relatively good judge of character, no matter what Josh insinuated. *I'm just jealous because she's so gorgeous.* However, BJ sensed it was more than that. Outside, BJ had felt that Linda was deliberately abrasive to the residents of Ashley Place, and why would she do that?

If it wasn't fairly obvious that Linda found Joshua attractive, BJ would have thought the blond woman was trying to sabotage the plan to rebuild Ashley Place. It was such a strange feeling that BJ shook her head as if to dislodge the thought. It had been a day for strange thoughts, she chided herself.

Before BJ could knock on the door to apartment number four again, a querulous older woman asked, "Who is it?"

BJ recognized Adella St. John's voice.

"It's me, Mrs. St. John. BJ Jones from the VanderWeil Foundation."

BJ heard the lock turn, followed by the door opening a small crack. Adella St. John peered closely at BJ, with the chain lock still in place.

"Oh, shoot!" Adella slapped her leg in annoyance.

She opened and allowed BJ to enter. She was an elderly woman with a beige complexion that carried the wrinkles of her eighty plus years well. Her hair was curly and white, pinned up into an elaborate french roll. Despite the straying tendrils, it was attractive on her. You could see that she'd once been a beauty. She wore colorful polyester lounging pajamas.

"You just missed him," Adella said as she grabbed for BJ's arm and dragged her into the apartment.

"Who?" BJ said as she flipped through her notebook for a clean page.

Actually she didn't pay much attention to Adella, having had many such conversations with the woman.

"Nathan, my grandson. Who'd you think? And how many times have I told you to call me Adella? Mrs. St. John is an old woman, which I am not."

"Oh, sorry," BJ said, finding a clean page and collecting her pen.

Ever since Adella had been her client, the older woman had been trying to match her up with a grandson. Anyone could see that Adella doted upon this grandson. It was the same old story as far as BJ was concerned—another person trying to hook her up. Since nothing ever came of it, BJ had dubbed Adella as harmless and chose to overlook the older woman's efforts. BJ sighed.

Indeed, it wasn't flattering that the whole world seemed to believe she couldn't find her own man. BJ didn't linger on this thought today because now she was considering other solutions to her life-style.

"I just can't get you two together," Adella fussed. "But I will, you'll see."

"Yes," BJ said, absently looking around.

BJ listened to Adella with only half her attention. She knew by experience that it would take a while for the older woman to settle down and talk about her current needs. The woman seemed to prefer treating BJ as if she were a guest rather than a social worker.

"Let's have a cup of tea," Adella said and bustled into the kitchen to prepare it.

Adella served the tea in an old-fashioned silver tea set, and they settled down to talk. The older woman was usually eager for company, and she loved to talk about her past. Today she brought out a box full of yellowed, old playbills and photographs. Together on the couch, they went through the papers.

BJ picked up one picture where a distinguished middle-aged man posed formally.

"That's my first husband, Harold. Now he was a fine gent. He ran a troupe of dancers and singers. I went to Paris with him. He was older than me." Adella gazed fondly at the picture of the older man. Girlishly, Adella twittered, "Harold doted on me."

Next Adella passed a battered shot of a young service-man. It had a signature and was followed by the year 1952. "That was Nathan, my second husband." Adella sighed. "We weren't married long. He died in a war that wasn't supposed to be a war. Korea. He was younger than me but we had our fun nevertheless. Handsome, right?"

"Yes, he is," BJ agreed, looking carefully at the picture before passing it back.

"He was Nathan's grandfather. I had only one child, and he was the father. Nathan looks just like him. Now this handsome gent here is Henry, husband number three. He was my last husband and the love of my life, too."

BJ looked closer at the old faded photograph. Adella was wearing black, both dress and hat. The hat was a large picture hat with a black veil.

"You look very elegant," BJ remarked.

"I always loved to dress, you know. And look at that hat. I still have it packed in my old steamer trunk. Wasn't I about as fine as I could be?"

"You certainly were," BJ said, laughing with Adella.

"You're lucky to have such things," BJ said. "These are rare collectibles now."

"Lord, you got to be kidding. These old things?" Adella laughed. "Well, if that's true, then the tenants of this house are wealthy."

BJ laughed. "Oh, yes?"

"That's right. I ain't kidding. Everyone in this house was in the theater many years back. There's trunks of this stuff in every apartment and even some locked away in storage down in the basement."

"Oh, no. Not the basement. They could be ruined," BJ said.

After BJ had looked at the pictures, Adella seemed loath to put them away. She sat and held them in her lap. BJ took a chance and tried to open the talk on Adella's life in the present.

"Do you have enough food till the end of the month?" BJ asked.

"I've got plenty of food," the older woman said with a bit of haughty elegance. "I've been feeding myself for many years, and I still have a good figure, too, if I do say so myself—even though I'm over seventy. I'm not a bag of bones, the way some of you young things are. I'm what you call voluptuous.''

The older woman had forgotten that BJ knew her date of birth from their records. Adella St. John wouldn't see seventy again, not in this lifetime. She was over eighty and still sprightly.

BJ sighed. It was nearly impossible to keep the woman on the subject, and usually when she became evasive, it was because she'd been playing lotto again. Adella could be exasperating. However, BJ didn't allow herself to become annoyed with Adella. The elderly woman's biggest flaw was her pride, which was in the end why she didn't always cooperate.

Despite an occasional touch of forgetfulness, and a more frequently seen tendency to spend much of her Social Security check playing the illegal numbers, Adella was one of BJ's more stabilized clients.

"Adella, please answer my questions. I don't want to think of you here not having enough food . . .''

"I already told you that I have plenty of food.''

BJ let it go, realizing that her own concentration was straying today, and it was all due to Joshua. Her thoughts kept straying to the fact that Joshua Hendricks had been with her all morning, and she still didn't have a clue as to what she was supposed to be doing. She was also annoyed about the conversation she'd had with Linda. They both knew more about the area than Josh had led her to believe.

A knock came on the door.

"Who's that?'' Adella demanded.

"Joshua Hendricks,'' was the answer.

"I'll get it.'' BJ went to the door.

"Why did you leave?'' Joshua asked when she let him in.

"I thought you had an appointment.''

"Later," he said as something caught his attention from behind her.

BJ turned to find Adella standing there, looking suspicious.

"Who are you?" Adella asked, frowning and looking askance at Joshua. "I hope you don't have designs on BJ here because she's almost engaged to my grandson. They don't need no dog in the manger."

"Adella!" BJ almost shrieked, wishing she could go through the floor. "This is Joshua Hendricks, a builder who's going to renovate Ashley Place."

"Renovate? I ain't heard nothing about no renovate."

BJ made a sign to Joshua, trying to convey that Adella wasn't always on target. She was also eager to explain that Adella was wrong when she'd said that BJ was engaged. Joshua didn't seem to be paying her any attention though. He probably couldn't have cared less.

"Madam," he said bending over Adella's hand, "enchanted."

"Oh, a charmer—good looking, too," Adella twittered. The older woman softened immediately. She took Josh's arm and led him into her living room. "Honey, you just come over here and sit so's we can talk."

Adella sat on a love seat and patted the cushion next to her. Joshua smiled broadly, lapping up Adella's outrageous flirtations. Already BJ felt dismissed as Adella turned the full megawatt of her smiles on Josh.

When Adella looked up at BJ, it was to say, "BJ, you sit over there," indicating a lumpy chair some distance away. However, just as BJ got comfortable, Adella leaned over and patted Joshua's hand. "Let me get you a drink."

"I'll bring another cup," BJ offered.

"No tea," the older woman admonished. "BJ, bring this handsome devil a beer."

Beer, BJ thought, as she went into the small kitchen. And she'd always thought that Adella was very hospitable to *her,* but obviously handsome men rated the royal treatment.

"Not that I wanted a beer," BJ muttered under her breath, as she puttered about in the tiny area. "But you'd think she would at least have offered."

Chapter Eight

What a flirt Adella is, and Joshua is no better. Look at him, preening for all he's worth. And since when does Adella have me fetching things around here?

It was the second time that day that BJ had gone into someone else's kitchen. And this time, same as the last, found her nosing around in the cabinets. Adella was right, there was enough food there. And no cat food, either, thank heavens. BJ had heard stories from other caseworkers about finding cat food in the homes of elderly clients who didn't own pets.

She found two bottles of beer in the refrigerator and took one to the living room. With Joshua there, they sat listening to Adella for a longer time than BJ had planned. Josh, who was the best listener that she'd ever come across, seemed mesmerized by the stories of the old black theater.

At one lull, BJ volunteered to make another pot of tea with Adella's consent. Joshua refused another beer but agreed to tea also.

BJ was in the kitchen again getting ready to fill the teapot

from the sink when Adella warned from the living room,
"Be careful of that faucet. The pipe underneath leaks. I
have a bucket to collect the runoff. Make sure it's not filled
to the brim."

BJ opened the cabinet doors to look under the sink and
was appalled at what she saw. She was standing there gaping
when Joshua came into the kitchen.

"Let me take a look at that," he said.

After pulling up his very fancy overcoat and rearranging
the crease in his pants, Joshua hunched down. He sat
agilely on the back of his heels to stare long and hard at
the sight there. He glanced quickly at BJ, then turned back
to scowl at the eroded plumbing.

There was a nearly filled bucket under the pipe, but it
wasn't to catch water from a mere leak. The pipe that ran
from the sink was not connected to anything but hung
free. If there had been no bucket, the water would have
flown freely into the cabinet and then to the floor.

Joshua stood up and pulled out the bucket. To empty
the contents, Adella directed him to the bathroom. When
he returned the pail, he looked exasperated.

Before seeing Joshua's expression, BJ had been feeling
sympathetic. Adella was a proud woman and a survivor.
The woman's efforts were pathetic, but somehow they
worked. It was so sad that BJ almost wanted to cry. That
single glance at Joshua made her compose herself. She
didn't feel like hearing him accuse her of being an enabler
or worse.

Like her, now that he was in the kitchen, he also nosed
around. But he wasn't interested in the contents of the
cabinets. Instead he examined the pipes behind the stove
and opened the oven to look inside. He inspected the
window sashes and tested the chains and locks. All the
time, he whistled tunelessly between his teeth.

"What are you two doing in there?" Adella queried from
the living room?

"Coming right now," BJ said, trying to get Joshua to follow. He waved her through as he continued, this time sitting on his heels to minutely examine the radiator valve. The man missed nothing.

BJ carried the tea, glancing backward and deliberately clearing her throat to remind Josh to follow. He seemed to take a long time, but BJ knew that was just her imagination.

"What's he doing?" Adella asked.

"Just checking," BJ answered, wishing Joshua would mind his own business and come out of Adella's kitchen. "I guess he's checking on what needs refurbishing."

"I ain't heard nothing about no refurbishing. Maybe tearing everything down but no refurbishing." Then Adella leaned toward her and whispered, "Is he from the first company or the second one?"

"What second company?" BJ asked.

"Shhh," Adella hissed just as Joshua came out, wiping his hands on a blinding white handkerchief.

"Adella, how would you like to have that sink fixed?" Joshua said on entering the living room. "I could have it finished by tonight."

His offer cheered Adella up immediately, BJ noticed. It made BJ feel softhearted, too.

"Oh, can you, dear boy?" Adella said.

"Sure," he answered. "Let me finish what I have to do today. Later I'll pick up a few things and be back this evening. We'll have you back in business in no time."

"Oh, that's wonderful. I can't remember the last time that old sink really worked," the older woman twittered. Then with a smug glance at BJ, added, "I always say it's good to have a man around the house."

BJ wanted to roll her eyes to heaven. Of course she had no doubt that the man Adella meant was the precious grandson. Still, BJ was glad to see Joshua's generosity to the old woman. He'd been strange and harsh with the beggar when a simple no would have sufficed.

The other thing his kindness did was alleviate the feeling that she'd had earlier—that she'd made a huge error in judging his character. In a really good gene pool, there would always be compassion, she thought.

When they left Adella's apartment, Josh offered to drive her back to her office, where she could pick up her own car. She still had a few hours and would have to work double hard to make up for some of the lost time.

"You don't think that woman needs someone to look after her?" Joshua said, when he'd stopped near her car.

"Not now. Maybe later," BJ answered before she became aware that there was more intensity in Josh's attitude than was necessary. "Adella's independent and only needs support like someone to shop and maybe one hot meal a day. Also someone to come in occasionally and clean. I check on her pretty regularly and see how things are going."

"You know she gambles?"

The question came from out of left field. She was quite chagrined. "How did you find that out?"

"She's got her policy slips all over the place. She plays the illegal numbers. How do you know she's not using all her income, or worse, in debt to some shark?"

"Because we talk, and she would tell me if that were true."

"Hah! Like you talked to that panhandler with your purse near an open car window?"

What is wrong with this man, BJ thought. "Don't tell me you think Adella's a big bad purse snatcher?"

"No, I don't think that," he said, sounding peeved. "But I do wonder about her living alone in that derelict building."

"It's not a derelict. Once it's been refurbished, everything will be fine. Besides, Adella has family and friends living near. It would be horrible to separate her from them."

"Why doesn't she move in with them?"

"You don't know how difficult it is for an elderly parent to move in with their children. Besides, the daughter's apartment is too small to accommodate another person. And as long as Adella's independent, why should she? Our foundation helps her maintain herself." Then she said something that told more about herself than she had planned. "I will personally see to it that she continues her independent life-style as long as she's able."

"Very noble of you. Maybe even quixotic? How about bleeding heart?"

"I am not a bleeding heart. Adella enjoys her life as it is."

"But is she safe?"

"Where do you suggest she live? In a nursing home?"

"She needs someone to take care of her."

"That would cost a fortune. Where would she get the money? Not everyone has your advantages." That got his attention. She was sorry that she'd said it, despite his calling her a bleeding heart. She added, feeling a bit lame, "Adella's not helpless."

"Safety is important," he said.

He didn't answer her retort about his advantages. Curiously enough, their voices had remained rigidly conversational during this, but she knew they were both angry.

A pulse jumped at Joshua's throat. He glanced out the window before he spoke again.

"What's this about your being engaged?"

The statement left her disorientated for a few moments before she remembered Adella's lie. "That's Adella's fantasy. She's always trying to hook me up with some grandson."

"Another matchmaker? You're surrounded by them, aren't you?"

This sudden turn in the conversation threw her for a loop, and somehow she resented having to explain to

Joshua. Just because she admired his chromosomes didn't mean she owed him anything.

"Well, I hope the tour has been informative," she said and held her hand out to shake before she escaped.

"It has," Josh said, taking her hand in both of his.

She withdrew, exiting his insulated luxury car and walked hurriedly to her own noisy and frequently unreliable vehicle. The car started after spluttering and wheezing only twice, allowing her to pull away quickly. BJ could see Joshua watch her drive away.

Great DNA or not, the man made her nervous.

Josh watched her drive away like a scalded cat in her eagerness to escape his foul mood. He had to admit the day hadn't turned out well. For one thing, he'd been too keyed up, remembering the last time he'd seen her.

He'd allowed himself to bask in her admiration of his work, that was why. He put the car in gear and moved out. What a fool a man could be when he was chasing a beautiful woman. But was that the only reason? Just chasing a desirable woman?

If that was the full extent of his feelings, why had her being so close to that beggar made him into a raging bull, protecting his territory? He remembered how unafraid she'd been on the basketball court. He wondered if her working out had made her overconfident. The thought made his gut twist.

Joshua knew more than he cared to admit that these streets were dangerous. With the trees and grass, they gave the illusion of safety, but danger came here as much as anyplace. America had changed in the last twenty years.

But if he was going to question today's irrationality, he'd also have to ask why he'd gotten so angry when the old woman had said BJ was engaged to someone else. Or maybe he should ask why he hadn't told her the truth, that he fully intended to raze Three Ashley Place.

The next day, BJ and Darlene went to lunch and from there decided to do a little window shopping. They were standing in front of one store, mooning over the clothes there.

"Let's go in and spend some money," Darlene said. "You need something besides those tank dresses."

"Tent dresses," BJ corrected automatically.

But BJ was getting really tired of defending her wardrobe. She wondered if Darlene was right as she followed her best friend into the rather expensive boutique.

"Oh, before I forget—here," Darlene said, after rummaging through her tote bag and pulling out a paper bag.

"Not another book?" BJ said, glancing at the package dubiously. "I haven't finished the one you gave me for Christmas yet."

"Why not? If it was a love story, you'd have read it twice by now. For heaven's sake, take it." She shoved the book into BJ's hands. "It's not a bomb. That's the same way you act with men. Don't you trust me?"

"Very little. I always keep in mind that you have a one-track mind," BJ responded.

"Tsk." Darlene sucked her teeth. "You should thank your lucky stars that you have me for a friend."

BJ gazed inside the brown paper bag and read the title, *"Using Your Mind Power to Get Your Man in Ten Easy Lessons*— Puleeze!"

"It's a gift. You can't give it back," Darlene insisted when BJ tried to hand it back. "Makes you look ungrateful."

"I *am* ungrateful," BJ said, pushing the book quickly down into Darlene's tote bag. She glanced around guiltily, fearing someone might have seen the title.

"Oh, no," Darlene said, taking the book to push into BJ's purse. As if on second thought, the plump woman extracted the book again. She tore off the wrapping, saying,

"You'd better read this! I bought it out of my house budget. I took food out of my family's mouth to buy it for my best friend. So you'd better read every word. I'll be questioning you."

"Okay, okay. Give it to me," BJ spoke in a whisper as she glanced around again.

"Only if you swear to read it." Darlene voice rose higher as she waved the book in the air and held it away.

"I swear, I'll read the darn thing. Now give it to me."

"Okay," Darlene said, mollified. "I'll take you at your word."

"Lord," BJ grumbled, shoving the book into her bag. "Why couldn't I have tall friends? Short people are such bullies."

"The world needs more short people. We save the rest of you. Look at Napoleon and Alexander the Great. What would the world have done without them? I'll bet even Shaka Zulu was short."

"The world would have lived in peace," BJ answered.

Another tsk from Darlene. A few moments later, Darlene was picking through a table with sexy lingerie when she asked, "Have you thought of what I suggested? About promising yourself to find a husband. This is about mind over matter. If you make up your mind to do something, and commit yourself, you'll accomplish it."

"Yeah, yeah," BJ said, looking at sweaters that were lying on one table.

"It's true. First you need to see it in your mind, and then you can accomplish it."

"How long you think I've been looking for a good man? Since college, that's all. And have I seen one? No!"

"Because you're too picky. Whatever happened to what's-his-name? The politician?"

"Max," BJ answered. "He's too short."

"Height doesn't count. Anyway, you're tall, so why does he need to be also?"

"All he ever did was talk about how many women were after him."

"Women do run after him. He's a catch."

"Let someone else catch whatever it is he's got.

"Do you have to sound so childish? This is serious business." Darlene sniffed.

"The last time I let myself be talked into dating him, he assumed that if he bought me dinner he'd purchased rights to my body, too."

"You could change his bad habits."

"I couldn't care less about him and his bad habits," BJ said.

"If he gets rambunctious, just say no." Darlene sounded so confident as she eyed a minute lace bikini brief against her rounded hips. She made pouty kisses at herself in the mirror.

"Thank you, Nancy Reagan," BJ said.

"Hold still, you've got a flake of pastry on your chin." Darlene retrieved a tissue from her purse and tried to wipe BJ's face.

"Would you stop that?" BJ said, trying to escape Darlene's efforts. "Stop treating me like a kid! Did you ever think you could be taking this motherhood role too hard?"

"I do it because sometimes you're like a big kid," Darlene said in her frustration and watched as BJ wiped her own face.

"I'm not a kid." BJ's voice seemed on the verge of tears. It stopped both of them. Darlene stared in wonder. Then BJ finished, saying, "I'm old enough to be someone's mother."

"All right. I'm sorry," Darlene said.

Although Darlene might have been willing to change the subject, BJ was not finished. Now that the pending tears had passed, BJ had moved on to annoyance. "No way would I ever consider getting involved with someone like Max. I want a man who goes to work during the week and spends his off hours with me. What politician do you know does that?''

''Max is going places, that's why the women are after him,'' Darlene spoke soothingly.

''So let him keep on going. That's not a good enough reason for me. He'd probably keep a harem on the side, anyway. That is, if anyone could get him to commit.''

''So, how about Norman Delaney?''

''You're always pushing him on me.''

''No. Forget about him. He's been divorced for only a year or so.''

''What's wrong with that?'' BJ asked.

''Divorced men are fine, but not Norman. Word around is that he's still recuperating from his ex-wife.''

''You're right,'' BJ agreed. ''He can be boring, too. Last time I went out with him, I fell asleep. But at least he's single. You know how many married men are always trying to hit on me?''

''Ignore them. They can't afford you. Oh, look at that!'' Darlene pointed to a beautiful red dress in a soft woolen fabric. She grabbed it off the rack and held it against BJ. ''Perfect!''

''That? Give me a break. It's too short. I'd freeze to death in this weather.''

''No, you won't. Just stick to cabs and make sure you don't drive that ghastly car of yours when you wear it. And it's red; you look good in red.'' Then Darlene looked slightly doubtful. ''Maybe it's too much like the one you bought last year?''

''I took that back,'' BJ mumbled.

''You took that dress back? No wonder I never saw you wear it. Then you have to buy this one, and don't exchange it, either, when my back is turned and go back to those tent dresses.''

''Tank dresses . . .'' then realizing how Darlene had

tricked her, BJ said, "I mean tent dresses are very comfortable. I don't have to worry about how I sit."

"There's nothing wrong with the way you sit. Here, take it," and she shoved the dress into BJ's overloaded arms. "You can wear it to my dinner party."

"I'll think about it," BJ grumbled, as she tried to sort the items that Darlene had pressed on her.

"Speaking of which, I invited Joshua Hendricks, too."

"What?" BJ yelped.

"You know, that gorgeous builder that we met at Lucy's office party. Oh, by the way, how did that tour go?"

"Okay," BJ said, trying to sound offhanded. She was dying to ask if Joshua had accepted the invitation.

"Did he look interested in getting anything on with you?"

"No!" BJ absolutely refused to talk about the dates with Joshua.

"He's got to be interested. You're probably deliberately turning him off."

BJ tried to keep her mouth shut and not ask the next question, but she couldn't stop the words. "Did Joshua agree to come?"

"Of course he did. No one wants to miss my parties."

"Why do you keep saying party? I thought it was a sit-down dinner for Tiffany."

"That's what I meant," Darlene said, wagging her eyebrows. "He asked about you."

"What did he say?" BJ turned away as if to search through skirts hanging on a nearby rack. She didn't want Darlene to see her face, but her heart felt as if it had jumped into her mouth.

"Just wanted to know if you were coming. That's a good sign."

"Darlene, if this is another of your matchmaking schemes, I'll never forgive you." BJ didn't want to be forced together with Josh. She blurted out, "Anyway, I'm not interested in him. He's too conceited."

"Joshua conceited?" Darlene thought on that for a moment then said, "Of course he is. Any woman not interested in him would have to be deaf, dumb, and blind. It makes sense that if Max gets chased so would a hunk like Joshua. That would make any man conceited."

"Did Lucy put you up to this?" BJ demanded.

Darlene started coughing. "Whatever made you think that?"

"Because the two of you are just alike. And don't think you've fooled me, either. I've noticed that both of you have been billing and cooing at each other since Christmas. Always trying to get me matched up with some guy that's absolutely horrible for me."

"Well, forget it. I've absolutely given up on you. You'll have to find your own man, period. And besides, Joshua Hendricks would be absolutely perfect for you."

"That's not what my clients at Ashley Place say."

"Oh, those old coots. They're trying to match you with their own candidates. Surely you wouldn't take their words when you have me and Lucy to run interference for you?"

"They're not old coots, and they're just trying to be helpful."

"You never say that about me."

"You just want me married with a child because you are."

"True. And I'm right, too. Marriage and children are rewarding, fulfilling responsibilities."

"And you used to be my feminist friend. What happened to you?"

Darlene sifted through a table of neatly folded colorful scarves. Within minutes, she moved on to the next table, leaving the display of scarves all jumbled together. An exasperated salesgirl rolled her eyes as she went to fold the scarves again.

"I'm still a feminist, but sometimes a compromise is the right way to go."

"I can't believe you said that."

"What's wrong with the men I picked for you?"

"Aside from Carlos, whom you had the good sense to marry yourself, they're all duds. Which doesn't surprise me, because all the men in New York are duds when I really think of it."

She was thinking of Joshua Hendricks, a very special New York man. While he might not be a dud, he certainly wasn't a man to fall in love with—no matter that he had moments when he seemed a pussycat. You could get too comfortable with a man like him. He was just the type to break your heart. Fortunately she only admired his genes and was safe from him otherwise. But why did her heart laugh at that statement?

"That's just a childish attitude," Darlene said, interrupting BJ's thoughts.

"I want a man like my dad," BJ said.

"The problem with you is that Basil soured you. You spent too much time waiting for that jerk."

"I agree, and I don't intend to spend another second waiting in a similar situation."

"That wouldn't happen again."

"Darn tooting, my friend," BJ said.

". . . because now you know better," Darlene filled in.

"That's exactly what I'm trying to tell you."

"But you shouldn't give up. If at first you don't succeed, you just have to try and try again."

"It's not my way. You have to start at the beginning with each relationship, and that could take me another hundred years to weed through to a good one."

"More than that," Darlene said cryptically, with a nod of her head, as she glanced out of the corner of her eye at BJ.

"Huh?" BJ wondered if she was missing something.

Darlene said, "It's going to take you even longer than a hundred years, because every time you go out with a guy, the first thing you want to know is how perfect is he. Then you take another year or two to gear up your courage, and then if some other woman hasn't snatched him away, maybe, just maybe, you'll go out with him. And then again, maybe you'll stay home and read a book."

"Don't knock it. At least I know exactly what's going to happen in my books."

"True, but in real life, you have to take chances."

"Not on any New York man."

"What's wrong with New York men? They're the same as men all over the world."

"No, they're not. They want to party all the time, and they want their women to be quiet and obedient."

Actually BJ had no idea whether Josh liked to party, and as for his wanting his women quiet, he certainly kept her blabbing her mouth off. She shook her head.

"Just as I said," Darlene piped in. "Men are the same all over the world."

Chapter Nine

Darlene's dinner was planned for later in the afternoon. It was still early when BJ's car spluttered, sneezed, and lay down to die. She could have spit, until it occurred to her that she could go with Joshua, who was also attending.

Two weeks had passed since she'd taken him to Ashley Place. While they'd had lunch once in the interim, and she had spoken with him several times at the site, she still hadn't adjusted to suddenly seeing him or having him speak over the telephone.

When she called and heard him on his answering machine, it rattled her. His incredibly seductive voice suddenly turned her to Jell-O. She was too flustered to speak and hung up foolishly. She stared at the phone, and it rang suddenly, startling her.

"Hello?" she said.

"Hi." Joshua's sexy tones rumbled into her ear. "I tried to reach you yesterday, but your machine put up one huge ruckus and then hung up on me."

"I guess I should buy another one. Everyone complains," she said.

"Darlene tells me you need a lift tonight. I'd be honored if you went with me."

The man's charm was lethal, she thought. Honored, he'd said. You couldn't fault him for manners.

"Thank you," she answered and they made a time. Then she remembered something that she'd meant to speak of before. "You know, Adella asked me if you were with the first company or the second one."

"A second company?" he asked.

"Yes, it was curious but I didn't take her too seriously. Just thought I should ask. I've learned that Adella doesn't knock herself out to keep her stories correct."

"Like your engagement?" he said softly.

BJ forced a little laugh. It was the first time he'd mentioned this in the last two weeks. She remembered her initial resentment over Josh's attitude. "Adella's trying to marry off her grandson."

"Yes," he replied. "I got that impression. And not only is she trying to marry him off, she's picked you for the bride."

She laughed again, and it sounded false. "You shouldn't listen to Adella, I don't."

"I always listen to what people tell me," he answered.

That was true enough, BJ thought. He certainly listened to every word she said.

He changed the subject with, "No more about Adella and no shop talk. This is Saturday, and we're going to have a great time."

"Yes," she said, forgetting everything in a happy glow.

Several hours later, BJ had just finished making a total mess of her bedroom in her two-and-a-half-room apartment, trying to get dressed. She had tried on everything in her closet, attempting to find the perfect outfit. Darlene had asked them to dress causally, so BJ had been looking for casual but sassy.

The red dress she'd bought at Darlene's suggestion caught her eye, and she tried it on. It fit her to perfection, and she was dying to wear it, but it was definitely not casual enough.

She had decided on a sweater and skirt when the doorbell rang. Leaving the bedroom to answer, she took a quick look in the mirror and felt she looked pretty good.

When she opened the door to Josh, on sight of him, her mind stopped functioning. She could barely breathe.

"Hello," he said.

"Oh," she answered, realizing that she was keeping him at the door. "Come in."

"Are you ready to go?" he asked.

She took a good look at what he was wearing and thought, Oh, no. Look at that outfit. He wore French-cut woolen slacks, a cable knit sweater, and a tweed jacket with leather patches on the sleeve. Okay, so it was more casual than she'd ever seen him before, but she couldn't help wondering if the whole ensemble wouldn't have cost as much as she earned in a month. *If this is dressing casually, I'll eat my hat.*

She looked down at her sweater and skirt. That one glance convinced her to change. She said, "No. I mean, I haven't finished dressing. I just threw this old thing on to answer the door."

Josh watched BJ's gently swinging hips as she left him in the living room. The sight played havoc with his imagination. He put his hands in his pockets and started looking at the original watercolors on the walls.

"How's Hannibal?" BJ called from her bedroom.

Joshua smiled. "That old faker is having the time of his

life. Of course he asked for you only this morning. He
wanted to know when you were coming to visit him."

He heard her chuckle at his sally. "Your dog asked for
me?"

"What can I say? He's got taste."

"Sure, I'll just bet. How's he getting along with his guard
dog duties?"

"Lousy. He doesn't even want to stay in the apartment
by himself sometimes."

"Well, don't be too hard on him," BJ said. "One thing
you can't complain about is that he has a loving nature."

"So do I," Joshua muttered too low for her to hear.

"What did you say?" she called.

"I said you're right. My dog loves me."

He glanced around at his surroundings. BJ's apartment
appeared to be a place where she expressed herself completely. There were trailing green plants at strategic spots.
Soft lighting seemed to radiate from everywhere. The furniture was comfortable and scaled to fit the rooms. A soft
area rug buffered his feet, while original watercolors hung
from the walls. He could see she had spent a lot of time
and energy on it.

She had managed to accomplish a terrific ambience in
the room. He judged that she was a homebody in her own
way.

He liked it. It said something about her. It made him
think of his own empty place. He would have liked to stay
in for a while and wished they weren't going out.

Josh was examining her bookshelf when BJ walked back
into the room. He turned and saw her. He felt as if someone
had hit him in the stomach.

She wore a slinky red dress that gently hugged her
shapely torso. His body responded immediately. He wished
they weren't going out for an entirely different reason. It
had nothing to do with her apartment but quite a bit to
do with her perfectly luscious body.

Previously she'd worn clothes that concealed her, and he'd only imagined. Now, just as on the night of the basketball game, he knew.

Strangely enough, he suddenly felt as if he didn't want her to show those curves to anyone else, and that thought made him pause. He'd never wanted a woman as much as he wanted BJ at that moment.

She gave him a big smile and said, "Isn't there something about if animals and babies love you, then you can't be all bad?"

He barely found the voice to respond, "Well, I don't know about babies because I hardly ever have contact with any. But if Hannibal's opinion counts, I guess I'm all right." He couldn't take his eyes off her.

"Well, will I do?" she said to his staring and turned around for his approval.

"Wow!" His voice sounded rough. "Yes, you certainly will do. But will you be warm enough?"

The words had slipped out before he'd realized that he was going to say them. He was amazed that he'd made even that much of a protest, because in that dress, he could see her long gorgeous legs.

"You think it's too much?" she said, looking down at herself.

She suddenly seemed doubtful. He wanted to hug her, and he could have kicked himself for saying that.

"No, you're perfect, and we'll be in the car," he tried to reassure her. As they left, he said, "Were you trying to tell me that I should be satisfied if my dog loves me and not to aim any higher?"

"What?" she said, looking puzzled.

"Never mind," he said. "Just a joke."

The weather was blustery on the drive to Darlene's house. BJ glanced upward at the heavily laden sky.

"It's supposed to snow," she said.

"Later tonight," he said. "We'll be fine now."

Yes, she thought, she did feel fine. She felt safe and protected with Joshua in his plush car. She glanced at his competent hands on the steering wheel. She had been inordinately pleased at his response to her dress. He glanced briefly at her and smiled before turning back to the road.

"I see you collect original art," he said.

"Yes, I like to think I'm helping striving young artists."

"You are," he said. "Also, it's an investment. Those pieces could be worth a mint at some future date."

"I guess so, but in truth, I never think of that. I simply buy what I like."

"Well"—he glanced at her again—"any woman who likes fine art can't be all bad, either."

"Touché," she said with a laugh. Then, becoming more serious, she said, "I think it was very nice of you to let Darlene rope you in to this. However, I want to warn you about something."

After a quick glance her way, he said, "Sounds ominous."

She took a deep breath and plunged in. "You remember our conversation at the Christmas party?"

"Yes?" he said.

"Darlene is like Lucy in some ways. . . ." She stopped, not knowing how to proceed.

"How's that?" he asked when she'd paused too long.

"You see, they're both usually trying to play matchmaker for me."

"Somehow you don't look like a woman who needs that much help." He smiled seductively.

She stared at his smile for a long time before realizing that she had meant to explain what this dinner at Darlene's house was about. She pulled her eyes away and cleared her throat.

"Ahem. Yes, well, you see, Darlene is trying to impress you with the joys of domesticity."

"What? You mean she's invited me with ulterior motives? Not for my charm and companionship?" he teased.

"I still say it was very nice of you, but please don't let her make a nuisance of herself. Once you get past Darlene's predilection to pick men for me, I know you'll have a good time."

"Okay, gotcha. And by the way," he said, "thanks for your willingness to cook dinner for Lucy and me."

"What dinner?" she asked.

"Lucy called me today and said that you were going to host a dinner for us next Friday. She didn't tell you?"

What could she say? She looked into Joshua's beautiful eyes and realized that she would really enjoy cooking for him—no matter that it was one of Lucy's machinations.

"Oh, yes," BJ answered. "I almost forgot."

"Good," Josh said. "I'm looking forward to it."

"Josh, you didn't tell them about us going to the basket-ball game, did you?"

"No," he said. "I thought you said you wanted to do it."

"Thank you." She breathed a sigh of relief. "I know it sounds foolish, but sometimes it's a nuisance when they get involved with things like that."

"It's all right," he said, effectively cutting off her uncomfortable attempt at explaining. "And I won't be the least bit upset if Darlene tries to match us together. You shouldn't be upset, either. It just means they care about you. Maybe they feel you need protection, and that marriage would provide that."

His words took her aback. She almost wondered if he thought she was incompetent and needed a husband, too. Probably, she guessed, but she was certain he wasn't interested in the job.

"Maybe they do, but they're wrong," she said.

"Even your client, Adella, wants to find a husband for you."

"Adella has been mixing in people's business all of her life. She just can't stop," she said, sounding more exasperated than she wanted.

"Okay, I know it's annoying, but they don't mean any harm."

"I'd like to hear what you'd say if someone was doing that to you."

"While I suggest not getting upset, I *do* think you should stop it if it bothers you," he clarified.

"I try," she said. "But they don't pay me any attention."

"Make them listen," he persisted. On a new note, he added, "I take it you're a woman who wants to be free of husband and family?"

"Not really, I would love to marry someday."

He glanced quickly at her. "You would?"

"Of course. I want children, a home, and family. Doesn't a husband go with all of that?"

"Not necessarily, but I agree that they certainly should. And I want to commend your honesty."

She glanced back at him because his statement sounded rather superior. "Why do you say it like that? As if my honesty was questionable? Is that because it's passé for a woman to even mention that she might want a husband? It's supposed to run the men away?"

"Ouch," he said. "You don't pull any punches, do you?"

"Well, is it?"

"Sorry if I rubbed you wrong there," he said, refusing to respond to her challenge. "But if you agree with your godmother, why is there a problem?"

"The problem is that she thinks I can't find a man for myself."

"I see," he said.

"Don't *you* expect to marry someday and have children?" she asked.

"Yes, of course. Though it will be a few years before that."

"Oh, sure," she said sarcastically.

How did we get on this topic? she wondered. She sighed with relief when they arrived at Darlene's house.

Darlene opened the door, saying, "Hi." After first hugging BJ with one arm and greeting Joshua, she said, "Let me have your coats."

BJ could see Tiffany, Darlene's adorable small daughter, hurriedly crawl to join them. When Tiffany reached them, she went immediately to Josh. There she pulled on his pants to stand. Once on her feet, she treated Joshua to a gorgeous dimpled smile that showed all of her six teeth. *Babies love him, too. This man is lethal on females.*

BJ went down to pick up the small child and rescue Josh's pants. "Oh, you little darling," she said as Tiffany transferred her attentions from Josh to BJ.

"Oh, no." Darlene stopped BJ by hoisting the child onto her own hip. "Not in that dress." Darlene looked at Joshua, saying, "Doesn't BJ look terrific today?"

"Puleeze," BJ said, trying to stop her best friend.

Josh gave BJ an appreciative look, saying, "Most definitely."

"Where's Carlos?" BJ asked to get off the topic.

"He went on an emergency call," Darlene explained, "but he'll be back soon."

"Carlos owns a heating oil company," BJ said to Joshua.

"He's the owner, number-one worker, and emergency deliverer, too," Darlene added.

"I know how that works," Joshua answered with a rueful expression.

Once they were inside the living room, BJ looked around and realized how cozy it all seemed. The room was warmly lit and had a fire in the fireplace. On the mantelpiece, Darlene still had her Kwanzaa candles displayed, as well as a small cornucopia of fresh fruits and nuts. Savory smells of dinner were in the air, including the smells of freshly baked apple pie.

Darlene, noticing BJ's glance at the Kwanzaa candles, said, "I know they're a month past their time, but I couldn't bear to take them down. Anyway, it's good for Tiffany. This was her first Christmas, and we're teaching her about her heritage."

Looking around Darlene's home, BJ suddenly felt full of yearning. So much for warning Joshua about Darlene's schemes, BJ thought, when she was also bemused by the signs of domestic bliss. It was like a picture that should have been on a Christmas card. Darlene, who'd never been particularly domestic to say the least, had outdone herself. Sometimes she envied her best friend's good fortune. BJ sighed.

Could such a thing ever happen for her? The time had passed so fast. It seemed only yesterday that she'd graduated from college. She couldn't help remembering all the fantastic dreams that she'd had. Both Darlene and herself had come to New York at Lucy's glowing description of what life was like in the North. They'd dreamed of having dazzling careers and setting the world on fire. They'd gotten jobs, herself working at the VanderWeil Foundation, while Darlene had gone into city government.

They were going to clean up all of New York's problems for the first three to five years, have great adventures, marry wonderful philanthropists, have the two point eight children, settle down with a picket fence, and live happily ever after.

They'd both loved Queens, despite its problems. Darlene had become familiar with people in the administration, and BJ had been glad to live near Lucy, who was also well established. It had been so much fun. Dancing every night, with summer weekends spent at beaches on Long Island.

Life had seemed so simple. Now here it was more than ten years later, and none of that had happened. True she still enjoyed her job, but her personal dreams were no closer than they'd ever been. And as for the man that she'd always believed would come along and sweep her into this life—she glanced at Joshua—he seemed as far away as the moon. Tears stung the back of her eyes.

Well, at least Darlene seemed to have captured the gold ring, BJ thought. That was something.

Darlene took that moment to say, "BJ, come on into the kitchen with me." Before BJ could answer, Darlene promptly plopped little Tiffany into Josh's lap, saying to the handsome man, "Carlos will be here in a minute, so you take Tiffany."

Josh's face was a study in shock. He had been caught unprepared.

BJ rolled her eyes heavenward at Darlene's tactics but didn't say anything. She stood to follow, planning to rescue Josh by taking Tiffany.

But when BJ tried to take Tiffany from Josh, Darlene grabbed her arm. "I told you, not in that dress." Darlene looked at Josh, who seemed near panic. "You're okay, right, Josh? I need BJ to help in the kitchen."

"Sure," Josh said, eyeing the child.

The sight of Joshua holding the little girl fascinated BJ, and when Darlene grabbed her hand and dragged her into the kitchen, BJ went. She was curious to see how he would handle the situation and allowed herself to leave him there.

In the kitchen, BJ turned on Darlene, whispering, "If you're going to act like that, I'm leaving."

"Act like what?" Darlene asked, looking far too innocent.

"Like dumping Tiffany on him."

"What's wrong with him holding my daughter? She's a sweet, even-tempered child."

"That's not what I mean, and you know it. You're trying

to make Josh see the pleasures of all this home-sweet-home and family bit.''

Darlene glanced around, looking smug. "It is nice, isn't it?"

"Stop trying to wriggle out of this. And I've already warned him against you. So it won't work."

"Why did you tell him? There's nothing wrong with reminding a man about the pleasures of home, hearth, and family."

"I don't want him to think that I've had a hand in this."

"Nonsense. And anyway, men gain more from marriage than women do. Men are the ones who invented marriage."

"Hah, I think they've forgotten that, or maybe they're just trying to invent something new, like being free to run with all the girls."

"That's why they need us to remind them of what they're missing. Do you think I didn't have to remind Carlos? He really believed he was happy when he was single. I had a hard time convincing him that he wasn't. I saved him from himself. And don't think I don't remind him of that, either."

"Carlos is a brave man. Anyone who'd promise to love you till death has got to be brave."

"Carlos is in love. That's why he's brave." Darlene turned her attention away from BJ to check a scrumptious-looking broiled fish in the broiler.

While Darlene's back was turned, BJ slipped over to the door and peeped around it, trying to see Josh. He was still sitting in the exact same position with his eyes totally focused on Tiffany, who was pulling on his tie and trying to put it into her mouth.

"Don't worry about him," Darlene said, sounding impatient. "You should thank me for this. This is how marriage is perpetuated. We married ones look out for you young single things."

"I'm older than you by several months."

"I don't mean literally. I mean in the sense that I'm a matron." That thought seemed to surprise Darlene, for she went off on a tangent. "Oh, Lord, forget I ever called myself that—a matron!"

Barbara Jean, however, wasn't really paying much attention and didn't bother to answer. She was gazing into the living room and was much too busy watching Josh with Tiffany on his lap. The sight created a strange longing inside her.

Joshua could hear the women's voices but not what they said. Once he looked up and saw Barbara Jean watching him. He smiled at her, hoping that his smile wasn't as feeble as it felt on his face.

"Are you all right?" BJ asked.

Josh contemplated the baby on his lap, who looked right back at him with glowing brown eyes and an adorable grin. He managed to answer BJ's question with a strangled, "Everything's under control out here."

However, he didn't have time to pay much attention to the luscious BJ, because suddenly he felt something wet creep down his hand and looked down to find that the squirming little bundle of humanity that was sitting on his lap had drool running down her chin—and missing her dress, ran straight to his hand. He was terrified of moving his hand, for fear that he'd drop her. He looked panicky at the door where BJ had been standing and found she was gone.

BJ turned back to the kitchen and Darlene. "So out with it. What happened at that luncheon with you and Lucy?" BJ thought Darlene looked strangely guilty at this.

"Didn't you ask me this before? I told you, it turned out very nice, thank you."

"You never mentioned what she wanted to see you about."

"Oh, we talked about the problems with city government. You know our departments are closely related."

"That's all?"

"What did you expect?"

"You've never done that before."

"So? Maybe it's time that we did."

"I thought you didn't even like Lucy."

"Of course I love your godmother. And she loves me, too."

"Hah, she didn't use to."

"That was when I was younger and sort of wild. Now that I've become a respectable—ahem—*young* matron, Lucy's a lot more understanding."

"Did she put you up to this?"

"Be real—I invited the man before I had lunch with Lucy."

"Okay, I just want to be sure. This could be a conflict of interest or something."

"Oh, give me a break. I can invite a dinner guest if I want to."

"You know something? I'm glad you've settled down. Now will you stop bothering me? And can't you talk about anything except men?"

"I'm only trying to help so you needn't be so snippy. And settled down is all right for me but not for you."

"Oh, glory," BJ said, rolling her eyes heavenward.

"You're wasting the best years of your life."

"I'm not like you. I'm a country girl."

"BJ, this is Jamaica, New York, not Columbia. How can you be a country girl in New York City?"

"I mean my attitude toward life."

"Am I asking you to give up your attitude, or am I asking you to make up your mind to get married this year? I read this thing about keeping a positive mental attitude."

"I do have a positive mental attitude."

"You have to be more determined. I want you to read that book that I bought for you."

"Which one? Oh, all right, I promise to read both of them. Now will you stop?"

"Okay, but don't think that I've totally let you off the hook."

Before BJ could answer this statement, Josh let out an "Ouch!" and they both hurried into the living room to see what was wrong.

Joshua looked around hastily for something to wipe the baby's mouth and found nothing. Finally, he looked back at the child and resigned himself to the inevitable when the drool proceeded to run down to his pants. His pants began to stick to his leg.

"Goo," the little charmer said and gave him a moist smile, showing pearly teeth.

"Back to you," Josh answered sotto voce.

At his voice, she smiled broadly and started bouncing up and down. His heart accelerated. She was small and wriggly, and he hadn't a clue to whether he was holding her right. The last thing he needed was to hurt her. With her dribbling on him, he wondered if she'd become too slippery and squirm out of his grasp.

Joshua glanced up at the doorway where BJ had stood, but she wasn't there. "I can do this," he said more in prayer than anything else.

Earlier Tiffany had found his tie attractive and kept a death's grip on it. Now she pulled herself up by it, bringing her face closer to his. She managed to free her other gooey fist and landed it right on his nose.

"Ouch," he let out involuntarily.

BJ and Darlene rushed out of the kitchen at this. He was ashamed to have made the noise. He felt totally incompetent, letting the baby get the best of him. He was also deliriously glad to see the two women again. The cooing noises they made to both the baby and to him were mollifying.

He sent a prayer up to heaven when Darlene took the squirming little bundle. That was also the moment when he realized the full implication of why his pants were sticking to his leg. The baby hadn't only drooled on him, she'd also wet her diaper, and it had leaked out on his pants.

"Oh, no," BJ commiserated.

"Quite all right," Josh said, trying to sound unconcerned as he pulled the damp fabric away from his leg.

Later he found himself having a new thought. While it was true that BJ always tried to warn him about Lucy and Darlene, somehow he often felt that she was in cahoots with the other women. Why not? It wasn't so strange that women pursued men. After all, hadn't *Ebony* and *Jet* magazines called him a good catch?

The thought of the sexy BJ trying to catch him made him feel quite mellow. It was an interesting possibility. She'd just been playing hard to get. He could wait until she was willing to admit it.

BJ glanced sadly at Joshua's pants. "It seems that every time we get together, you wind up with a cleaning bill."

Joshua responded with, "Don't worry yourself about it," and gave her one of his sexiest smiles.

While she was pleased that he took it so well, something about his response sounded condescending. It made her wonder what he had to be smug about. But Carlos, Darlene's husband, happened to return at that moment so she didn't dwell on Joshua's attitude.

"Here's Carlos, the love of my life," Darlene said, introducing the two men.

With Carlos's return, they sat for a while in the living

room. The rest of the evening went without hitch, save two incidents. One occurred when Lucy's name was mentioned.

Carlos said something to the effect that Lucy, the godmother, always reminded him of the old movie, *The Godfather*—likening Lucy to a mafioso don. It was supposed to be a joke, but BJ was slightly hurt.

Despite all of her own complaints about Lucy, she really loved the sprightly, small woman. As the four of them moved to the dining room, BJ was still trying to make them understand.

"It isn't that Lucy's manipulative, it's just that she's always trying to help people," BJ said.

"I'm glad you brought that up," Darlene said, bringing out large steaming dishes to set on the table. "Your godmother said I should remind you about the dinner next Friday night. You'll be there too, right, Josh?"

"Yes," he answered.

Oh, no, BJ thought. Did Lucy tell the whole world? Wouldn't you know it. And here she was trying to defend Lucy's reputation, which was impossible. The woman ought to run for mayor.

BJ glanced across at Josh, who was listening to Carlos, and thought, why not? She liked him after all, and for once didn't mind Lucy's and Darlene's choice. Having a dinner would be nice.

"BJ!" Darlene shrieked, breaking into BJ's reverie. "Watch your elbow. You almost pushed that dish off the table."

BJ suddenly jumped and indeed almost did drop the dish. It was Josh's coming to her rescue that saved the near accident. However, he seemed annoyed.

"Leave her alone," he said to Darlene. "She can handle that."

Everyone looked at him. Even Joshua seemed disconcerted by his own outburst. Without further ado, they started eating their soup. Darlene saved the day by launching into one of her favorite stories, a long-winded version of the fourteen-hour delivery of Tiffany.

BJ realized that this was several times that Josh had jumped in to defend her. She was bemused.

Later, while going to bed that night, Darlene said to Carlos, "Did you notice how Joshua rushed to BJ's defense tonight?"

"I don't blame him, you need to stop mothering her," Carlos said.

"Not mother BJ after all these years?"

"Maybe she doesn't like it."

"Of course she does. She loves it."

"Darlene, soul mate of mine, you almost tucked BJ's napkin under her chin tonight."

"I was only being a friend and trying to help."

"Why don't you come over here and be a friend and help me?" Carlos leered.

Darlene giggled as she slipped under the covers to lie with her husband.

Later she asked Carlos, "Do you really think BJ doesn't like me to mother her?"

"I don't know about BJ, but I sure as hell think Josh didn't like the way you're inclined to bully her," Carlos mumbled sleepily.

"Bully BJ? Me? It's just that she needs someone to look out for her."

"Maybe Josh wants to be the one who does that."

"Carlos, don't you think there was something queer about them tonight? Like they knew each other more than we thought?"

"BJ and Joshua? Naw. Don't forget they toured Ashley Place, so of course they know each other. She'd have told you if there was more than that."

"You're right. BJ never keeps secrets from me," Darlene said and turned over to sleep. But just before she dozed off, her eyes opened as she realized that BJ hadn't worn one of her old tent dresses. *Wonder what that means?*

Now that BJ had been convinced to cook for Lucy and Josh, she was eager to do a good job. So the next day she began to plan a menu. True, the holiday season was over, but what with Darlene's giving a dinner, it seemed to be prolonged. It felt good to be entertaining, something that she hadn't done in a long time.

She went shopping and enjoyed every moment of buying delicious foods to feed Joshua's hunger. She dreamt about appeasing other hungers. She cleaned her apartment until it gleamed. She bought herself a pair of lounging pajamas, making certain that it wasn't too fabulous, which would look foolish in her tiny apartment.

By Friday morning, she'd had her hair shampooed and set as well as having splurged on all the extras and had a manicure, pedicure, and facial. She felt ready for anything.

"Gee, I'm sorry," Lucy said, sounding sincere . "Something's come up with the mayor, and I couldn't get out of it."

"It's okay," BJ said, but she was indeed very disappointed. She'd been looking forward to it all week.

"I haven't even had time to call Joshua yet."

Something made BJ answer, "Oh, don't worry about that. I'll call him."

When she put the phone down, she looked around at the apartment, which did her proud. Although it was true that at first she hadn't wanted to do it, now she was eager to have Josh in her home to entertain and feed with food she'd prepared with her own hands. The idea had touched some elemental part of her self. It was a real letdown to have everything canceled now.

Then an errant thought insinuated itself into her thoughts. Did she *have* to cancel?

Chapter Ten

When Joshua tried to contact BJ, the line was busy, and he glanced at his watch. Before he could dial again, his own secretary transferred a call in. It was going to be a long day, he thought. Linda walked in at that point. "Linda, call Lucy McPhearson and confirm that dinner for tonight."

"I didn't know you had a dinner appointment with Lucy McPhearson tonight," Linda said. "Is Mrs. McPhearson thinking of making you her boy-toy?"

He was getting sick of Linda's tendency to interfere. "I don't think Chairwoman McPhearson is the boy-toy type. Nor for that matter am I a boy."

"Well, excuse me," she answered.

"You don't expect to know about every dinner engagement I have, do you?"

"No, of course not," she said stiffly. "But you watch what I'm telling you. Don't forget the way she tried to throw that overgrown goddaughter at you." She huffed out of his office.

Josh picked up a pencil to tap on the blotter. Linda's

words made him remember that first day and the appalled
expression on BJ's face when Lucy threw them together. BJ
looked ready to die over Lucy's very obvious matchmaking
efforts. The memory made him want to chuckle despite
his annoyance with Linda.

And he was getting fed up with Linda. Part of him hated
to be sharp with her. He remembered her when they'd
gone to school, but he resented her acting as if she had
some claim, other than friendship, on him. Lately she
seemed to insinuate herself too much into his life. He
deliberately hadn't mentioned the dinner because BJ was
involved, and he didn't want to hear Linda's snide remarks.

The truth was that he wasn't quite as sure of himself as
he would have liked. Barbara Jean Jones brought out some
strange behavior in him, and he didn't want more people
to know about it until he'd figured it out himself. He'd
made a fool of himself several times already over her.

A delightful image of BJ's long, lithesome frame slipped
into his mind, with memories of her full lips curving into
her mind-blowing smile. It made everything else flee from
his thoughts. The image also made his groin tighten. He
couldn't get the night they'd played hoops off his mind.
While it had been a basketball game, it was as arousing as
if it had been foreplay.

Linda returned to his office, saying, "I just spoke with
Mrs. McPhearson's secretary, who says the dinner's been
canceled. Mrs. McPhearson can't make it this evening.
Good thing I called."

Joshua sat up, puzzled. "Strange that the secretary didn't
notify me earlier." He reached out for the phone, but
before he could pick it up, it rang. He motioned to Linda
that he'd pick it up.

It was BJ. Joshua waved to Linda as she left again, saying,
"I'll see you later." She closed the door behind her.

"Hello," he said, leaning back to get comfortable.

"Hi," BJ said. "Just calling to confirm the dinner with Lucy for tonight."

"Ah," he said and sat up again. "Did you speak with her today?"

"Yes, just a moment ago. You don't need to call her. Everything's still on."

This threw him for a moment. Then he thought, maybe the secretary was wrong. "Good," he said to BJ, "I'm looking forward to it."

"Umm," she sounded.

"Yes?" he urged her on.

"Lucy still doesn't know that we've seen each other on our own. I haven't told her. . . ." Her voice faded away.

"Okay," he said. "But care to tell me why?"

"I started to tell her," she rushed on, "but I was afraid it would start her on her usual goals." He chuckled. BJ laughed with him, but she sounded tense and ill at ease even over the telephone. "She means well but all her efforts fail miserably because . . ." She paused.

"Go on," he encouraged.

"It usually scares the men and makes them bolt."

"Have there been a lot to bolt?"

She didn't answer right away, and when she did speak it was to say, "Well, see you tonight." She disconnected.

Joshua stared at the telephone after hanging up. He sat forward, fingers tented and tried to figure out what had just happened. Now both BJ and Lucy said they'd just spoken together. And either they misunderstood each other, or one of them told him a lie. *Lucy says dinner is off but the lovely BJ says everything is still moving straight ahead.* She had even innocently warned him against Lucy's matchmaking efforts.

This was sounding very interesting. He always felt good whenever he talked to BJ, but today was better than most. There was no way he'd miss that dinner tonight.

He rubbed his palms together. "Hot dog."

Wonder if Ms. Barbara Jean Jones is setting me up? Who knows, maybe I'm about to be seduced. Could I be that lucky? Good things come to those who wait. Suddenly he felt like an adolescent boy. He wanted the day to pass quickly so that he could be with BJ, but he was also a bit unsure. He'd never felt this way about a woman before. He knew it wasn't just the promise of sex. There was more.

Later, when Joshua knocked and BJ opened the door, he wanted more than anything to take her into his arms. The warm light radiated from a source behind her. She wore a small pink ruffled apron over a black lounging outfit with a long slim skirt. The skirt gave an occasional glimpse of a long, burnished ebony leg. He couldn't believe how enticing she looked.

He felt as if he stood at the entrance of an oasis of human warmth and comfort. He had an incredibly powerful urge to step up to her and clasp her to him. He wanted to feel her curvy body lean on him. To hold her tight—to take her to bed.

He restrained himself, knowing that Lucy McPhearson might be inside, and if she wasn't already there, she could soon come. Besides, this was BJ's show. Let *her* make the moves tonight.

He walked in when she stepped aside and looked around. It was warm and cozy, just as he'd thought on his first visit. He turned to face her. He realized that he'd been unconsciously tapping the wrapper on the bouquet of hothouse flowers that he'd brought. He felt like a besotted boy at that moment. He moved slowly when he handed them to her. Joshua didn't want to startle her. He didn't want anything to go wrong and thrust him out of paradise.

"Thanks," she said and put her face to the blossoms.

"Don't put your nose into them," he said with a hand on her chin.

"I was going to smell them."

"Sometimes they have small insects."

"Well," she said and held the package away from her. "Thanks for ruining my illusions."

She glanced up at him from the corner of her eyes. It made her appear incredibly seductive. His groin ached. She shifted as if sensing the change in his manner. He couldn't take his eyes away.

They stood that way for several moments before she seemed to catch herself and say, "I'll put them in water."

He exhaled deeply and realized that he'd been holding his breath. "Where's Lucy?" he said.

"She should be here any minute now."

"No problem," he said, spreading his hands. He wasn't sure why he hadn't mentioned that he'd called Lucy's office also, but he started looking around her apartment.

"Let me take your coat."

He slipped his arms from the sleeves, and she moved in back of him to help. It was a small commonplace gesture, but it knocked him for a loop. He wondered if he was going to break out in a sweat.

"Do you mind?" He indicated that he wanted to loosen his collar.

She glanced at his shirt as if he'd asked for much more than he had. After a quick tremulous smile, she said, "No, please do." Her voice sounded husky, too.

He opened his shirt at the top and rolled the sleeves up to his forearms. She watched for a moment before saying, "I'll just hang these up."

He was sorry when she left. He resented the separation. But the few moments gave him time to get himself under control. Only God knew why sh disturbed him this way. And he suspected that although he was extremely attracted to her, it wasn't only a sexual thing.

Although he'd been in her apartment before, this was totally different. Previously they'd been in a rush to go to Darlene's dinner. Now he knew that unless Lucy showed up, and he certainly doubted that, there was going to be only the two of them—at least for dinner.

He looked at her bookshelves again. He had a natural curiosity about what she read. There were a stack of sociology texts and some literary hardbacks. It was the paperbacks that made him smile. They were mostly romance books. Tucked in an out of the way spot were two how to get your man books. He was tempted to chuckle. He picked up one and flicked through to scan the pages.

"Oh, those are gifts from Darlene," she said hastily, looking terribly embarrassed when she returned and realized what he was reading." He sensed she wanted to grab it from his hands.

"You've done a nice job here," he said, pushing the book back on the shelf. "Puts my place to shame."

BJ grinned shyly as she ducked her head and shifted feet before she could compose herself. His chest felt tight.

"Thanks," she said and moved away hastily. "I'll bring in the appetizers."

He followed her into the kitchen and realized that the move startled her, but she seemed to recover quickly. She was standing over a tray of intricate hors d'oeuvres, covered with a sheet of waxed paper. He looked around before going closer to see the tray.

She raised the cover, saying, "Try one."

He popped one into his mouth. "It's good," he said, taking another.

He noticed her hand shake as she covered the tray again. She looked stiff and tense.

"Well, I don't know what's happened to Lucy," she said, and it sounded false.

"You're not worried about your godmother, are you?" he asked, taking another small puffed cracker from the tray. "It's still early."

"Usually she comes early," BJ said.

"Everything's going to be all right." He wondered what she thought he meant by that statement.

"Let's sit in the living room," BJ said hastily when he'd tried to reassure her.

She wondered if he sensed she was uncomfortable standing in the small kitchen with him. He picked up the tray and gestured for her to go first. She indicated the coffee table, and he set down the tray of appetizers. She was glad that he'd offered to carry it, because she felt all thumbs. She was too aware of how much she wanted him. She didn't want to have another of her accidents. *Not tonight,* she prayed.

She poured a white wine into fluted glasses, and they talked about nothing in particular. He watched her. Joshua's intensity always made her edgy, and this night was no different. She wondered what he thought about Lucy's not being there. Her hands shook so badly that several times she'd almost spilled her wine. He seemed to be waiting for something.

She glanced ostensibly at her watch. The pretense made her feel coiled as tight as a spring. Finally she said, "Well, I guess we shouldn't wait dinner any longer. No telling where Lucy is."

She had set up a card table, which she covered with a fine embroidered linen tablecloth. There were linen napkins to match. It had been an expensive splurge, but she was glad she'd done it. Fine bone china finished off the table.

She served a succulently broiled chicken, with salad and thick slices of a hard-dough bread from the Caribbean— and more white wine.

"This is delicious," he said, taking more food on his plate.

She enjoyed watching him eat, though her own appetite for food had waned. Everything about him seemed wonderful. She enjoyed every little nuance. He looked strange with his shirtsleeves rolled up his forearms. She was tempted to touch the hairs on his corded arms. Watching him made her yearn to hold him.

After dinner he helped with the dishes and cleaning. The longer he was in the apartment, the more charged the atmosphere seemed to become. And the more she wanted him. The whole evening had been shot through with a barely contained sexuality.

She had been expecting it to break through any minute, and it finally occurred in the kitchen. It was her nerves that broke first. She'd been a wreck ever since she'd told Joshua that the dinner was still on. Her hands shook visibly as she washed the dishes.

Once when she almost dropped a plate, Joshua caught it and put the plate into the dish drainer.

"I don't know what's wrong with me tonight," she said.

But that wasn't true. She did know. She knew how much she wanted him.

He put the towel down and drew her against him. Gently he cupped her chin in his hand and kissed her. The kiss was gentle, but she recognized his controlled passion. It frightened her, because suddenly she realized she was getting herself into more than she'd expected.

"Well," she said, moving away from his hardened body, "let's have the coffee now."

"Okay," he said on a long drawn-out breath.

She took a deep breath when they went back into the living room, knowing the time had come. However, instead of moving to the couch, he sat in the large wing chair. He sat quietly for a few moments. His eyes had gone from glittering brown to a smoky color.

Finally he spoke, bidding her a husky, "Come over here."

She poured a cup of coffee and took it to him. He placed the cup on the table, and taking her hand, gently pulled her to sit on his lap.

She was reluctant. It wasn't that she weighed that much,

but at five foot ten she wasn't a flyweight either. She hadn't sat on a man's lap since she was a kid. And that man had been her father.

"I don't think so"—she pulled back—"I'm a big girl."

He continued to tug, insisting, "It's all right." When she was sitting gingerly on his lap, he said, "Now let's see what Lucy meant when she said you always curl up into a small ball."

They sat that way, and soon she relaxed because he didn't seem uncomfortable. It was incredibly seductive to feel cherished in this way. They kissed, and he put his hand on her stocking-clad leg where her skirt had fallen open. His fingers tapped out their own rhythm. Soon his hand advanced an inch under her skirt. When she realized what he was doing, she got up.

"Maybe I'd better sit on my own chair," BJ said.

At first she couldn't figure why she'd stopped him. He was finally doing what she'd been dreaming of since she'd first laid eyes on him. She trembled, remembering how she'd maneuvered for him to come tonight. But she knew what it was—she was scared. She was afraid that she would disappoint him.

Joshua stood up also, his hands in his pockets. He started walking around the apartment again, gazing once again at the paintings before moving on to the bookcase. When he noticed the book he'd been perusing before, he pivoted toward her.

Joshua's glittering, jewel brown eyes had darkened again. He gazed intently at her, holding her motionless. He seemed to have some power to keep her enthralled. She felt as if he could see right into her soul. The feeling was moving. It was also uncomfortable, for she felt vulnerable and helpless.

Suddenly she regretted his being alone in her apartment. There was an element of the inevitable about the time. She was sorry that she'd brought him here tonight.

"If I'm going to leave here tonight, it's got to be now," he said quietly.

With a sigh, BJ rose and went to get his coat. He exhaled, she thought, with disappointment. She held his coat out to him when she returned; a sudden heavily laden pain settled into her. He took the coat and let it fall on a nearby chair.

His hands grasped her arms, and he kissed her hard. "Let's have the truth," he said softly. "Lucy's not coming, is she?"

"No," she admitted.

"You knew that when you spoke to me this afternoon, didn't you?"

"Yes," she whispered.

He grunted in triumph before kissing her long and hard. She felt his erection against her stomach. It seemed as if all strength leached from her bones. She leaned into him, kissing him back with a fervor that told him how much she needed him.

"Tell me what you want," he demanded. She felt as if she'd moved beyond speech and pressed herself against him in a mute appeal. "Tell me you want this."

"I do. I do," she pleaded.

"No. Not good enough. Say it," he whispered harshly.

"I want you. I want you . . . to love me," she said with more ardor than she could have believed.

He laughed triumphantly and said, "Ah, yes. That I fully intend to do."

With trembling fingers, she attempted to open his shirt. When she fumbled, he opened it for her, letting it slip off his shoulders. She placed her palms on his chest, feeling the wonderfully swirling hairs there. She bent forward to kiss him there, and he gasped. His skin was warm and inviting. She felt his heart speed up under her lips.

With one finger under her chin, he lifted her face to touch his lips on hers. "I want you," he muttered.

With their mouths cleaved together, he rolled her blouse up slowly and broke the kiss to sweep it over her head. His mouth went to her breast over her bra. Then he unhooked the bra and took each nipple into his hot wet mouth to suckle. Hot flashes of sensation went straight to her feminine core. She pressed herself against him, and his hand went to the apex of her thighs. He covered her with one hand and squeezed gently. It drove her mad, and her knees grew weak. She craved his touch and moaned like a crazed woman under his hand.

He rained kisses upon her mouth, her throat, and trailed small bites down the side of her jaw. He seemed ready to devour her. She exposed more of her flesh to his ravaging mouth. First, her skirt fell to the floor, and then he went to his knees, and her panties soon followed. He kissed her there, and her knees buckled.

Joshua surged upward, grabbing her up into his arms and wended his way into her bedroom. He laid her on the covers, and she held on to him, too eager to let him go. He moved to her, shedding the rest of his clothes.

He took a moment to sheath himself, and then he came to her. She remembered that she had thought of him as a sperm donor. That, she thought, was going to be impossible. But nothing mattered at that moment except Joshua. She wanted Joshua the man, not Joshua the sperm donor.

He spread her legs and moved between them. There he touched her quivering flesh, and she cried out. She was wet and ready. Heat seemed to envelop her.

When he joined his body to hers, she gasped in joy at their union. She raised up, winding her legs around him. After a short pause, he began to move within her, and she cried out at every stroke. He put his mouth over hers to mute the sounds that emitted from her. She ground herself into him with all her heart. Each thrust brought an increase in the exquisite pleasure that was so intense, it was almost unbearable. Finally everything broke, and she held on to him as she sailed into that exquisite moment. Joshua joined her with his own gasp.

When it was over, she suddenly burst out crying. It came as a shock to both of them. He pulled her close, and she cried on his shoulder, feeling like a total fool.

She blubbered, "I don't know why I'm doing this." She tried to explain, as her nose ran, and she tried to wipe the tears with her hands.

Joshua pulled up the covers and took her down to lie on his chest. She had never felt more at home, despite their bodies being slick with perspiration. He wiped her face with the edge of the sheet.

"Okay," he soothed, "it's okay."

He caressed her, running a finger down the side of her face in a smooth continuous movement. He continued, and soon she stopped crying. She felt so comfortable that she dozed.

Somewhere during the night, he woke her with more caresses, ready to make love again. "I couldn't wait before," he said.

"You didn't have to," she murmured with a smile.

He laughed and kissed her slowly. "We're going to have to do that again."

"Again?" she said.

"Oh, yes," he answered. "Again and again. I've been wanting you too much to be easily satisfied. Now, where were we?" he asked.

BJ woke that morning and glanced over at Joshua, who slept sound as a baby. Light from the window slanted through the blinds. She shifted quietly to watch him. He had a shadow of a beard, which made him look even sexier if that was possible.

Last night, she feared, had been a mistake. Everything

had seemed so simple that afternoon. She had decided that the best way to get him out of her system was to have sex with him. In truth, she'd thought she could even use him as a sperm donor. He was gorgeous, brilliant, and charming. What more could a child want in the genetic department, she thought. Joshua would have made a perfect donor.

When Lucy had canceled at the last moment, it had seemed a perfect opportunity. She hadn't expected him to come with his own protection.

It just showed what an amateur she was. Her only experience had been with Basil, and theirs had been an established relationship. Her hopes of conceiving last night had definitely been put to rest. Still, she liked him better for it.

She had never been good at causal affairs, and she wondered if she'd survive this one. Though whether it was a mistake or not, she couldn't regret it. She hadn't known such feelings existed, not at that intensity.

She went to the bathroom to freshen up, and when she returned, Joshua was awake. He pushed several pillows up at his back and sat up. His tightly curled hair was rumpled, and his golden brown skin seemed polished by the early morning sunlight. One strong muscular hand came from under the sheet. Her throat closed at his male beauty.

"Come here," he said, patting the bedside. She sat beside him, yielding as he pulled her to kiss him. He opened her robe and laid his hands on her breasts.

She wasn't as comfortable in this role as she'd have liked and before thinking blurted out, "That was very considerate of you to use . . ." She stopped.

BJ had trouble getting it out and felt like a fool. People talked about things like condoms all the time—they had to. So why was she hesitating? She took a deep breath, but before she could speak, Joshua tilted her face with his finger under her chin. He placed a gentle kiss that lingered on her lips. When he drew back, he smiled gently at her.

"Condoms," he said for her.

"Yes," she said and glanced nervously around the room. "So how's your health?" she blurted out into that tender moment.

Joshua fell back on the pillows and laughed. "Well, I guess you *can* speak your mind when you need."

"Umm, you see . . ."

"I see and I understand. I'm in good health, and I don't take chances. Actually I seem to be too busy to take chances. But I do have regular physicals. How about you?" he threw back at her.

"Me?!" She was slightly indignant. *Does he think I do this regularly?* She was quite taken aback before she realized how silly it sounded. If she had a right to know, then he certainly did. "I'm in perfect health. I have regular physicals and . . . I *have* been too busy . . ."

"Okay, okay," he soothed. "Of course we should have asked before, despite our using . . ."

"Yes."

She felt so good after their little talk that it made her brave. Talking about condoms had been very simple, so surely she could now talk even more freely.

"Look, I'm sorry about Lucy's not coming last night and I suppose—"

Joshua took her into his arms and placed a kiss on her forehead. Considering the lovemaking of last night, it was a peculiarly chaste kiss.

"No more pretenses." He stopped her with a finger on her lips. "I already knew that Lucy wasn't coming."

"You knew?" BJ's face felt suddenly hot. It was worse than she'd hoped.

"I called her yesterday. I also knew that the two of you had spoken together." She didn't know what to say. "We can be honest with each other now. A woman who made the move on me like you did last night doesn't need to play coy."

Despite wishing she could curl up and die, she was glad to have the truth out at last. "Well . . ." She sat up and tried to laugh it off.

She eluded his grasping hands and stood up, clasping the robe together hastily. Although she was relieved to stop lying, somehow Josh's knowing about her trick made her feel naked, vulnerable. He'd seen her cover herself and shifted to rest on one elbow to watch her.

"Don't you think it's a bit late for you to do that?" he asked as she tied the sash. He reached for her hand, bringing her to sit back on the bed. He said, "You never need to be afraid or doubt yourself."

"I'm sorry about that . . ." she started.

"Don't be. I'm not."

"I mean for tricking you . . ."

"Hey, do I look damaged? Trick me anytime." He put his face into the curve of her neck. "I wanted you more than you can imagine. I've been running after you since the beginning."

"No, you haven't," she said, her head on his. She inhaled his unique smell. "You've been waiting for me to run after you."

He laughed at that. "All you had to do was ask."

"Ask what?" she said, knowing exactly what he was saying. She sat up.

The man had enough ego for two, but he was right, she thought. He was a good-looking man, a hunk, and well aware of it. He'd have had to be deaf, dumb, and blind to miss how women's eyes followed every move he made. She'd been really glad that Lucy had been up to her usual machinations when it caught Joshua.

"Ask me to come over," he added.

Joshua took her hand and tried to gently pull her back into the bed. She wanted to acquiesce. It was Saturday morning, after all. She had the day off, and maybe he did also. They could loll around in bed for as long as they wanted. They could walk through the park, see a film, go to the museum. Why not? Why shouldn't she accept the gift of the day as it came.

Reluctantly she pulled away and stood up. "I'll fix us something to eat," she said and walked to the door.

"I'm more hungry for you than for bacon and eggs," he called after her, and she spun about to glance at him again.

Abruptly she realized that good looks weren't enough. Not even his fantastic lovemaking was enough.

Joshua Hendricks was the most incredible man that she'd ever known, but she'd passed the point in her life when she could take the time and spend a couple of years loving him and maybe having him break her heart. Thirty-five was a point at which you had to make serious choices. She wasn't going to be menopausal tomorrow, not as far as she knew, but she did want a family, and she wanted to be young enough to enjoy her children. Just because a man was handsome, ambitious, and rich didn't mean he'd make a good husband and father. And considering Joshua in that light was very foolish. He wasn't the least bit interested in either role. And why should he be? A man could make babies into his dotage, while a woman had a certain number of years before that phase of her life passed.

The passion was something to be savored for the moment and remembered for a lifetime. But you couldn't build your life on something as transitory as passion.

She didn't say any of that, what she said was, "Keep this up, and I won't be able to walk for a week."

He laughed and jumped out of bed to follow her into the kitchen, watching as she prepared breakfast.

"I guess I'll have to go easy on you if I want this to continue," he said.

She wondered what that meant to Joshua but swore to

herself that she wouldn't ask. She picked up fixings for breakfast and thought, he probably thinks that now he can keep me on the side for a year or two. *Well, he can't.* Sudden tears stung her eyes.

"You're not going to cry again, are you?" Josh said.

"No, I never cry!" she insisted, furious that he'd noticed and reminded her of the crazy crying jag she had gone through last night.

"If you say so," he said, sounding edgy.

"What do you see our relationship as?" she asked and realized that she'd said it despite promising herself that she wouldn't.

"Why do we have to decide that right now?" he asked.

"You're the one who brought this up." She knew that wasn't fair. He had only been making a joke.

"Why can't we just allow it to happen? To unfold as it would naturally?"

"You mean like we date for a while?" she asked.

"Right," he said, looking comfortable with their talk now.

For some reason, BJ couldn't allow things to be comfortable at that moment.

"I've seen these sorts of relationships go on for years."

"Yeah," he said quickly in agreement. "That way, we'll get to know each other."

That was not what she wanted to hear. She had a sudden urge to scream.

"All right, if honesty is what you want, let's give it full chance," she said, knowing that she was in danger of letting her mouth go before her brains.

"Umm," Joshua said.

"No, don't chicken out now. You want honesty, and I want you to have the whole story. Do you know what Lucy's trying to do?"

"Find you a date?"

"Date? Lucy? I know you know better than that. Does

Lucy look like a woman who'd take half a loaf if she could get the whole thing? I told you, she wants to find me a husband.''

"Okay, but even Lucy must know that it takes time to go from a date to marriage.'' He raised one eyebrow.

He managed to look supremely smug, as if he'd just spoken some great world-resounding male wisdom. She was suddenly angry enough to want to antagonize. Yes, she knew her pressuring him this morning was foolish and even tacky, but it didn't help the way she felt.

"Darlene is also aiming to get me married. And she's already suggested that I should start with twins to make up for lost time.'' It was true, BJ consoled herself.

"Twins?'' he managed to say, but he moved out of the kitchen into the living room and she followed.

He picked up his pants from here he'd tossed them last night and stepped into them.

"Right, twins. And you want to hear the real joke?''

But before she could tell him what the real joke was, he was buttoning his shirt. He picked up his silk tie but hesitated.

"Look, BJ,'' he said, "this allowing Lucy and Darlene to make these decisions for you is a mistake. You can't let them railroad you into marriage on their whims. You're a grown woman and deserve the best.'' He came to hold her.

She went into his arms, pathetically glad that he'd stopped dressing. He caressed her neck, pushing her hair back. She felt his erection pushing against her abdomen when he kissed her, exploring her mouth with his tongue. She turned weak with desire and need.

"This is between us, right?'' he asked.

"Yes,'' she answered.

"We've been wanting each other since the beginning, since you sent me that hot look across a crowded room, right?''

"Yes."

He looked so smug that she wished she could slap him. Yet maybe he was right. She'd never get pregnant if he insisted on using condoms.

"There's nothing wrong with that. We don't need anyone to dictate what we do."

"Yes," she agreed. "You're right."

"Now," he said, untying the sash of her robe. "Tell me what you want," he whispered.

"I want a baby."

Chapter Eleven

"What?"

"A baby," she repeated.

"I heard that! What the hell are you talking about?"

He put the tie on and knotted it in record time, following quickly with shoes and socks.

She looked away. "I agree with you about marriage, but I do want a baby."

"We just met, for pete's sake. You don't even know me," he said.

"You sound very old fashioned—"

"I *am* old fashioned," he retorted.

". . . but you're wrong, I do know you. At least I know your type."

"Meaning?"

"You're the son of an upper-middle-class family. You were raised to have it all." Joshua was in her closet, looking for his jacket and overcoat. He hadn't even asked her to get them for him. "I chose you because of your obviously

excellent gene pool.'' Somehow that didn't sound as bus
nesslike as she would have preferred.

Her mention of gene pool had stopped him in his tracks
At her statement, he stared at her and rocked on his heels

"My gene pool? Now I've heard it all." He looked awa
from her for a moment before coming back. "Is that al
you want for your child? A good gene pool? Not asking
much, are you? What the hell is wrong with you, woman?"

Suddenly he was moving again and had his jacket and
coat from the closet.

"I'm not asking you to marry me just for a baby."

"Is this what you've been offering the men you've been
dating?"

"I haven't been dating."

"Smart guys."

That hurt, but she was absolutely determined. "You
wouldn't have to worry about anything. I wouldn't even
bother you again."

He was dressed and ready to go. She couldn't believe
how quickly he had managed it. He opened the door but
hesitated with his back toward her.

She managed to say, "I thought we'd have the whole
day together."

"I have things to do."

Although he turned his head in her direction, he didn't
meet her eyes, and his hand remained on the doorknob.

"Really?" She doubted that. She took a deep breath.
"Joshua, wait. You're right about Lucy and Darlene, and
I do intend to stop both of them immediately. And as I
said, I really don't need a husband."

"Okay?" He said it long and drawn out.

"But I *do* want a baby." She looked totally earnest.

"With the economic situation the way it is, how do you
expect to take care of a baby on your own?"

"Nowadays women do that all the time, or haven't you
noticed?" His eyes narrowed as he watched her, but he

didn't answer. "What about it?" she asked again. He was in the hall, standing with both hands in his pockets.

"No way," he said and eyed the stairs.

"Well, I had to ask, didn't I?" She had followed him into the hallway.

"If you say so." He put his hand on the bannister.

"I want to ask one more thing," she said.

She could see that he wanted to bolt but managed to stand his ground. "What?" he snapped impatiently.

"That you keep this conversation private from Lucy or Darlene."

That stopped him momentarily. He stood there as if he wanted to say more. When he continued, he took the stairs two at a time. Then he was gone. Something about his hasty retreat made her think he escaped as if a few special demons were after him. Part of her could understand his reaction, but that didn't stop the disappointment.

She listened to his footfalls as they moved down the stairs and heard the door close. Her chest felt tight. Her stomach was sore and quivery from last night's tension. Her hands trembled. She wanted to cry—but after crying last night and coming so close to repeating herself this morning, she took a deep breath, and the pending weeping subsided.

I'll clean the house, she thought, that ought to be therapeutic. She went inside her apartment and closed the door. She spent the next hour polishing all the same things that she'd already done for last night's dinner. It was an exercise in futility.

"I don't give a hoot about fancy-pants Joshua Hendricks. And with his conceit, he probably thinks I'll pine away with a broken heart. Well, he can just go have another think," BJ thought, shampooing the bathroom rug. She'd shampooed it only two days ago. "If it wasn't for his DNA, I wouldn't have even glanced his way. He caught me at a weakened moment." She thought of his gorgeous eyes and suddenly wanted to cry. She paused and took several deep breaths until she was calmer.

Joshua had done the maximum going back to Manhattan. In his apartment, he was a seething caldron of frustration. The thing that alarmed him was that when BJ said she wanted a baby, his groin had filled instantaneously. Even after having made love all night, he'd been raring to go. There had been no gentle arousal, no sleepy urge to explore—just ready-freddy. He'd never been more ready in his life, and he'd never wanted a woman more than he had BJ at that moment.

She had blown him away. He'd known he had to get out of there immediately, otherwise he was going to sink himself into her with no holds barred. And considering how horny her request had made him, she probably *would* have had twins in nine months. He'd dressed hurriedly in a race against his own body that was working in conjunction with his imagination. There was no doubt which would win in that sort of battle. His good sense had barely been able to hold on long enough to get out. All he wanted to do now was take the trip right back to her house.

He stared at the telephone for a while before picking it up to dial BJ's number. Somehow he wanted to explain what had happened. The phone rang, triggering the answering machine. He swore if the cursed appliance hung up on him this time, he'd go over there and break it.

"BJ, I know you're there," he yelled through the machine, "because I just left, and I know you haven't gone out, either. Pick up—or I'll come right back." That was some threat, he thought. The only one who'd be in trouble would be himself.

She answered the phone. "Yes, what is it?" she said, cool as ice.

"Look, I'm sorry about the way I ran out on you this morning."

"No problem. Is that what you called for? I've already forgotten about the whole incident."

There was no way he was going to believe that, but he didn't want to argue, either. "I didn't mean it the way it sounded."

"Yes, you did," BJ Jones had the nerve to say.

"Little chit," he muttered under his breath.

"Did you forget something, Joshua? Otherwise I'm very busy and want to hang up."

"What are you going to do?" he said, and his mouth was dry.

"What do you care?"

"Just promise me you won't do anything rash," he said.

"Like what? Cut my wrists because you dumped me? You are so impossibly egotistical."

Egotistical! "What I mean . . ." he said and paused awkwardly.

"I really don't think we need to talk any further about this. I understand you perfectly, and you needn't worry."

"Just because you're feeling rejected is no reason to do something crazy." He talked fast before she could hang up.

Problem was that he was saying all the wrong things. That's why he always preferred her to do the talking.

"Don't worry, I have no intention of doing anything crazy. I am merely cleaning my apartment—"

"You are out of your mind. That apartment gleams already."

". . . and now, if you don't mind—"

"BJ, don't you hang up—!"

When Joshua heard the dial tone, he had what almost amounted to an irritable urge to pull the telephone out of the wall.

* * *

The next time the phone rang, BJ stared, wishing *she* could pull it out the wall. Please, she prayed, don't let it be Joshua. *I don't think I could take another bout with him.*

"BJ, this is Mother—pick up, baby-girl."

It was her parents. She was so glad to talk to them that she picked up the phone immediately. Connecting with her family in Columbia always made her feel as if things would work out.

"Momma, Daddy, how are you?" BJ said, incredibly relieved it wasn't Joshua.

"We're doing fine here," her dad answered from the other extension.

She breathed a sigh of relief, and they filled each other in on the week's events.

"Baby-girl," her mother said, "when are you coming home?"

"Well, I've been so busy lately . . ." BJ hedged.

Her dad's voice saved her from having to answer when he said, "Your mother's been up to her usual tricks, spending my money as if it grew on trees. Now she wants to pay someone to shovel snow off *my* sidewalk. As if I'd allow any of those young devils to touch my sidewalk."

"Albert, would you hush," her mother admonished her father. "You know you're too old to be out shoveling snow."

"Did you hear that, baby-girl? Called me old. There's no end to the insults I suffer at that woman's hands."

"You old coot," her mother said to her dad. "Leave baby-girl out of this. Do you think she's going to be your little girl forever?"

"And why not, I want to know?" her father asked. "Is there any law that says a man's daughter can't be his little girl forever?"

At this point, BJ knew that neither of them were talking

to her. She turned on the speakerphone and went back
to cleaning. Her parents' voices droned on as she continued with her own thoughts. She felt almost as if she was
there with them. This thought came as she was busy scrubbing her small hallway. She was on her knees and using a
small toothbrush to remove every speck of dust in the
cracks. Actually this had been done a few days before, also.

"Ain't that right, sugar?" her father asked her.

It was his calling her sugar that broke through all her
resolutions to carry on despite everything that had gone
wrong that morning. Sugar was her dad's special name for
her. It went along with kisses on skinned knees and long
talks on cool summer evenings. When her father called
her sugar, there was no doubt he was speaking to her.

Unexpectedly BJ started crying.

She'd had no idea that she was going to get tearful, but
just hearing her father speak to her in that voice reminded
her of the days when he really did fix all her problems. Or
maybe it was the fight she'd had with Joshua that morning,
especially as it followed last night's lovemaking.

"Baby-girl?" Her mother sounded alarmed. "Is that you
crying?"

BJ rose and stumbled to the phone, where she punched
in the button to disconnect the speaker. She covered the
phone as she tried to bring herself to answer and reassure
her parents. She couldn't seem to stop the tears.

"You see?" her father said, "now you got her crying."

Her mother said, "Me? You mean *you* got her crying."
To BJ the older woman said, "I want you to come right
home, baby-girl, you hear? I want you to come home immediately!"

"That's right," her father said, for once in total
agreement with her mother. "You listen to what your
mother says. You come right home."

"Yes," BJ said, "I'll be there as soon as I can. Maybe by
this evening."

It was a decision made in an instant. She was glad to go home, where both her parents would fuss over her for a while. There she could take a few days and get some semblance of good sense. She needed to think this out. There was no reason for her to be this upset over Joshua. Or was there?

Besides, it *was* nice to stop scrubbing her apartment.

Although it was Saturday, BJ took the liberty of calling Cody VanderWeil at home. He was reluctant at first but did finally okay her taking several days emergency leave. With that done, she called Lucy and Darlene, who were both puzzled by the suddenness of the decision.

"But I don't understand," BJ's godmother complained.

"I suppose I forgot to mention it," BJ said airily. "You know I like to go to Columbia as often as I can."

"Yes . . . but . . ." Lucy said.

"Okay, see you when I get back," BJ said, glad to get off the phone.

BJ left three hours later. She dared not drive to Maryland in her unreliable car, so she took the bus to Washington, D.C., where her parents picked her up.

"Hi, Daddy, Momma." She kissed them as they walked back to the car.

"Barbara Jean," her mother said with a hug, and when her father surreptitiously elbowed her mother, BJ realized they were both on their good behavior.

BJ suspected they'd both decided not to call her baby-girl today. She wanted to smile because her parents were both trying to be careful in case the nickname should bring more tears. It almost made her laugh that her parents still thought her a girl who would cry over a nickname. But it also reminded her of telling Joshua about it on the first day they met. And sure enough, she didn't laugh but *was* tempted to cry. However, she didn't.

Of course she had to undergo her mother's scrutiny.

"Humph," her mother said. "You look like you're going to dry up and blow away."

BJ had her first genuine laugh that day, as she hugged her mother. It was one of their few disagreements. Her mother liked BJ to be more padded than she wanted for herself. When her mother tried to fatten her up, BJ would return to New York and work out to get rid of the extra pounds.

With a quick glance at her dad, BJ wondered if he looked a little grayer. But he had hopped spryly enough out of the car to wrestle with her bags.

"Oh, Daddy, I can do that," BJ protested, trying to hold on to her luggage.

It seemed so unnecessary for her father to be lifting her weekender, when at five foot ten she was younger and definitely strong enough to contend with her own baggage. But what could she do?

"Nonsense"—he pulled the bag out of her hand—"I'll put this right in the trunk. You just get in the car and talk to your mother." In a whisper, he added, "Psst, we'll talk later. You go be with your mother now. She got a little upset when she heard you cry."

"I'm sorry, Daddy."

"It's okay, whatever it is, we'll handle it," he promised.

On the thirty-minute drive to Columbia, BJ watched the rolling hillsides. Already she felt renewed. It was good to be back with her roots. Many of her extended family were no farther than an hour's drive away. Some were in the Washington, D.C., area, where they'd all lived at one time.

She took a deep breath with pleasure. Here the air was cleaner, and life simply seemed quieter, although that wasn't totally true. Many of the residents worked in the D.C. area and also lived relatively hectic lives.

Until they'd retired, both her parents had commuted to government jobs. Columbia was built around the same time her parents had married and had her. They'd bought their home when the area was originally being surveyed for development. It reminded her that Ashley Place would soon go into its renovated phase.

It didn't take long in Columbia before BJ was able to make some sense of her jumbled feelings. By Sunday morning, she felt she had a handle on things.

"I'm lonely, of course," BJ told her reflection in the mirror as she combed her hair that next day.

"My last date was almost two years ago. So naturally I feel strange when I'm around Joshua. And of course, I shouldn't have gone to bed with him. That was the mistake of a decade. I was never one of those girls who could do that kind of thing. Worse of all, he's too much like Basil. I'd just spend years waiting for Basil to say the word. And Joshua looked like act two of the same show. No way.

"What I should have done was approach it rationally and motionlessly. Just tell him that I wanted a baby. No, on second thought, I don't think that would have worked, either," BJ said aloud. She remembered the way he'd rushed out of her apartment.

The smartest thing for me to do is stay away from the man. He's too sexually lethal for his own good. Besides, it wouldn't be any great loss with his gigantic ego. Imagine that he'd known all the time, and just let me make the move on him. He might as well have said that he thought I was desperate. *I ought to show him I can have a dozen men.*

Yeah, wouldn't that be a big change for me? But being as such things never happen, let's stop the daydreaming, she told herself.

BJ spent the next few hours having lunch with an old teacher and visiting the Smithsonian museum. By the time she arrived back at the house, she was ready for a nap but went looking for her parents first. Her father was in the living room, watching a news program. He hadn't seen her, so busy was he fussing with the television reporter.

He looked so annoyed that BJ decided to leave without speaking. Upstairs in her room, she prepared to shower.

"BJ. There's a call for you," her mother said from the downstairs hallway.

BJ picked up to find Lucy on the line. "Girl, I was scared out of my wits. Why did you hang up so quickly yesterday?" Lucy complained.

"Lucy, I didn't want to discuss my trip with anyone. I simply wanted to come home," BJ said.

"You could have explained more," Lucy said.

"Then I might have missed my bus."

"What's this about your crying? Your father acts as if I've been beating you with rusty chains."

That stopped her. Of course her dad wouldn't think twice of questioning Lucy about that. "It didn't mean anything. A little PMS."

"You never had that before."

"What's the big deal? I've been visiting my parents all the time. What are you worried about?"

"I don't know. You seem different these past few months."

BJ certainly didn't want to go into any occurrences during the recent past. No way. "You're just imagining things. We'll talk when I get back." By then, BJ figured, she'd have something to reassure the older woman. "I have to go now."

"See what I mean? You hardly ever have time to talk with me lately."

"I have a pot on the stove that's boiling over," BJ said, rolling her eyes to heaven.

"Since when has your mother let you take over her kitchen?" Lucy was not willing to let her go.

"Lucy, please. We'll talk when I get home."

"All I'm asking for is an explanation for your rushing off to Columbia the way you did. Is that too much? And you might as well tell me."

"Okay," BJ said to appease Lucy. "I'll call you back later."

"You'd better," Lucy said.

BJ went into the shower. When she came out, she lay down for a few minutes only to awake an hour later. With a hasty glance at her watch, she went downstairs. Her mother was in the den, chatting on the phone, and her father was in the kitchen. He looked much more pleased, she thought, as he dried the dishes and whistled to himself.

"Oh, there you are," he said, looking slyly. He chuckled happily. She didn't get a chance to question his mood before her mother called.

"BJ, another call."

Lucy again, BJ thought, as she entered the den and took the phone from her mother. For some reason, her mother looked smug, too.

"Lucy," BJ said with no preamble, "I don't have another word to say about it. I wanted to come home, and when Cody okayed it, I packed and left. At my age, I can do exactly as I please."

"How old are you?" Joshua asked.

"Oh," BJ said in shock, and there was a long pause. "I didn't realize it was you."

"I wondered how you were doing."

"Great!" she rattled back to him. "I mean that I'm doing fine." She glanced around guiltily, not wanting her parents to hear this conversation.

"Family all right?"

"Yes, of course."

"Good," he said.

There was a prolonged silence.

"Why did you call?" she asked, trying to keep her voice low.

"Just wondering if everything was all right."

"Well, you needn't worry yourself. I'm just fine. You didn't break my heart in the least bit."

"You have to admit that you left suddenly."

"It didn't mean a thing. I always do that. How did you get this number?"

"Lucy."

"I should have guessed," she said.

"She was worried, too. She said that it wasn't like you to do things this precipitously."

"For heavens sake. Coming to see my parents isn't something that I have to plan for weeks."

"No, but Lucy didn't want you running around on the rebound."

"On the rebound? All we did was . . . Did you tell Lucy?"

"Only what I had to," he answered.

"You didn't have to tell her anything."

"When Lucy and Darlene became worried about you, I had to explain—"

"You didn't have to explain a thing to her. All she ever does is get me into trouble. Oh, never mind."

"All right, I didn't tell her anything," he admitted then. "It was me who didn't want you to get caught up in any rash behavior."

"Like what? Jump off my parents' garage?"

"I don't think of you as a tragic heroine or anything like that." He paused then added, "I was thinking more of any sudden rash behavior with men."

"Really, Josh, you take yourself much too seriously."

"Well, with your birthday and your recent depression."

"What birthday? My birthday was months ago."

"Darlene said you were depressed."

"Darlene? You spoke with Darlene, too?" BJ forgot to lower her voice for that moment.

"Yes," he answered.

BJ spoke in a near whisper. "Darlene is wrong. I am not depressed, and I enjoyed my birthday. However, what I am not enjoying is this telephone conversation—not one iota."

"I told them you were probably all right," he said.

"Goodbye, Josh," and she banged the receiver onto the phone.

The phone began to make the sound that it hadn't been seated on the receiver right, and she caught it and banged it purposefully.

"Who was that?" her mother queried.

"No one," BJ snapped with more emotion than she intended.

"Really? He said that he worked with you and—"

"He does not work with me," BJ said angrily and banged the receiver again when the grating noise started again.

"He also said you were very good friends, and that the last time you talked you argued—"

"He said what?" BJ wanted to howl, and she started to bang down the phone once again. Instead she mentally calmed herself and gently placed the receiver correctly. Once she was sure this was done, she turned to her mother. More than anything, she wanted to ask her mother exactly what Josh had said, but somehow while her mother's one eyebrow was raised, BJ suddenly lost her courage. Maybe she really didn't want to know what he'd told her mother.

Chapter Twelve

When BJ hung up on him this time, Joshua swore he was going to drive immediately to Columbia, Maryland. The woman was an absolute bewildering mass of contradictions.

He was so peeved that he left his apartment, deciding to go to his office despite its being Sunday. In the foul mood he was in, looking at the bare walls only made it worse. He'd even brought Hannibal on the drive to the office, figuring if the apartment bothered him, it should have bothered the dog, too. *Some watchdog—I have to rescue him from my bare apartment.*

Joshua stepped into his offices and found Linda Collins going through his files. She looked incredibly uncomfortable on being caught, for some reason. Hannibal, who'd never been to the office before, growled.

"What are you doing here?" he asked.

"I had a few loose ends to tie up and thought I'd come in today," Linda replied.

Joshua removed his coat, hung it up, and sat down

behind his large chrome and glass desk. He sensed Linda shifting as if to leave.

"You ever hear your biological clock ticking?" Joshua asked on impulse.

Linda frowned. "No way. Why should I?"

"You don't want children?"

"You kidding? And have my whole life turned upside down with a bunch of snotty-nosed brats? Why are you asking? You were never interested in kids before."

"Me? I'm not interested in kids, I was simply asking a hypothetical question." He waved for her to leave.

He watched his assistant exit. Something about the scene that he'd just witnessed didn't sit too well with him. Linda had actually looked guilty when he'd caught her going through his files.

But Josh was in no mood for Linda today. He had other fish to fry. His thoughts had already traveled back to BJ. She ruined his clothes, maligned his background, and seemed to be making a real habit of banging the phone in his ear. So why hadn't he simply washed his hands of her? Only heaven knew.

He was sick of feeling as disturbed as he'd been since Saturday morning. That was only about thirty-six hours ago, he realized. However, neither his heart nor his body was the least bit sick of the lovely BJ. He was as indecisive as he'd ever been in his life. It was infuriating. No matter how patient he was with that woman, she always managed to make him feel like an ax murderer or something equally as bad. Was there anything equally as bad, he wondered.

And as for why he allowed her so many liberties—he stood in the middle of the floor to spread his arms—he had absolutely no idea. He should have gone out and found himself a woman. Problem was that no woman seemed to catch his attention. If he wasn't trying to sneak a glance at BJ's legs, he was watching her every move. Now since

aturday, he was trying to imagine how their children
ould look.

"That woman has jinxed me," he said aloud.

She's got me running after her like a greyhound chasing
rabbit. I thought she was supposed to be after me.

He stopped that trend of thought by promising that he
vouldn't permit BJ's aggravating habits to get to him. She'll
ome around, he thought. There aren't many men like
ne, who'd have shown the mercy toward her that I did.
:gad! She asked to have my child! But no, I better not think
f that, because then I will drive to Columbia.

Best to think how fortunate I am. How glad I am to have
scaped from her crazy ideas. Sperm donor! Twins? It was
>etter this way.

The woman called him names at the drop of a hat—
gotistical, arrogant—me? Was that true? he wondered.
iuddenly he wondered if he had injured her feminine
>ride or something like that. You never knew with women.
)ne minute they'd be tough as nails, and next thing you
:new, wham! They'd be crying.

A second positively ghastly thought insinuated itself into
iis brain. Suppose she wasn't going to change? Suppose
ihe was going to slip away from him? Suppose it was he
vho had to change for BJ?

That he didn't like at all. Ahh, she'll come around, he
nsisted again. This time he'd make sure, and he reached
or the phone to dial Lucy.

As for Lucy and Darlene, he hated to think of himself
as falling so low as to need them to set him up with BJ.
He'd never live that one down. But then this would just
>e a friendly little chat. Knowing Lucy, she'd bring it up,
and then he could act innocent.

It was while waiting for Lucy to answer that the third
awful thought occurred. He wondered how serious the
problems with BJ would be when she discovered that he
was going to raze Ashley Place and start from scratch.

Lucy knew already, as did Cody VanderWeil, about the
real plans.

"Hello, Lucy." He thought he sounded pretty cool,
although it *was* his third call to the woman in one day.

"Why, Joshua, what a nice surprise for you to call again,"
Lucy said. "Darlene just hung up. We're both still worried
about BJ . . ."

Joshua wondered if it was just his imagination, or if
Chairwoman Lucy McPhearson did manage to sound sly
and knowing on the phone.

"How long have you two been friends?" BJ's mother
asked.

"I am not friends with that man," BJ said emphatically.

"Well, he certainly seemed to think that you two were
very close."

"I'll kill him," BJ muttered.

"What did you say, darling?"

"Oh, really, Mother, you shouldn't worry. We've been
doing some work together, that's all. He's not my boy-
friend."

"For some reason, I thought it was more personal."

"Well, it's not."

Just at that moment, her father came in, and he was
drying a dish clumsily. Ever since he'd retired and proved
a nuisance around the house, her mother made certain
that he helped with the housework. He loved it, although
he loved to complain almost more than actually doing the
work.

"Did you get the call from Josh?" Oh, no, BJ thought.
Don't tell me Josh spoke to Daddy, too. "Seems like a
pretty smart young man for a New Yorker and for someone
who knows Lucy. He called earlier. Said he wanted to
surprise you."

"Yes, I'll bet he did," BJ groused, remembering how

cheerfully her father had been whistling when she came downstairs.

"That's what I was just trying to tell her," her mother chimed in. "He's much more sensible than her other friend was."

BJ knew only too well which other friend her mother was speaking of. Neither of them ever liked Basil. They thought him too citified, and of course they'd both been right, too. But for them to not see that Joshua and Basil were both cut from the same cloth was unusual.

When her father had left, her mother said, "Ready to tell me what happened—why you were crying yesterday?"

"It wasn't anything important. Maybe I was just premenstrual."

"That I don't believe. But maybe if you told me it was a man, I might take that more serious. Was it a man?"

In a way, BJ wanted to open up to her mother and admit that she'd been crying her eyes out because of Joshua's rejection. But it wasn't something she wanted to discuss now. Having admitted to herself how much she wanted a baby was something she still had to deal with. Soon she might have to tell her parents that she'd decided to have a baby sans husband. That would be enough for her parents to deal with. They didn't need to hear about her sex life, too.

"I don't want to talk about it now, Mom. Give me a little time."

"Okay, but you know your father's not as relaxed about you as I am. You near scared him out of ten years' growth."

"Yes, I know. And I'm sorry, too," BJ said, looking away from her mother.

"Hah! Well, don't worry too much. Your dad loves a little excitement in his life. That's why I like to give him a hard time. But you know you were always his darling, beautiful child."

BJ raised her eyes to her mother. "I never felt so beautiful, though I do admit that you and Daddy both used to tell me that. All I remember is shooting up so fast that I thought my knees and elbows would be declared lethal weapons. It seemed all the princesses were small and dainty and frequently blonde.

Her mother chuckled. "I know you were bewildered when you grew taller than most of the boys in your class, but you adjusted."

"Playing ball helped," BJ said. "Of course I did love it that everyone thought I'd be a model. That made me very happy until I began to fill out across the breasts and bottom."

"Shoot! I was glad when you did, too. Think I wanted my baby-girl looking gaunt, like she never had a decent meal? Besides, you were never plump, just curvy, which is nice."

They both laughed at that. BJ said, "Well, at least my mother approves of me."

"You better believe it," her mother responded. "But you know something, honey?" her mother said as if an after-thought. "And don't get touchy now, but this is something that I've got to say."

Huh, BJ thought, now she's got something bad to tell me. "What is it, Mom?"

"You always had a funny little thing about you that I know you don't like to talk about. But you see how Lucy and Darlene are always trying to mother you?"

"Yes?" Actually BJ knew exactly what her mother was going to say. She'd said it before.

"You need to look at that, honey. Why do you think you're a target for people like that?"

"Mom, don't tell me it's all *my* fault."

"Maybe not all your fault, but you're responsible for part of it. You've been doing it since you were a small girl—ever since you shot up so tall. Somehow you get yourself into a small ball, and everyone rushes to save you."

Unexpectedly BJ thought of playing basketball with Joshua. She'd hammed it up a little when she'd fallen, and poor Josh had near died. Was that what her mother meant? But that was just a little game. Wasn't it? It had gotten her thoroughly kissed, too, she remembered.

"Okay, I'll think about what you've said," BJ answered. "Is that good enough?"

"That's good enough for now."

BJ's mother then proceeded to dish out a healthy plate and set it in front of BJ. As she looked down, BJ wanted to smile. *My mother is still making certain that I don't look gaunt.* But it was good to have her parents fuss over her, so she dug in and ate everything. Soon enough when she returned to Long Island to cut back again.

Later her mother said, "BJ, I know you just told me that you didn't want to discuss it, but I need to say this. You've been avoiding dating since you broke up with that Basil. Honey, that was two years ago. You can't let him sour you on men. He wasn't good enough for you to begin with."

"Oh, Mom," and she put her arms around her mother. "Don't worry, I'm long over him. It's just that—maybe I need to make my own decisions about this."

"Don't take too long. That's all I'm asking."

She's right, BJ thought. Basil did have me running scared for longer than I wish to remember. But I've been over him a long time. However, it wasn't until Joshua that I began to want a baby. And as for my response to him that night, who would have thought that would happen?

When she left her mother in the kitchen, she found her father in the living room, sitting in front of the television. He had a pipe in his mouth.

"Daddy, are you smoking that pipe! You know Mom will give you hell," BJ said.

"Watch your language, girl. And no, I ain't smoked since you were a little spud. Your mom used to have such caterwauling fits that I couldn't even enjoy my occasional pipe smoking. That's why I like to keep it in my mouth sometimes, just so she can see what I gave up for her.'' He leaned over and pulled the hassock toward him. ''Come on and sit over here by Daddy.''

As BJ sat next to him, looking upward from the hassock, she suddenly felt incredibly comforted. It reminded her of so many talks they'd had in the living room. While her mother might better understand her emotions, it was her father who had taught her the way of the world.

''BJ, all I'm going to say is that you don't have to get married if you don't want to, no matter what anyone says. And you're a beautiful woman, a treasure of great worth. Some man will see that—the right man.''

''Oh, Daddy.''

''Now don't tell your mother what I said. She'll be fussing after me for weeks.''

BJ hugged and kissed him as if she were still ten years old. Maybe today's wisdom hadn't been world shaking, but it had been nice to hear.

As for her not telling her mother, it wasn't long before she heard him in the kitchen, picking a squabble with his wife about what he'd just said. BJ had a fleeting moment of wondering if she'd ever find such a mate for herself. One that she could fight with and still love with all her heart in the years to come.

Curiously enough, despite having a wonderful time with her family, by Monday evening she was ready to go home to Long Island. She was concerned about her clients at Ashley Place. She also wondered what Darlene and Lucy were up to. And thoughts of Josh had stayed with her throughout the entire three days.

When BJ unwound her long legs and stepped off the bus from Columbia, she was ready. The time spent in Maryland had rejuvenated her. In the days away, she'd rested, talked to both parents several times, taken a side trip or two, and made important decisions for her life.

If Darlene wanted a New Year's resolution, she had it, albeit a little late. If Lucy wanted her to be better informed about the world, was Lucy going to be surprised. . . . She was going to read more and watch the television news, too.

BJ was going to turn over a new leaf. Actually she had planned on turning over a whole forest of new leaves. All blind dates were a thing of the past. And as soon as she hung up her clothes, she pulled out all her old tank dresses—oops—make that tent dresses. Into the GoodWill boxes they all went.

"Never could stand them, anyway."

Last but not least, she was going to date. She'd show Mr. Perfect. He might think she was a hopeless case, prone to commit suicide, but she'd show him. Let him watch her dust.

She was also going to find out what was happening at Ashley Place. Someone was going to give her a few answers and soon. All of this lasted until she went to work on Wednesday morning and found four new caseloads on her desk.

"Cody, what am I supposed to do with these? They won't even fit into my file cabinet."

"I'm sure you'll think of something," Cody said.

"They're at the other end of town. When will I get to see the clients at Ashley Place?"

"You'll just have to prioritize carefully. Ashley Place isn't your only site. Everyone has to bite the bullet."

Later Darlene came over, looking slightly sulky. She sat at BJ's desk. "So how was the trip?"

"Just fine," BJ answered, pouring over the new cases.

"You could have told me before you went traipsing off like that. It near scared me to death."

BJ glanced at Darlene, remembering what her mother had said. Was her mother right? Had she become so spoiled

by her friend and her godmother that she sometimes
allowed them to fuss over her?

"You miss me?" BJ asked, ruffling Darlene's hair.

"Never mind," Darlene said, straightening her hair, but
she did appear less sulky and more relaxed. "How were
your parents?"

"Oh, good, good," BJ said.

"You know, the weirdest thing happened this weekend,"
Darlene started, sounding facetious. "Joshua Hendricks
called every day, something he's never done before. I
didn't even know we were that kind of friends."

"Really?" BJ said as she ducked back into the files.

"Yes, and I don't think he's suddenly developed a burn-
ing desire to hear *my* voice, either. He asked for your
telephone number in Columbia that first day."

"Oh, that? Yes, he *did* call."

"And so . . ." Darlene encouraged.

"He only wanted more information about Ashley Place.
You remember, we did that little orientation tour."

"Mmm," Darlene said. "I think he's ready. This could
be your year. Come on, say it. What's the matter with you?"

"Darlene, please. Let's not start with that again."

"It's true. Joshua is ready to fall right into your lap."

"He's too big to sit in my lap."

"So you sit in his. Look at how hot he got under the
collar, just because I made a little suggestion to you. Even
Carlos agrees."

"I'm sure that had nothing to do with me." BJ wanted
to squirm under Darlene's gaze. She felt guilty about not
telling Darlene anything about the relationship with
Joshua. But what was to tell? That she'd had a one-night
stand with Joshua? Yet BJ knew she could have mentioned
that they'd dated. It was just that, for once, she wanted
something private. Even though there was little possibility
of anything, other than their one-night stand, she wanted
it to be personal. She wasn't ready to share it yet. "Maybe

he simply likes clowns who fall on their face," BJ said, wanting to change the subject.

"BJ, you were never a clown, maybe a little clumsy but never a clown."

"Thank you for a few crumbs, best friend."

Darlene ignored that. "Did you ever call him about the shirt?"

"Which one?" popped out of BJ's mouth before she thought.

Fortunately Darlene didn't seem to hear. "I can't understand why it doesn't take. You two are perfect for each other."

"No, not him," BJ said, feeling uncomfortable as the conversation continued.

"What's wrong with him? He's got to be the best I ever sicced on you."

"I'm glad you're admitting you did sic him on me. But although he's all right, he's not my type."

"You could change him if you tried."

"What about his assistant, Linda? She's more his type than I am." BJ was curious to hear Darlene's assessment of the other woman.

"Linda? She's not even in the running."

"How do you know that? I think she wants him."

"So what if she does? He needs a nice girl like you."

BJ groaned. "Nice? Puleeze! That makes me sound so boring."

"He doesn't look bored to me. Don't you want a husband and babies, too?"

"So misery can have company?"

"I am not miserable, and this is serious. Answer my question."

"Yes, but . . . I don't need a husband to have babies."

"Shhh." Darlene put her finger to her lips and looked guilty as she furtively glanced around. "Suppose someone heard you? Come on, let's go to lunch. Hunger is turning your brain to mush.''

A few minutes later in the elevator going down, Darlene said, ''I can't believe you said that.''

Several hours later, BJ was on the phone with Lucy and wondered how they could be having the same conversation that she'd had earlier with Darlene.

''Lucy, I'm not going out with anyone, so stop trying to hook me up with those guys. They're never my type.''

''What about Joshua?'' Lucy snapped back. ''I can't for the life of me understand why you two never got together. He's always asking for you.''

''That's very nice of him,'' BJ said.

''He's obviously interested. I'll bet if you played your cards right, you could land him.''

''Like he's a fish?'' BJ asked facetiously.

''Sometimes catching a husband is like fishing or maybe even like a tiger hunt. You have to beat the bushes.''

BJ wanted to chuckle. A lot Lucy knew about tiger hunts. But she didn't laugh. Instead, she said, ''Maybe I don't want a husband. Maybe what I want is a child.''

At first there was total silence. Then Lucy said, ''Omigod! Suppose your mother had heard that? She'd blame it all on me and swear I'd been a bad influence. Being a bad influence on two generations of females in your family is more than I can handle. For that matter, so would your father . . . everyone in Columbia and D.C. . . . perish that thought, would blame me, too. I don't want to even think on this.''

''Lucy, I'm not a child. I *can* make my own decisions. No one would blame you.'' All she could hear was Lucy groaning in the background. Lucy was inclined toward dramatics when all else failed. BJ spoke into the phone, ''I only said a husband wasn't necessary.''

"I have to go now," Lucy said, "You've given me a headache."

"Lucy?" This time it was Lucy who hung up. BJ felt a little guilty, but the truth was that she *had* been thinking of having a baby. She was mature and could afford to raise one. It was something that would come up again.

BJ sighed. If Josh had agreed, she might have already been pregnant. The thought made her yearn.

Only a few moments later, the phone rang again. "So you finally got home?" Joshua's sexy voice came over the line. She almost felt as if she had called him up by magic.

"Yes, although I don't think it's any of your business," BJ answered.

"How could you tell poor Lucy that you were thinking of having a baby sans husband," Joshua said.

"You already knew that. And what are you doing talking to Lucy about that?" *What's with this poor Lucy?* Were the three of them discussing everything about her over the phone? BJ wondered.

"She's positively distraught." Joshua's voice dripped disapproval.

"All I said was that I didn't need a man to have babies," BJ said. Joshua's annoyance was quite satisfying.

"Would you stop saying that!" he yelled. She had to take the phone away from her ear. "Are you losing your mind?"

"I am quite sane, and this is my choice," BJ said.

"Are you saying that to other men? You need a keeper, that's what you need!"

When he took a few moments to catch his breath, BJ put the phone back to her ear. "This has nothing to do with you. You've already had your chance."

She could hear him drop something as he cursed and spluttered. "Now you're going to hell and back with this," he snarled.

"Why not? *You* are no longer in the running." Lord, she was enjoying this.

"I don't want to be in the running. Think I'd saddle myself with a wife and a dozen crumb snatchers?"

Chapter Thirteen

"There, you see? Who said anything about a wife, and I already told you I would take full responsibility. And last but not least, no man had ever better call any child of mine a crumb snatcher. Furthermore"—she had to stop to catch *her* breath—"when did Lucy, 'the Mafia godmother,' become 'poor Lucy'?"

"She's different where you're concerned. She only wants what's best for you," Joshua said, sounding calmer now that they were talking about Lucy.

"Don't let my godmother fool you. She's always got her own agenda," BJ said, recognizing on some level that she was being ambivalent.

"Why haven't you told Lucy and Darlene that we've been seeing each other?" he asked.

"Seeing each other? Or do you mean our one-night stand?" she asked facetiously. Then added, "Why didn't you?"

"What do I look like? A kid? Besides, you swore me to secrecy."

"So you think *I'm* a kid? Anyway, Lucy is really very old fashioned."

"So am I, if you'd bothered to notice," he said. Then added, "What about Darlene? I thought women told their best friends everything?"

"Oh, puleeze. My sex life is nobody's business. Everybody would be trying to marry us off."

"Maybe we could see each other," he said, surprising her after the fireworks he'd sent over the telephone wires at her.

"You mean so that we can repeat that night?"

"I didn't say that."

"You don't have to. I know what you mean."

"What are you, a mind reader?"

"No, but I sure know what's on your mind."

"Maybe I spoke too hastily that day. You have to remember you did throw it at me suddenly. It's not an everyday occurrence for a woman to ask me for a baby. Usually I'd think marriage would come first."

"Marriage was not an option," she said.

"I thought you wanted to get married and have a family. That's what you said before."

"I've changed my mind. Anyway, forget it. That's the least of the problem."

"It is?"

"Our very philosophies are different. Didn't *you* notice?"

"Notice? When?"

"When you rudely ran off that poor beggar."

"He was trying to take advantage of your soft heart." Joshua sounded totally without remorse.

Well, at least he hadn't said her soft head. "How could you know what he was trying to do? Now you're the mind reader? Perhaps you should remember that good DNA will always include compassion."

"Compassion?" Joshua spluttered.

"I have nothing more to say, Josh, except goodbye."

"Wait!" he stopped grousing long enough to say, "I know this is none of my business, but this situation does alarm me."

"Please say exactly what you mean before I hang up."

"I'm talking about Lucy and all those blind dates. You're falling right into your godmother's hands."

"How's that?"

"She's putting a lot of pressure on you. Choosing a father for your child should be done carefully."

"And?" she drew the word out.

"At least I could give you time to look for your child's father at your leisure."

"Why would you be so kind to me?"

"I'd hate to see you back with Lucy and Darlene setting up blind dates for you, which is what will happen without me squiring you around."

"Not necessarily. I could simply go out with men of my own choice," she said and thought, wouldn't that be a joke. I haven't even met a man in months.

"When's the last time you had such a choice? Good men are hard to find," Joshua Hendricks informed her.

She felt as if the top of her head exploded. Rather she felt as if the top of her head exploded, and he'd just read her mind.

"What did you say!" BJ said softly. But before he could answer, she went on. "Surely you aren't implying that I can't find a date for myself?"

"When was the last time you did?"

Lord, she thought, it's a good thing I can't get my hands on the man, I'd probably throw something at him. "As it happens," she lied smoothly, "I'm going out tonight."

"Yeah, sure, I believe that. A woman who hasn't been out in months has a long line of dates waiting," he said. "Look, maybe we need to talk. How about dinner tonight?"

"Joshua, I wouldn't eat with you if you were the last man alive," she hissed. "You'd give me indigestion."

"Now, now, don't get yourself all riled up," he said in a voice that would have annoyed a saint in heaven. "Who did you say you were seeing tonight?"

Aha! He had heard her, but maybe she shouldn't say tonight. "I didn't exactly say tonight."

"I'm absolutely certain that's what you said."

"I meant to say tomorrow night."

"Tomorrow with whom?"

Now she had him, she thought triumphantly. "The next thing you hear will be a dial tone," she said sweetly, before gently lowering the phone.

Now that she'd hung up, BJ realized she hadn't felt this good for a long time. She was out to show that arrogant stuck on himself man. It was positively wonderful. Of course she wasn't personally interested in him for anything except his gene pool, but, ah well, who knew?

Nevertheless BJ fully intended to ignore Joshua. She knew fully well that his main complaint was a bruised ego. Today she would embark on a plan to find her own date, whether nice or obnoxious, to prove once and for all that she didn't need anyone to find a man for her. Unfortunately she would have to act fast if she was going to have a date by tomorrow night. Who in God's name could she convince to take her out between now and then?

She swivelled in her chair and looked around the huge open office. The first person she saw was Norman Delaney, one of her co-workers. Aha, she thought, the perfect candidate.

Although he was fairly good looking and a very nice man, almost every single woman in the office had a Norman story. Norman had been divorced for two years, and the only woman he was really interested in was his ex-wife. Most of the women avoided him. BJ sighed, but she couldn't afford to be choosey.

She kept her eyes on him until something made him look up. Then she smiled. He looked inordinately pleased and smiled back. A few minutes later, Norman got up and walked across the room toward her.

BJ chatted with Norman for a few minutes before she got up the courage to invite him to a play she wanted to see that was appearing at an off-Broadway theater.

"Ah, I can't," Norman said, sounding regretful. "I've scheduled evening visits for tomorrow. But what about Saturday?"

"That would be nice," BJ agreed.

After Norman was gone, she realized that she still needed a date for tomorrow. The immediate success with Norman emboldened BJ to try again. There was no way she wouldn't have a date for tomorrow. She'd show Joshua if it killed her. She rifled through her address book until she came to Max Hawkins's number.

Max Hawkins was a political hanger-on with big ambitions. She'd met him some time ago through Lucy. Under ordinary circumstances, she would never have gone out with Max but extraordinary circumstances called for extraordinary action. She dialed Max's work number.

"BJ?" Max sounded surprised when he realized who she was. "Well, well, what can I do for you?" His voice sounded oily and sly.

"I was wondering if you had a little time tomorrow evening. I wanted to discuss something with you."

"You know I always have time for you. I have to be at the Democratic Center for a while, but you can meet me there."

Hearing they'd be in the Community Center was good news, because the last time she'd gone out with Max, he'd become a bit amorous.

"Oh, that's great," BJ said, knowing she sounded too eager. But for once, she didn't care. She felt like she'd just put one over on Josh. Now, she thought, all I need to do is find something important to warrant my calling Max up like this.

When she hung up, Lucy called again.

"What's this about your having a date for tomorrow?" the older woman demanded.

"Who told you that?" BJ almost shrieked.

What was this—telephone tag they were all playing? Joshua must have hung up on her and immediately called her godmother. BJ absolutely couldn't believe this. Were all her family and friends talking to Joshua about her? What traitors.

"Joshua did," Lucy answered.

"Since when do you talk to him about me?" BJ was so annoyed that she added, "It just so happens that I do have an appointment—with Max Hawkins."

"Max Hawkins? Whatever for?" Lucy asked.

"Why are you asking? You're the one who introduced us."

"So what? I introduced you to Joshua, too, and I don't see you going out with him. I thought you hated Max?"

"Nonsense. Whatever gave you that idea?"

"*You* did, after you kept calling him a creep."

After work, BJ and Darlene as usual went down the elevator together.

"You look like the cat that swallowed the canary," Darlene remarked. "What are you up to?"

BJ's first response to Darlene's question was to wonder if she'd been talking to Lucy or Joshua. But obviously it wasn't true. *Just my imagination.*

"No big deal. I just made plans to see Max Hawkins tomorrow night," BJ said smugly.

"Max? I thought you said you almost punched his lights out last time."

"Did I say that? I guess I was taking things too seriously."

"BJ!" Darlene was flabbergasted.

"Don't worry, we're meeting at the Community Center, and then we'll eat at a local eatery. Nothing more, and it will be dutch."

"What about later, when he takes you home?"

"He won't take me home, I'll drive my own car."

"I don't think you—"

"Max knows not to try anything. I'm taller than he. And Saturday, Norman Delaney is taking me to see . . ." BJ paused. "We haven't decided where we're going," BJ said, feeling suddenly cagey.

"Norman Delaney? I thought you said you fell asleep the last time you went out with him."

"Maybe I was tired. Talk to you tomorrow," BJ said and got into her car.

Fortunately the engine turned over, and she was able to make a graceful exit. In the rearview mirror, she watched as Darlene gazed after her. It made BJ want to laugh. That ought to teach all of them that she could handle her own dates. Of course both men had been introduced by Lucy and Darlene, but at least these appointments were her own.

The next night after work, BJ drove her car to the Community Center to meet Max. She wasn't looking forward to it because the last time she'd dated Max, she'd sworn never again.

As soon as she walked in, she knew it had been a mistake. Max gave her a lecherous look and smiled as if he'd won the numbers. Max was a short, slightly plump, fair-skinned man who ambulated with a slightly rolling gait. He had two major conversational gambits. The first was how many women wanted him, and the second was all the famous people who needed him.

Fortunately Max couldn't leave right away. She spent

the next three hours stuffing envelopes for the district political club. She certainly preferred working for the community than listening to Max talk about himself. The problem was that it went on longer than she planned, and she was beginning to long for her bed. The local eatery they'd spoken of wound up being the neighborhood's fast-food burger joint, where a group of noisy teenagers were acting up. She was staring around at them when Max led her to their table.

"So what's so important that you had to talk with me?" Max asked.

"Oh," she said stupidly before she remembered. "I was wondering if you knew anything about the plans for renovating Ashley Place."

Max smirked. "Why not ask Lucy?" he asked. "She's the expert on that."

BJ suspected he thought her question was only a ploy to get him out tonight, and indeed he would be right. That didn't stop her from wanting to poke him nevertheless.

"I thought that you might be able to add something to what Lucy said," she answered.

"Something more than Lucy? Your faith in me is very flattering." He looked around importantly.

He put one moist hand over hers and smiled slyly. As soon as she could, she moved her hand and picked up her burger.

"Just wondering," she said.

Now she wished she hadn't done this. Not even Joshua was worth having to put up with Max.

"I'll ask around—just for you—you understand," he said with a suggestive wink.

"Yes," she said, "I'd appreciate that."

"How much would you appreciate it?"

Egad, she thought, the man's still a creep. She glanced surreptitiously at her watch. "Oh, look at the time," she said. "I really must be going."

As luck would have it, her car wouldn't start. Max stood there, watching her futile efforts with a big greasy smile on his face.

"Don't worry your little head about it," he said. "I'll take you home."

She would have preferred calling a car service but thought that would have been rude. She had asked the man to see her. Besides, if he tried anything, he'd be sorry.

"Okay," she said.

Max took her home and walked her to the door despite her trying to stop him. She had pulled out her keys in the car, wanting them handy to avoid any wrestling matches when they said good night.

At her door, Max tried to kiss her. BJ turned her cheek.

"Why don't you invite me up for a drink?" he said.

"Sorry, I have to get up early for work tomorrow," she said, turning the key.

When the door opened, Max pushed in with her and smiled up at her. He stood with his back to the door and tried to push it shut without turning around, but the door resisted his efforts.

"You know you didn't want to talk about Ashley Place. I know what you really want," Max said.

BJ didn't like the sound of that. She spoke through clenched teeth: "It was very generous of you to see me tonight, but I really have to go now."

Instead of leaving, he grabbed her arm and tried to press his mouth against hers. She was disgusted. It was bad enough to have him force a kiss on her, but he was shorter and had dragged her head down to do it. First, she tried to shove him away, and when that didn't work, she kicked him in the shins.

"Yikes!" he let out, releasing her to grab his shins. "Why you little—"

Joshua's voice seemed to come from nowhere. "I think you'd better leave her alone."

Max and BJ turned to stare in shock at Joshua standing with his foot holding the door open.

"What are you doing here?" BJ asked, bewildered by this turn of events.

"Who are you?" Max said, switching his attention from her to the tall man.

"A friend of Barbara Jean's," Joshua answered.

BJ was on the verge of saying that Joshua was no friend of hers but realized she didn't have any desire to explain anything to Max Hawkins. And although she was embarrassed that Josh had seen her having to fend off the short man, she was also glad to see him.

There they stood, Josh closest to the open door, with Max between them.

"Well, good night to both of you," she said, trying to encourage them to leave by pushing the door. Joshua looked surprised, but he moved backward and was now standing outside. It was Max who tried to stand his ground.

"Now just a minute," Max said. "You're the one who invited me."

"Max, you've already had a free envelope-stuffer and even a hamburger. That's the full treatment. Now please go," BJ said. She'd really had it for one night.

"You know you wanted more than that," Max's voice said insultingly.

She couldn't stop the impulse of a quick glance at Josh. This was going to make her look like a really desperate woman. Josh frowned, looking like a thundercloud ready to burst. She managed to stand her ground with Max but wondered what Joshua thought of all this.

"If I did," she said with as much aplomb as she could manage, "I've changed my mind."

Josh stepped in, saying, "I guess that means goodbye for you, buddy."

"Goodbye for me? What about you?" Max said.

"Maybe you should worry about your own problems," Josh said, towering over the shorter man.

Somehow Josh managed to look menacing, with very little effort. After a split second of doubt, Max hustled back to his car and drove off.

"Who the hell is the runt? I can't believe you let him bring you home. Haven't you ever heard of date rape? He looks just the type to me."

"Did anyone ask for your opinion?" BJ snapped. "Anyway, he works in Lucy's office."

"Not another blind date?"

"No, it isn't. Besides, it's none of your business."

"You can't be serious about this hunting for a sperm donor?" Josh said.

"Why can't I?"

"Look at him, he's got bad feet," Josh said.

"It's his character that counts, not his feet."

"Character! That guy's already sold his soul for a vote, and he'll never run for office."

"You don't know a thing about this."

"Anybody can see it. Okay, forget about his feet, but think about those beady eyes. It would be different if you were in love. Would you deliberately give your child those eyes?" Josh asked.

It was the perfect thing for Josh to say. She looked into his glorious brown eyes, and her insides quivered. She knew the eyes she wanted her children to have.

"That has nothing to do with you. Besides, what are you doing here?" BJ said, returning to a safer topic.

"You should thank your lucky stars that I was here," he said. "Lucy was worried about you."

"Lucy!" BJ realized she was disappointed. She had wanted him to say that he'd come on his own.

* * *

Joshua didn't call her the next two days, and she was slightly put out about it. On Friday she called Darlene about going to lunch—something they had done almost every day for ten years.

"Yes," Darlene said when she picked up.

"How about Chinese today," BJ said. "I'll treat you."

"Oh, BJ," Darlene said. "I meant to call you before. I have a previous commitment today."

"Oh?" BJ said, curious. "I hope it's not Lucy again."

"No, it's Joshua," Darlene said with total aplomb.

"Joshua!"

"Yes, he called earlier. You'll be all right. Right?" Darlene said.

"Of course," BJ said, trying to sound totally unconcerned.

She went and had a soggy frank from the local heartburn wagon and fumed about Darlene dining—probably at some upscale restaurant with Joshua.

Saturday BJ went shopping and bought herself a sexy black knit dress. When she got home, she fell across the bed, wanting nothing more than to sleep and never move again, but she couldn't.

Tonight was the night that she and Norman Delaney were going to the theater and have dinner afterward. She should have been pleased for the chance. It was an off-Broadway show that she wanted to see. After that fiasco with Maxwell Hawkins, tonight would certainly prove to everyone that she could find her own man.

And it would show Joshua Hendricks that she had no intention of chasing after him. Imagine him playing bird dog for Lucy and spying on her with Max. He'd even offered himself as a martyr, as if she needed him to play big brother to her. And if he thought that she'd go along with some long-term, nebulous relationship in which she'd wait for him to make up his mind, he could think again.

When she'd been wrestling with Max and looked up to see Joshua looking like her personal avenger, she'd been incredibly glad. Not that she couldn't have handled Max— but it was so much nicer to have Joshua scare him away.

Time to dress, she realized. She would have loved to wear exactly what she had on, but quickly nixed that idea. If she was going to make a success of this, she had to do it right. BJ rolled over onto her back and stared at the ceiling for a few minutes before making herself sit. A few moments later, she started dressing.

She donned the new dress and realized that out of the showroom it suddenly looked much too brief, showing a great deal of leg and cleavage. It reminded her of the red dress she'd purchased at Darlene's instigation. She had a few moments of hesitation, wondering if she should wear it. But Norman wasn't Max.

True, Norman was still very emotionally attached to his ex-wife to be much of a date, but at least he was a gentle-man. That decided her, and she kept the dress on. For her hair, she pulled it all to the side and applied mousse. After a quick look, she added a comb. Finally she applied makeup. She looked quite sophisticated, she thought, but decided to take Darlene's advice and keep to cabs. No sense freezing to death for Norman. He'd probably never notice.

But when Norman picked her up, he was quite apprecia-tive of the efforts she'd taken to look nice. Hmm, she thought, looks like Norman's finally recovering from his ex-wife. She was pleased that she'd changed. To avoid a repeat of the night with Max, BJ suggested they leave immediately and was glad that she had when Norman looked slightly disappointed. For Norman, who'd once gotten into a crying jag while out with her, this was real improvement.

As they sat in the off-Broadway theater, she looked around surreptitiously, almost expecting to see Joshua, but she knew it was just paranoia. There was no way Mr. Fancy-Pants could find her, because she hadn't told anyone where they were going.

This ought to show everyone that she could do it—especially Joshua. Still, she was almost disappointed that Joshua wouldn't appear like the cavalry tonight.

After the theater, they went downtown to a Chinese restaurant in Manhattan's financial district. This was Norm's idea, and he drove. BJ's car was still with the mechanic. BJ suddenly wished she hadn't come, because she remembered that first Sunday when Joshua had called and they'd gone to lunch.

They had already eaten and were talking over coffee. BJ was holding on to the cup as if it were a lifeline. She seriously needed the caffeine.

For one thing, this was her second late night that week, and she was used to retiring early. And while at first Norman had been quite scintillating, something in the show had reminded him of his ex-wife, Lola. For the last hour he'd been droning on and on about his failed marriage. Her eyes kept closing, and she was seriously trying not to fall asleep.

It wasn't that she hadn't enjoyed the evening with Norman, because she had. He was truly a nice man, and the play had been good. It was just that he was so boring. She couldn't believe she'd put herself into this date just to prove that she could find her own man. The only way she stayed awake was by planning how she would tell everyone how much fun she was having. *How can I make sure Joshua hears all without mentioning Norman's dull conversation?*

She glanced down at the long expanse of leg under her black dress and thought, too bad Joshua couldn't see this outfit, too. She tried to daintily cover her mouth with a napkin when she yawned.

"You know," Norman said, "Lola was almost as tall as you are. You even resemble her in other ways." He stared at BJ with his chin propped on one hand.

"Yes," BJ said, "so you've told me." Another yawn threatened to unhinge her jawbone. It was only the twentieth time that he'd mentioned it, BJ thought.

"We were together for five years." Norman sighed heavily, his chest heaving, and shook his head.

"Yes, you mentioned that, too," BJ reminded him and glanced covertly at her watch, wondering how much longer before she said she had to go home.

No wonder I fell asleep on him last time. Some small contretemps at the door caught BJ's attention. She watched as the waiter spoke to a tall man in a camel hair coat. Suddenly she straightened up as the man walked toward them.

At first, she figured it was only her wishful thinking. Something about the way the man's shoulders swayed made her take a real look. It definitely looked very much like Joshua approaching!

That seemed impossible. While she had mentioned Norman to Darlene, she hadn't known they'd come here. The restaurant had been Norman's choice.

"Oh, no," BJ groaned.

Her heart hammered against her ribs. BJ told herself that the only reason she was so glad to see Joshua was because she wanted him to see her dress. She hoped that was all it meant.

She also admitted that she was glad to see him for another reason. She was truly sick of listening to Norman. Joshua's entry hadn't been a moment too soon. She remembered to hide the big grin that threatened to spread over her face. She even tried a bit of the short girl's decorum and daintily crossed her ankles. She didn't expect Joshua's reaction.

"Barbara Jean, sweetheart," Joshua said loudly as if they were long lost lovers.

Sweetheart? BJ wondered what brought that on. Joshua came to embrace her. Norman looked puzzled.

"How did you know I was here?"

"Darlene told me," Joshua answered.

"How did she know?" BJ wondered aloud.

"She asked me," Norman said innocently, "and I told her."

"I'll kill her," BJ said. Joshua tried to hug her again, and BJ said, "Would you stop that?"

"Stop what, my darling?"

"For starters, stop calling me darling. What are you doing here?" she hissed, wishing that Norman didn't have to hear.

"Precious, I couldn't stay away. When I came home and found you missing, I had to look for you. I was worried."

Chapter Fourteen

"Came home?" Norman joined the conversation, speaking to Joshua. "You live together?"

"No, we don't!" BJ jumped in to stop Joshua's upsetting Norman. "He's making that up."

"She's right," Joshua said and took a loud deep sigh as if he could barely continue. "It was Barbara Jeans' decision. She wanted her—space."

"Her space?" The word seemed to strangle Norman.

Actually up until this point, BJ had been having a little fun. It served Norman right for talking about nothing but his ex-wife all evening. As for Joshua, he was a gorgeous man, and she could see the women watching him. Norman was sort of cute, too. Being fussed over by two men made her look pretty good, BJ thought.

That was until Joshua pulled an empty chair from another table and joined them. He leaned close to BJ, and she had to duck his placing a proprietary hand on her knee.

BJ said, "Well, as you can see, I'm perfectly all right, so

you needn't worry any further.'' She was hoping to get rid of Joshua. She glanced at Norman, who looked more bewildered than ever.

"How can I help it?" Josh said, refusing to let go. "Lucy, Darlene, and our baby, Tiffany, sent me."

"Your baby, Tiffany?" Norman said, looking askance.

"It's always the innocent that suffer," Joshua responded aside to Norman.

"You didn't tell me you had a child," Norman said. His glance shot to BJ.

"I don't!" BJ said.

"It's a secret," Joshua said in a stage whisper.

BJ, still trying to dislodge Joshua's hand from her knee, as well as cut into the conversation that had started between the two men, said to Joshua, "Would you please leave and stop being such a nuisance?"

"It's breaking my heart that you want to leave me after all these years," Joshua said.

"How could you be so cruel?" Norman said to BJ. He dropped his napkin to the table. "Have a little mercy on the man. I thought you were a warm, sensitive woman. Not like Lola . . . " Norman choked up.

"I *am* a warm and sensitive woman," BJ said.

Joshua knelt at her feet, while Norman leaned closer to watch with a pained expression on his face. Joshua didn't look the least bit pained. He looked smug, with one hand on his heart. People sitting at tables around them had stopped eating to watch. Any idea that this was fun had evaporated. BJ was humiliated. Josh was worse than Lucy and Darlene together.

"Norman, he's lying. He's trying to get a builders' permit from Lucy, and he'll do anything for it."

Norman looked at Joshua at this, and Joshua managed to look absolutely distraught.

"She's grown coldhearted toward me," Joshua explained, as he pulled a pristine white handkerchief from his pocket. He held the handkerchief up to his eyes, as if to hide his tears.

"You poor man," Norman said, looking as if *he* were really going to cry. "I can't stand this." Norman touched his hand to his forehead, then he pushed his chair back from the table.

This seemed Joshua's cue to stand up and pass the handkerchief to Norman, who took it and immediately proceeded in putting it to his own glassy eyes. In the end, Joshua stood comforting Norman with gentle pats on the shoulder.

"I understand," Josh said to Norman, sounding so sympathetic that if BJ hadn't known better, she'd have believed him.

Norman's voice trembled as he said, "This reminds me of Lola. Please understand, I have to leave."

"No problem," Joshua said, helping Norman to struggle up from his chair.

"Norman?" BJ said, when she realized he was going to just leave her there in Joshua's clutches.

"You just go right ahead," Joshua reassured him. "I'll see Barbara Jean home. Keep the handkerchief."

Norman stumbled from the table, asking for his coat. By that time, his eyes were absolutely glassy. BJ stood up to follow after first batting Josh off again.

The waiter was right on their heels, apparently determined that no matter what their domestic fracas might be, they would pay their bill.

"Don't you worry, honey-cakes, I'll take care of this," Joshua said, as he reached for his wallet.

Honey-cakes? BJ rounded on Josh. "You should take care of it, you ruined my evening. So don't expect any gratitude." She stalked away, trying to catch up with Norman.

Hastily Josh placed money in the waiter's outstretched hand. The tip must have been hefty, for the waiter smiled and babbled, "Thank ye, sir. Thank ye."

BJ was still trying to talk to Norman. "Don't listen to Josh," she told the nearly weeping man. "He doesn't mean a word he's saying. He will exploit any opening."

Norman turned around as he was putting on his coat. "No, he really loves you. Just the way I still love Lola. I can see it."

BJ turned around, and Joshua was on their backs, looking as innocent as one man could possibly manage to look.

"Give him a chance," Norman said, taking both her hands in his. "For the child's sake." This brought the threatened tears closer. Norman choked and couldn't say anything more. He staggered out the door.

"Norman, are you going to be all right?" BJ called after him as she signaled for her own coat. BJ stood with arms akimbo, glaring at Joshua. She was livid. "Look at what you did! You made Norman cry."

Josh looked exasperated. She would have gladly kicked Joshua in the shins, except all the patrons already looked so traumatized that she figured they'd call the police if she did. She wanted to catch up with Norman so that he could at least drop her off at a subway.

It was Josh who retrieved her coat and held it for her. She lurched to grab it out of his hands, and he snatched it out of her reach.

"How could you do that?" she demanded of a Joshua who was attempting to push her arms into the sleeves.

"Sorry, darling. I couldn't help myself," Josh said.

People were still staring, and he sounded so innocent as he played for the other patrons' benefit.

"Would you stop calling me that?"

BJ happened to catch an occasional envying look from some of the women. It was the last straw. Here she was—a woman who couldn't even beg up a sperm donor—and someone thought she had something to envy.

The maitre d' came, saying, "Please, can you take this outside?"

BJ was so mortified that she quickly stepped through the door. Joshua followed on her heels, still trying to shove her arms through the sleeves of her coat. She had been pushing him away until they were outside, and the freezing wind hit her exposed legs under the short dress. Suddenly she was glad to let him help her with the coat. But when he started buttoning her up, as if she were a child, she slapped him away again.

"Would you stop that!" she shrieked.

BJ looked in all directions and couldn't find Norman. She was so angry that now *she* wanted to cry. In Manhattan's City Hall district, the streets were dimly lit and deserted. It was an area that closed down after dark, and in the winter darkness fell early.

"Want a ride?" Joshua's self-satisfied voice said from over her shoulder.

"No! Haven't you done enough damage for one night?" He slipped an arm through hers to lead her away, and she pulled away. "Just leave me alone."

She started walking fast and knew that he followed right behind. She was really angry, but she kept her head up as she tried to march away with a dignified tread.

"You'll be sorry you didn't take me up on my offer when those very lovely legs turn into blocks of ice."

She wouldn't deign to answer that, however he made her nervous. Also, her ankles were a bit wobbly because she'd worn a pair of heels. She hadn't done much of that lately.

"You'd better not try following me," she said, as she skirted a puddle of dirty water.

"I'll take you home," he said, maneuvering around the same puddle.

"There's a law against stalking people," she said.

"I'm not stalking you. I'm only trying to help out Lucy."

"You'll do anything to get your hands on that property."

"That isn't true. It's just that I think you're irrational now, and that you need someone to look after you."

"You?"

"Yes, me," Joshua said.

"Wouldn't that be like sending the wolf out to guard the sheep?" BJ asked.

"I feel responsible for this misunderstanding."

"There's no misunderstanding. I have simply decided to follow through on my plan."

"Look, if you really want to get married so soon, maybe I should marry you instead of your running after all these weirdo types," Josh said.

BJ stopped and glared at him. "Are you crazy? Did I say anything about marriage? Did Lucy tell you to say this?" BJ stopped to confront Josh.

"Lucy has nothing to do with it. I'm not you."

"What does that mean?"

"You'd think I'd let Lucy bulldoze me into those crazy blind dates like she does you?"

"Lucy has nothing to do with my dates any longer."

"Yes, and that's too bad, too, because now you don't even know how to pick a man for yourself," Joshua said.

"Watch me figure it out."

"Look at who you picked. First a potential rapist—"

"Max may have been a mistake," she conceded.

" . . . then a guy who strands you in City Hall in the middle of the night."

"There's nothing wrong with Norman. He was fooled by your lies, that's all."

"That's why he's a twerp. You think I'd let some other man convince me to leave you stranded?"

"You are so smug. You think you're perfect."

"I didn't say I was perfect, but I'm certainly too smart to let some other guy get away with that. All he can think about is his ex-wife."

That was surely true, BJ thought, but there was no way she'd open her mouth and say that he was right.

"How can you ask me to marry you, even in a jest, when you know Linda cares for you as she does."

"Linda? What are you talking about?" Joshua said.

"Don't play dumb. You're so sure that you're the cock of the walk, and you haven't noticed Linda?"

"Don't be silly—Linda and I have been friends since school."

"She bristles every time I come near you. I know a jealous woman when I see one."

"You're misreading her. She simply resents your slowing down progress."

"I don't think so. There's more to it than that."

"Would you get real? There's never been anything between Linda and me."

"You don't have to explain anything to me."

"If that's true, then why are you so hot about it? Look, Linda used to date a buddy of mine, and he dumped her. I felt he was too hard on her, and I took her side. Does that make us soul mates to you? The curious thing is that she used to blame me. I was just as surprised as anyone when she applied for the position as my assistant a few months ago."

"A few months ago? I thought she'd been working with you for years."

"No."

"Well"—she tried to look unconcerned—"it doesn't mean anything to me."

"Good, the subject is closed then."

"Would you just leave me alone? None of that matters, and I have nothing more to say to you."

"Well then, answer my question."

"What question?" BJ said.

"I asked you to marry me."

"Joshua, I'm in no mood for your pitiful sense of humor."

"What do you mean, my pitiful sense of humor? What's wrong with my sense of humor?"

"Well, let me say it like this. I wouldn't marry you no matter how much of a joke it was."

"Why not?" Joshua said, sounding piqued.

"You talk about me letting Lucy bully me, you're actually proposing marriage because you're trying to get on her good side."

"My dealings with Lucy are simply business. It's not why I asked you to marry me."

"No? Then why are you making such an obscene proposition?"

"Obscene?"

"That's right. Tell me exactly why you're making such a disgusting suggestion to me if it's not meant to be a joke."

"Well, it's . . . umm, umm." It seemed to be taking him a long time to decide why he'd suggested marriage to her.

"Yes? Go on. This can't be the very articulate Joshua Hendricks speaking, could it?"

Instead of answering her question, he challenged, "I think it's pathetic for a woman as old as you are to be so inept."

"Pathetic? inept?"

"You know what I mean. And with me as your fiancé, at least everyone would give you a break, and you'd have time to get your thoughts straightened out before you really do start dating."

"So you think I'm so pathetically inept that I can't handle my own life, and to show how perfect you are, you're willing to sacrifice yourself just to help me?"

"Now don't start getting yourself all upset, that's not quite the way I meant it."

"Who cares how you meant it? I have plans of my own, and you're just trying to mess them up."

"Plans like what? Not Norman? Don't tell me you've checked out *his* DNA, too?"

"There's nothing wrong with Norman."

"Not if you want to have children by a crybaby."

"There's nothing wrong with men who cry."

"Oh, forget it. You two would probably make a great couple. Your children could inherit your bleeding heart and his overactive tear glands. I don't know why I tried to save you from yourself anyway. Come on, I'll take you home."

"No, thank you. I'll call a cab," she said.

"No cab," he said, taking her elbow he tried to move her away from the puddle.

She snatched her arm away. "You can report back to Lucy and Darlene that I'll never forgive them for ruining my evening."

"Hah, ruined your evening, my eye. You mean I rescued you. You looked bored out of your skull when I came in. Your eyes were closing, and in another moment you'd have fallen asleep."

"I was not bored. Norman is an interesting conversationalist and—"

"Who talks about his ex-wife all the time," Joshua finished.

"How did you know that?"

"Darlene told me," Josh said.

"You deliberately upset that poor man." Just at that moment, BJ spied a lone yellow cab a block away on the deserted street. It was bearing down on them. She waved to it. "Taxi!" Turning to Joshua, she said, "Now please unhand me."

The cab swerved to her and stopped. Joshua released her arm and than began to swagger as if intoxicated. "Just a minute," Joshua slurred to the driver, "why didn't you stop over here?"

It was common knowledge in New York that taxis were notoriously rude to black men. Frequently this took the form of their refusing to pick up a black man as a fare after dark. Joshua had been well aware of this when he'd pretended to be drunk.

After one look at Joshua, who now appeared to be a stumbling drunk, the cab driver took off with screeching tires.

"Now look at what you've done," BJ said as she stared after the escaping taxi. She'd been talking about his scaring the cab off.

"You mean, look what *he* did," Josh said.

BJ turned back to see Josh's overcoat and pants were wet from where dirty water from the puddle had been splashed when the cab raced away. Josh stared quietly at his ruined topcoat and pants.

She felt incredibly sorry for him, but somehow when she opened her mouth, it was to say, "Well, don't stand there looking as if you've lost your last friend. It was your own fault."

Joshua glanced irritably at her. "I'll take you home," he said, sounding as if he'd throw her over his shoulder and put her in the car if she didn't agree.

BJ's legs were beginning to feel numb from the cold. She hunched her shoulders, which seemed to leave more of her legs victim to the windchill factor. There simply didn't seem to be enough warmth to cover more of her body. She glanced around the darkened street that now looked menacing. BJ reminded herself that she was no fool.

"Okay," she said haughtily, trying unsuccessfully to toss her moussed hair.

They were both quiet on the drive into Queens. As they neared her apartment, she spoke: "Why are you concern-

ing yourself with my dates? There's no use for your suck-
ering up to me. I have absolutely no influence on Lucy's
decisions where her job is concerned."

"I didn't do it for any damn permit. I did it to keep you
from making a fool of yourself and also because Lucy asked
me to," he said.

"Lucy is only taking advantage. I told you how she was."

"You told me that it was Lucy who was trying to match
a husband for you. What you didn't tell me was that you
had your own agenda. It was you who used Lucy as an
excuse to get me up to your apartment. You're just annoyed
that your ploy fell through."

"You sound like your virtue was threatened," she said,
disgusted.

"That's a dirty trick to play on a man."

"Leave me alone, Joshua." She was getting too tired to
fight.

"Do you know that in the six weeks since I've met you,
my wardrobe has been decimated? Talk about bad luck—
you're a jinx."

She was really sorry about his clothes. They were a sodden mess. He sat gingerly to keep from messing up the
car's upholstery. But it was his own fault. Besides, it seemed
a waste for her to lavish sympathy on Joshua, which was
probably why she said, "No one told you to stalk me. And
why do you always wear those clothes?"

"What's wrong with my clothes." His voice should have
made icicles form on his lips.

"Why do you always have to look as if you're going to
a formal wedding or something?"

"A businessman has to be well dressed."

"Even if he's just going to the supermarket?"

"You think I should dress like you?"

"What's wrong with the way I dress?"

"Nothing tonight. I realize that you wanted to look beautiful for Norman. You're lucky he didn't cry on it. Then

that damn dress would have shrunk up and let you freeze
for sure."

"Are you jealous?" she asked.

"Yes. Why shouldn't I be? For me, you wear your little
fortress dresses. I don't know why I care about what you
do. You're a bad-tempered, quixotic, enabling bleeding
heart. It's only that I feel sorry for you that I try to rescue
you from your own bad judgment."

Afterward Joshua watched her slam the passenger door
and walk across the pavement. *I ought to be glad she's gone.*
God knew, he needed to pay more attention to his business
and less to Barbara Jean Jones. Besides, he thought, why
am I bugging her about who she dates?

He opened his door and quickly got out. He walked
across the pavement, where she turned to wait for him.
Without a word, he took her shoulders and leaned toward
her to place his mouth softly on hers.

Joshua's kiss started gently, but when he touched her,
she went up in fire. She kissed him back, holding his head
to hers. He grunted satisfaction and picked her up with
his arms around her thighs to move into the shelter of the
hallway. Once inside they went at each other as if they
were starving. She was.

He opened the top buttons of her coat, baring her
throat. His mouth sought her there, raining hungry moist
kisses wherever he could. A powerful shudder tore through
her body. The bulk of their overcoats and other clothing
frustrated their efforts to be close. She was desperate to
feel his skin on hers, to be united in their flesh. Their
mutual frustration mounted, and she could hear Josh
mutter.

"Upstairs," he said.

"Yes," she breathed back.

She turned to run up, but suddenly he grabbed her to throw her over his shoulder. He ran up the stairs. Once on the landing, he set her on her feet. They kissed as she fumbled to open the door.

Once inside, he kicked the door shut, and they came together in a hungry passionate kiss as they both hurriedly pulled each other's clothes off. They were only partially undressed when he lifted her against the wall. In their mutual desperation, they were soon joined together. Their release came quick, and Joshua sank to the floor, still joined with her. Within a short time, he was urging her up again where they stumbled, arms around each other, into her bedroom. There they made love again, this time slower, savoring every moment.

When they had satiated themselves, and both lay unwilling to move, Joshua said, "I can't believe I did that."

"You mean you forgot your condoms?" she said.

"Yes, that's exactly what I mean."

"Don't worry about it. It's the wrong time of the month," she said on a delicious yawn.

"Please don't tell me that's your birth control method."

"Oh, Joshua, let's not get onto this right now. Why didn't *you* bring protection?" she asked.

"I don't walk the streets with condoms in my pockets, waiting for sex."

She liked him better for that. Actually she liked him for many things. Why not admit the truth? She loved him. She loved him for herself, too, even if there was never any chance for a baby.

Chapter Fifteen

Sunday morning, BJ had been deep in a dream about her and Joshua. Suddenly there were children everywhere—all with bright brown eyes—and all calling her Mommy. She was enjoying the whole thing so much that when something began to tickle her nose, she tried to hold on to the dream as she swatted it away. Unfortunately whatever it was kept coming back to tickle her nose.

When she opened her eyes, it was to find Joshua caressing her nose with the tip of a sheet.

"Good morning," he said.

Seeing his face was as good as the dream. She smiled up at him, and he gently touched her mouth with his. She stretched, feeling as wonderful as it was possible to feel.

"I guess you want breakfast?" she said.

"Later," he said and kissed her again.

She reached up to run her fingers over his jaw. It was scratchy, with a shadow of beard, and terribly sexy. He took her hand and kissed her palm.

He looked at her and held her hand close to his chest. "Will you marry me?" he asked.

She hadn't expected that and instinctively snatched her hand back.

"Are we back to that? You needn't keep up with these farcical proposals."

"This is not farcical."

"Surely, even for you, marriage is a bit far to go for a builders' permit?"

"This is not about a permit. And it's not about my sacrificing myself, either." He looked a bit sheepish at that last.

"Why are you asking?"

"We're good together," he said.

"When we're not fighting," she qualified.

"Even when we're fighting," he finished off. "And I've always planned to marry and have children."

"Before you're forty-five?"

"All right, have fun with this."

"No, I'm not laughing, and I want to think about what you've offered." She turned to glance at him from the corner of her eye and said, "Just accept that I'm not going to wait around for years on any long engagement."

"Good, now tell me what want—" Joshua stopped. "Never mind about that. Forget I asked."

Monday morning, while at work, BJ was staring out the window thinking of how much she already missed Joshua. She'd been working on bringing her files up to date but was having trouble concentrating on work.

She kept thinking of tonight's planned dinner at Shu-Fly Restaurant. After work she planned to rush home, change into something sexy, and meet Joshua there. It was as if they were celebrating the anniversary of their first date. She smiled at that.

She kept remembering how wonderful yesterday had

been. Joshua had stayed with her the whole time. He hadn't gone back to his own place until that morning, when he'd left to change clothes for work. Trust Josh to think of his appearance. She smiled at that.

They'd talked about her wanting children, and although he'd admitted he needed time to get used to the idea, he hadn't run as he'd done before. He'd said he wanted to cement the relationship first—whatever that meant.

Oh, yes, they'd both finally admitted that it was a relationship. She thought of how she'd deliberately gone about making him jealous and wanted to chuckle out loud. That thought made her look across the room toward Norman, who'd outright snubbed her that morning. And although he'd finally spoken, he still refused to glance her way. Ah, well, Norman might forgive her in time.

She had discovered that morning when she awoke that there was no danger of anything happening that month. She wasn't pregnant.

There was one thing that made her pause. Was her mother right? Had she deliberately manipulated Joshua into the relationship?

She'd think about that later. Now she'd allow herself to be gloriously happy. She still hadn't told anyone, but that was next on her agenda.

She pulled her attention back to the file in front of her just as the phone rang.

"Is this BJ?" the woman's voice asked.

Despite the pressured speech, BJ immediately recognized it as Adella St. John's voice. Some instinct made her uneasy.

"Yes, Adella?"

"We have some very important things to discuss with you. When are you coming to see us?" the older woman asked.

"Us?" BJ queried.

"Mr. Green and I," Adella filled in.

"Is there an emergency?" BJ was alert instantly. It was rare for the clients at Ashley Place to seek her out unless there were serious problems, and never before had there been two of them seeking her together.

"No, but we need to see you as soon as you can make it."

Although her next visit had been planned for next week, BJ felt the call warranted quick action. She leaned over the pile of folders on her desk to check her calendar. It was certainly full, but most of her appointments could be condensed to make a little time for Ashley Place later that evening.

"I'll come today," BJ said and scheduled time for later that evening.

When BJ stepped into Adella's home, she expected to see Mr. Green. What she was not prepared for was the sizeable group that eyed her suspiciously as she entered the living room from the small foyer.

Aside from the tenants of the building, there were several unfamiliar faces as well. BJ sensed these were residents of other houses on the street. All eyes had turned to observe her.

Quick introductions followed in which BJ realized she had guessed right, the people were tenants and homeowners of Ashley Place. She sat in the vacant seat at the front.

Mr. Green spoke first. "We're curious about that Hendricks man. We wanted to hear more about his plans to develop this street. Do you know anything?"

BJ had the feeling that she was on the hot seat. Her emotions warred with each other. First, she was incredibly curious. As Joshua would soon be working in the area, she understood their interest but wondered what had caused the tense hostile atmosphere. What had happened to bring them all together like this?

She answered carefully, wanting to help but feeling

uncomfortable with the situation. "I know very little about the technicalities. The area will be renovated—"

"Ain't nobody said nothing about no renovation," Adella cut in.

"Did someone use that word?" one of the other men challenged her.

The way they'd attacked BJ's few words unhinged her. She tried to recall who had mentioned renovation. Somehow she couldn't remember. She wanted to believe it had been Joshua, but he'd said that the area's needs would determine what would be done.

"Well . . . " she said.

"Tsk." One of the younger women sucked her teeth in annoyance before adding, "She don't know nothing."

"Why are we asking *her?*" another woman insisted. "She's probably on *his* side."

"Give her a chance," Mr. Green said.

Now BJ knew the seat she sat on could definitely burn her bottom. "Do you mind telling me what this is all about?" BJ spoke, realizing that she had better know what was happening before she said anything more.

"Is Joshua Hendricks going to throw me out on the street?" Adella said flatly. "I thought he was such a nice man when he fixed my old sink." She ended on a wistful disappointed note, and several people shifted impatiently.

"Throw you out?" BJ repeated. She glanced around the room as everyone seemed to sit forward. "No, of course not. No one could just come in here and do that. Our foundation wouldn't allow it." Her statement seemed to loosen the floodgates.

"Are we going to be paid for our homes?" one middle-aged woman demanded.

"We don't want our homes razed," a man that BJ didn't know said. "We need low-cost loans to repair our property, not someone to come in and throw us out."

"That's right," several voices said in accord.

"Yes, of course. I agree with you," BJ asserted. "But I don't think there's any danger of—"

"Are you going to protect us?" Adella queried.

The older woman's usual perky demeanor seemed dampened today. BJ looked around before saying, "You met Mr. Hendricks. There's no reason for you not to ask him. He will explain much better than I can. He's done wonderful things in the city. I've spoken with him several times, and he never said that he was going to tear things down."

Mr. Green cleared his throat and spoke calmly. "Me, I don't trust the city *not* to do exactly as it wants. Somebody needs to look into this and find out what's going to be done."

"I've heard it's supposed to be an apartment complex, nothing about renovations," one of the women challenged.

It was a strange moment. At mention of an apartment complex, an image of a model of such buildings appeared in her mind. It was the same model she'd glimpsed in Joshua's apartment. It had been weeks since she'd seen it, but she recalled it perfectly. A shiver ran up her spine, but she pushed the idea away.

"They'd have to publish their intent," BJ excused.

"Someone told me there was a notice in the *Law Registry* some time back," an older man said.

"*Law Registry?*" BJ repeated. Suddenly she remembered hearing this before. "Surely that wouldn't be a good enough notice. That's an eastern Long Island paper. They'd have to publish it in one of the big dailies or at least one of the local papers."

"What about the second company?" Adella said.

"There's no second company," one woman said, looking exasperated. "She's just confused."

Being called confused made Adella angry. "I'll tell you who's confused," the older woman snapped. It was the

first time that Adella had sounded like herself since the
meeting began, BJ thought.

"All right, all right." Mr. Green took over. "It's the
Hendricks Development Corporation that we're discussing
here. Let's not get off track."

However, the small contretemps had effectively stopped
the meeting. BJ glanced at her watch, knowing she had to
leave.

"I'll see what I can find out and get back to you," BJ
promised.

As BJ left, Adella accompanied her to the door. The
woman glanced around, apparently to assure they wouldn't
be overheard. Placing a frail, veined hand on BJ's arm,
Adella whispered, "There's going to be a meeting next
week. I want you to come."

"Okay," BJ said.

"You're going to look out for me, right?"

BJ was flustered. "Of course, I always do," she answered.

"Don't you let Joshua Hendricks put me out."

"He's not going to do that."

But Adella whispered on, "He'll listen to you. He likes
you."

"Adella, I'm sure Joshua won't throw you out of your
home, but it's not because of anything I'll say—"

"You talk to him. That will stop him. Promise me."

"All right. I'll talk to him," BJ promised before she left.

She glanced at her watch, realizing it was nearly time to
meet Josh at the Shu-Fly. She didn't have time to go home
and change.

She sat in her car a few moments before starting the
engine, searching for aspirin in her purse. The meeting
had given her a splitting headache. She knew the moment
it had started—when she had remembered the model
buildings she'd seen in Joshua's apartment.

On the drive to Shu-Fly, she kept reassuring herself that
there was nothing to fear. Many of the residents were older

people and inclined to be supervigilant about everything. They saw bogey men in every shadow. They simply needed to be informed, she thought. That way, they'd stop believing the worst.

She swallowed the two aspirins dry.

Josh was already there when she arrived. "Hi, baby," he smiled and greeted her.

He stood up to pull out her chair, planting a kiss on her ear when she sat. It sent a spasm of desire straight through her.

"What kept you?" he asked once he was back in his seat.

"I got a call from Three Ashley Place," she said.

"Oh," he spoke softly, picking up a menu.

"I promised them that I'd talk with you about some of their fears."

He looked sharply at her and then glanced away. Slowly he placed the large menu on the table. He seemed to gird himself as he asked, "Fears about what?"

"They're worried, especially Adella, about what's going to happen to their homes. I told them you'd be explaining everything, and I told them about the work you've done before."

It was a long moment before he answered. "We don't have all the paperwork yet, so in a way there's nothing to fear. And before we do anything, we do meet with the residents."

"I told them that, too. Also, the Foundation has been trying to get the area fixed up for a long time. Adella's seeing companies coming to demolish her home out of every corner."

"Companies?"

"She thinks there's two."

He frowned at that. "Yes, you said that before."

It wasn't what she'd expected him to say. "Is Adella right? Are there more companies? I thought you were going to do it."

"Well, not unless I get the permits," he said.

BJ took a deep breath. "Joshua, what is going to happen to Ashley Place? Are you going to renovate or . . . " Somehow she couldn't say it.

He sat up with both hands flat on the table. "BJ," he started, "that area is in sorry shape—"

"I know," she cut in, "but it's not hopeless," she said, and when he didn't answer, she added, "Is it?"

"My permit is for rebuilding," he said, not really answering her question.

"But you said—"

"That property can't survive without major structural repairs."

"You could do it," BJ said. When her hand felt cramped, she looked down to find she'd been crumpling her napkin into a wrinkled mess.

"I don't do that kind of thing anymore, and the owners couldn't afford it."

"Yes, but some of the more beautiful architecture is here, and we shouldn't just pull it down and stack up boxes one on top of the other."

"I don't build boxes." He sounded irritated at her words.

"You know what I mean," she said.

"Unfortunately I know exactly what you mean. I intend to put up quality housing for middle-income families."

"Why couldn't you do something like Strivers' Row?"

"You mean Harlem at One Hundred Thirty-eighth and One Hundred Thirty-ninth streets?" He looked askance.

"Yes, of course."

"That's very different from Ashley Place."

"If it worked one place, it can work in others. They were able to reclaim that area," she said.

"BJ, that was many years ago and in Manhattan." He hit the table, and she jumped. "This is totally different."

"Why?"

"Strivers' Row was owned by upper-middle-class African Americans, and even very rich blacks during the Harlem Renaissance. The owners were prize fighters, dentists, and surgeons . . ."

" . . . not all of them."

" . . . the houses have been kept up during all this time. Unlike that ramshackle white elephant—"

" . . . houses cared for by simple people with a desire to preserve their history and culture. People who are not rich—"

"They sure as hell weren't a batch of the poor and elderly, barely surviving on pensions and Social Security checks."

"They could do it with help—your help."

"Who'd maintain it? Besides, Strivers' Row has landmark status, while Ashley Place does not. And if it did, do you know how difficult it is to make repairs and maintain such a property?"

"For pete's sake, I'm tired of hearing about Strivers' Row. That's two blocks in a huge area of problems. Have you any idea what a problem that property has been? They have to do the repairs within the landmark's rules. They've had problems regulating the rents so that the owners won't go broke. And at least the owners are in better financial straits than are the people of Ashley Place.

"The people of Ashley Place couldn't possibly renovate those properties. And what of the other homeowners in that neighborhood? Queens is a simple bedroom community, and the people have worked hard to maintain the best life-style that they're capable of. It's one of the few areas in this country where blacks are the high earners."

"Three Ashely Place looks pretty good," she kept trying.

"Cosmetically but it's a mess. The plumbing's hopeless."

"That's what you were doing in Adella's kitchen, sneaking a look at her plumbing."

"I wasn't sneaking. And it's not just the plumbing. It's

the roof, the windows, the electrical wiring. The list goes on forever. As for the other houses on the street, most of them are in the same shape.''

"Josh, listen to me. It's worth being repaired. There are cities that have torn down their historical buildings and regretted it later. New York is a tourist city, attracting people from all over the world.''

"Since when have tourists been making trips to Ashley Place?''

"Oh, forget the tourists. What about the children of the area? What about the schools? Those houses are a part of *our* history. Everyone suffers when we lose places of historical interest,'' she said.

"History is wonderful,'' Joshua responded. "But people need to live each day as it comes. Those tenants are elderly, and why should they cope with such poor living conditions? I could have new buildings there in no time, while the people live in temporary housing. Then they'd have first choice to move into the new places.''

"What about their families and friends? How would you like to move away from all your support systems?''

"Their family and friends should accept it because their elderly will be better off in the long run.''

"It wouldn't be the same. They'd be away too long. And those people love their homes.'' She was disheartened by his obstinacy.

"They'll love their new ones, too,'' he answered calmly.

BJ wanted to cry. The longer they talked, the more she realized how far apart they were. She couldn't believe he was capable of compromising the people of Three Ashley Place when he knew her feelings about it.

She stared at him long and hard, realizing how unscrupulously he'd dealt with her.

"If you had your way, you'd tear everything down to a rubbish heap and put up some little housing complex with no character or history.''

"You're damn right I'd level it!" Joshua said, a reddened tinge appearing across his nose. Her calling his work "boxes" had finally gotten to his ego. "The whole place is an eyesore, and it's attractive to all the worst elements. It's a danger to every decent person trying to make a life there. It's like a weed, creating a harbor for snakes."

She was shocked by the magnitude of his disapproval. There was no talking sense to him on this issue.

"You believe that because you've never been poor. Decent people live there as well. You can't legislate neighbors. That's what they tried to do when they first built projects and look what happened."

"What I intend to build can't be compared to that."

"It is the same. No one saw what would happen to projects in the beginning. No one expected them to turn out as they did."

"Why do you keep talking about projects? This isn't the same. When buildings fall down like they're doing on that block, the very worst elements feel free to take over. At least by redoing them, they won't be attractive to a bunch of vicious, lazy punks who prey on people who can't fight back."

"Joshua, that isn't true. Those houses are occupied by simple people. And what about moving someone as old as Adella?"

"Adella has no business trying to live in that house. It isn't safe," he said.

"She has family in the area. If she's relocated, she'll be moved too far away from her children and grandchildren."

"Adella is like a beacon for any vicious mugger who sees her. She's elderly and vulnerable."

"Yes, but that's another reason why she needs to remain in familiar circumstances."

"What do you mean?"

"Adella functions very high for a person her age, and so do most of those elderly who live there. They've grown accustomed to their surroundings, and they often have family or friends who come in to help.

"Like hell they do. Most of their families are totally disinterested," he said contemptuously.

"Some of them, I admit, but not all. They help each other. As long as they can remain independent, we should do everything we can to assist them. Moving into a totally new environment, where they haven't established their network, could undermine their independence."

"If that old shack were to be totally demised by a tornado today, everyone would say, good riddance!" Josh said.

"Everyone, except for the tenants of Number Three," BJ said sadly.

"That bunch of hardheaded, old curmudgeons should be glad there's someone to think of what's right for them."

"You let me think that you were going to do the same thing that you'd done on the Upper East Side—refurbish."

"You assumed that. I never said it."

"You never denied it. Why not, if you were really being honest? You were aware of what I thought you were doing. I feel like a fool."

"Developing neighborhoods is a competitive business. You never tell your plans before you have the right of way." His voice softened as he said, "BJ, this is reality knocking at the door. Those people can't fix the problems of that block, and no flower garden is going to do it. The neighbors want them gone because of falling property values, and the city is ready to act."

"Why didn't you tell me?"

"I figured you'd act just the way you are now."

"Like an enabler?" she spit out. "Like a bleeding heart."

"BJ?" Joshua said and reached across the table to place his hand over hers. She snatched away as if she'd been burned.

She was ready to cry. She felt betrayed, used. He'd wanted to take her to bed and was willing to lie to do it.

BJ realized that she had no one to blame but herself. Lucy and Darlene were right when they accused her of being out of touch. Even after she'd come back from Columbia, she'd focused on handling her increased caseload and hadn't changed her habits as she had promised herself that she would.

When she'd talked to Joshua about renovating, he'd never said that's what he'd do. He'd tricked her so that he could soften her up for sex.

No, she couldn't even say *that*. She'd sensed something was wrong—right from the beginning. It was her own fault. It had all been an exercise in self-deception. She hadn't wanted to hear the truth. She'd wanted Joshua too much.

He was right about their relationship, too. She had done everything she could to attract him, ever since that first day when she'd flirted with him from across the room. Her mother had insinuated that BJ manipulated people, and this was one time when it had backfired on her, she realized.

"So," he said after the long silence. "Tell me what you're thinking."

How dare he say that! Hadn't she told him just about everything she ever thought of because he was always encouraging her to talk about herself? She'd never been so furious with Joshua Hendricks in the whole time since she'd known him.

"Not another word," she told him with pure fury. "I have nothing else to say."

"Wait," he said and rose when she stood to collect her purse.

"What for?" BJ said. You can't understand what you're doing. How could you? You were born with a silver spoon in your mouth. Look at you. You dress like a fop and act like you can walk on water. What would you know about people's love for their homes—"

Joshua tried to stop her. "Don't do anything you'll regret—"

She went on as if he hadn't spoken. "Would you like to know why you stay in that sterile empty apartment? Because your life is sterile and empty.

"As for your offer of marriage, forget it. And I wouldn't have a child by you if you were the last man on earth. Any man who'd throw elderly people out on the street in the cold is not eligible to father my child."

Finally she stood up and said, "I don't know why I thought your gene pool was worth copying."

"BJ, wait," he said.

"Why? Haven't we said it all?" she asked.

"BJ, don't be foolish," Joshua said as she walked out.

Joshua thought of what she'd said as he watched her leave. He realized that her words had hurt more than he could have anticipated. *I must have leaked a few brain cells somewhere since I met Barbara Jean Jones.*

That next day, as soon as BJ was at her desk, she called Mr. Green and told him that he was right, Joshua fully intended to tear down Ashley Place and put new buildings up.

"Well," he answered, "this means we'll have to go to plan B."

"Plan B?" BJ asked.

"We're going to fight him."

"Great!" BJ responded, feeling better now than she had in days. "I'll support you fully. What are you going to do?"

"We have some ideas, which I'd like you to hear. And of course, you can help by feeding us whatever information you can."

Layle Giusto

"No problem, but count me in to do more than that," she said.

"That's not such a good idea. You're part of the Vander-Weil Foundation. Any help from you will have to be unofficial."

"The Foundation will be glad to help wherever it can."

"I think not," Mr. Green said. "But if you want to find out, make sure you go easy in the beginning."

BJ didn't argue, but she was certain that the man was wrong. Next she called Lucy.

"BJ, where have you been? I've been trying to catch up with you."

"I've been very busy," BJ answered. "Lucy, there's something I want to know."

"Shoot," Lucy said.

"Exactly what is Joshua's permit for?"

"He's to remove the existing structures there and replace them with an apartment complex. What's the problem?"

"Did anyone consider that the residents of that street will be displaced with this plan?"

"Of course, that's how one does this. They'll be in temporary housing."

"Such as?"

"There's several options. Why are you asking?"

"What about the people on that street, whose life-styles are marginal. This type of situation could land them on the street, undomiciled."

"I seriously doubt that could happen here."

"What about the elderly of Three Ashley Place?"

"Some of those people need to be in nursing homes."

"Over my dead body," BJ said.

"BJ, that sounds like you're considering doing something very foolish."

"Call it what you want," BJ said. "I am not going to allow those people to be forced out of their homes."

* * *

That weekend, when BJ called her parents, she mentioned the problems.

"Oh, yes, you mean Joshua's project," her mother said.

"Who told you about it?"

"Lucy did," her mother said.

"You have no idea what he's trying to do. He wants to throw Adella St. John and all the other tenants out on the street. I won't allow it."

"I thought he was going to relocate her to a safe environment. At least that's what he said."

"Adella shouldn't be relocated. She's over eighty years old." She paused as her mother's words slowly sank into her brain. "What do you mean Joshua said? When did you hear about him mentioning relocation?"

BJ simply couldn't believe her mother read the *Law Registry*. Did the whole world read that paper? She was so annoyed with that thought that she almost didn't hear her mother's words.

"He called."

"Relocating Adella and some of the other tenants could cause serious difficulty for them. I simply won't—what do you mean, he called?" BJ demanded.

"Joshua did and explained the whole thing."

"Joshua called you?"

"Of course. He's called every week since you were here."

"Every week?"

Chapter Sixteen

"We always have a nice chat, although your father as usual tried to monopolize the conversation," BJ's mother said.

"Daddy talked to Joshua, too? Why did he call?" BJ asked.

"Oh, just to chat for a while," her mother responded with total aplomb.

"I don't believe it. Don't talk to him."

"Really, BJ, you're just like your dad sometimes. Why shouldn't I talk to Joshua?"

"Because he's a selfish man who runs roughshod over other people, that's why."

"Nonsense. Joshua's a perfect gentleman. Even your dad agrees. I heard all about the problems between you two. You should read the papers."

"Momma, he deliberately confused the issue. He had me defending him to the tenants. Can you imagine how humiliated I was when I found out?"

"You should pay more attention. You have to be open-minded about these things. Joshua has a good idea. Columbia was built from scratch only thirty-five years ago.''

"It's not the same thing. Columbia didn't displace people when they built it.''

"Remember those farmers? They were displaced. Anyway, I'm sure that when the people see all those new apartments, they'll simply love them.''

"Momma, that building has a history that will be lost forever if Joshua Hendricks is allowed to pull it down.''

"I don't see anything you can do to stop him. His is a big company, after all,'' her mother said.

"Other people have stopped developers from building huge conglomerates around their ears,'' BJ said.

"From what I've heard, it's not exactly huge.''

"How long did you talk to him?''

"Not long this weekend. He said he had some company business to do.''

"You shouldn't listen to him. He's absolutely unscrupulous. And he's so conceited and full of himself that if you really knew him, you'd hate him. Just like I do.''

"Nonsense, everyone knows you don't hate Joshua. You're just like your dad—always running with the gun half-cocked. Joshua is a real doll. Even your dad says so.''

Were they talking about the same man? A doll? What could she say? She'd called him a pussycat, herself. Now she knew he was more like a rabid wolf.

"All he needs is a little careful tending,'' her mother said.

At that moment, her father picked up the phone. "What are you two talking about?'' he demanded.

"I was just telling baby-girl about our last talk with Joshua.''

"Oh,'' Dad said, "a fine young man. Reminds me of myself at that age.''

"Humph,'' her mother answered.

"Mona,'' her father said to her mother, "I don't know

what you're humphing about. And don't think I haven't noticed your flirting with Joshua, either."

"Goes to show what you know. I thank you, Mr. Expert-on-everything. I was not flirting."

This was another of their favorite topics. Her father always swore that her mother flirted, while her mother adamantly denied it.

Of course, at this time, BJ knew that her participation in the conversation was unnecessary. From here on, she'd barely get a word in edgewise.

"You leave Joshua alone, he's BJ's beau."

"Daddy, Joshua Hendricks is not my beau." BJ knew it was a waste of time now, no matter what she said.

"Alfred, you've got the most active imagination of any man I've ever known. . . ." Her mother launched into the conversation.

"Listen, Mom and Dad, I hear someone at the bell. I'll talk to you later." It was the only way to get out of the conversation.

When she hung up, she spent a long time thinking of what her mother had said. She couldn't believe Joshua had called her family after their last conversation. What was he up to?

Two weeks later, BJ was eminently better informed than she'd been with Joshua the night they'd confronted each other at Shu-Fly. She'd spent the time researching how to save Ashley Place.

Cody VanderWeil had been on vacation during that time, so she hadn't approached him regarding the problem, but she was prepared for his full assistance. The Foundation was dedicated to maintaining its clients.

By the time she could speak with Cody, she was ready to take on city government, and Joshua Hendricks, single-handedly.

She dropped some photocopied sheets on Cody's desk, saying, "Look at this. It's about a case in another state where a group of community people were able to stop a developer by just pointing out that he'd filed notice in an inappropriate, little-known newspaper," BJ said.

Cody, who appeared to be scanning one of those little known inappropriate newspapers, folded the paper and sat up. He peered nearsightedly through foggy, wire-rimmed eyeglasses. "Am I to assume we're discussing the Hendricks Corporation and Ashley Place?"

"Who else?" BJ asked impatiently. "Why can't Ashley Place take him to court and do the same thing."

"Because," Cody said, proving that he knew exactly what she was referring to, "first, you'd never be able to get the residents together long enough for them to cooperate, let alone appear in court."

"How do you know that?"

"Most of them are too busy planning what they'd do with Joshua Hendricks's money, for one thing. And second, the *Law Registry* is neither little known nor inappropriate for this sort of ad."

"You know exactly what I mean. Nobody reads that paper."

He looked askance. "I read it."

"I mean no real people," and when Cody began to look chagrined, she changed to, "No one at Ashley Place read it." Actually she knew this wasn't true, but she was too revved up at that moment.

"Just because you don't, doesn't mean that none of those residents didn't."

"How can I read anything? You just doubled my case-load," BJ said, mentioning her other current pet peeve.

Cody countered with, "You're exaggerating. Getting back to the subject, I've heard the Hendricks Corporation is offering top money to the owners. I'd say it was a good investment for them."

BJ turned to Cody. "You knew about this?"

"Doesn't everybody?"

"Why didn't you tell me? It may be too late to stop him now."

"Why? Who wants to stop him?" Cody looked up again, and the light reflected off the circles of glasses. "He's going to pull down the block and build new apartments for moderate-income housing. I think that's recommendable."

"What about the people already there?"

"Relocate. What else? It's been done before. It's not the end of the world."

"Relocate Adella? She's close to ninety if she's a day. Sticking her into a totally new environment could undermine her."

"So what can you do? Sometimes you have to compromise."

"Compromise is all right when it doesn't mean robbing elderly people of their last few years."

"He's not going to kill them," Cody said sharply.

"You can't really predict what this will do to them. Every developer promises the original tenants will have preferential treatment with new housing. But when the time comes, the original people can't afford the rents. Are we going to stand by and let him get away with that in our territory?"

"There's nothing for us to do. That's prime real estate. It was only a matter of time before this area came to the attention of developers."

"For what? An ugly apartment complex? None of the nearby streets have anything like that.

"It doesn't have to be ugly. There are already blocks of town houses in that area," Cody said reasonably.

"Town houses are not complexes," BJ snapped back.

"Well, there are several in nearby areas. And I'd say they've been well done."

"Sure, the architects turned their backs for a few minutes, the kids wrote graffiti on them, and it was a huge improvement."

"Not true," Cody responded with his usual literal thinking. "There's no graffiti in that area."

"Don't you see? That's because the kids are proud of their neighborhood."

"BJ, you're getting upset over nothing. Indeed, you sound almost nihilistic."

"There's nothing nihilistic about what I just said." She turned and walked back to her desk, where she grabbed her purse and folder.

"BJ," Cody called. He hurried to catch her before she went down in the elevator. Usually seeing Cody run with his long lanky body would have brought a smile to her lips. Today she was too angry to smile.

"Where are you going?" Cody asked out of breath.

"To see if they're still in the area."

"What for? You'd better be careful. You know what our policy is about sticking to the things that the Foundation can do and leaving the rest alone."

"Never mind the policy. These are real people, not case studies in a textbook."

"BJ, I'm ordering you to leave this alone. You interfere any further, and the Foundation will have to consider disciplinary actions for a conflict of interest," Cody said.

She couldn't believe it. Cody had never ordered her to do anything in all the years she'd worked there.

"Now it's a conflict of interest? You didn't mention that when you okayed my orientating him to the area."

"That was different," he said with a straight face. "Do you understand?

"Yes," she answered. "I understand perfectly. If you're finished, I have some visits to make."

As she walked away, BJ was disappointed that the Foundation hadn't run to the street's rescue as she'd been dreaming they would. Different, Cody had said. Sure it was, she thought, because the VanderWeils said it was. But there was no sense in letting herself get off on a tangent now.

But one thing she knew—there was no way she'd allow Cody, the Foundation, Lucy, or Joshua keep her from helping Ashley Place.

Outside the weather had taken a turn for the best. It had warmed up a bit and convinced you that spring was near. BJ drove to Ashley Place in her newly repaired car and parked. There was a group of people standing on the street in the warmer temperatures. They talked among themselves. BJ got out and walked toward them.

"What's going on?" she asked.

"The developers have been here all morning. You going to see them?" one woman said.

"Is Joshua Hendricks here?" BJ asked.

"You got it," the woman said. "He went into that second house on the corner."

BJ glanced at the house the woman had pointed to. Nearby she heard two other women talking. "So I told him, 'You ain't that cute, honey . . .'"

"Hush up, girl. You ain't told him nothing of the sort. You were too busy drooling."

"No way. Just because he's a hunk, don't mean I'll take money for something that's precious to me. Then he had the nerve to give me that heartbreaker smile. Humph, I'm on to him. Though, truth to tell, I wouldn't mind taking him on." They laughed at that.

BJ suspected they were talking about Joshua. When the second woman caught a glimpse of BJ and poked the speaker, BJ knew she'd guessed right. The two women put their heads together and laughed louder.

BJ glanced at Three Ashley Place and decided to see Adella first, leaving the confrontation with Josh for later.

Upstairs, Adella said, "That Joshua went and bought me a bag of groceries."

"Joshua Hendricks?" BJ repeated.

"Who else are we talking about? You need to listen when I talk."

"He was here?" BJ still asked.

With all Adella's fears and complaints about losing her home, she still adored Joshua. He deluded people, BJ thought. He'd managed to charm Lucy, Darlene, and even her parents. *What did I expect? He certainly deluded me right from the start.*

"That's right," Adella said. "And at least *he* listens when I talk. He offered me a good piece of money, too, besides buying the groceries. He was here earlier—before you came."

"What's he doing now?" BJ spoke more to herself than Adella.

However, it was Adella who answered. "He's buying up the whole block for one of his new uppity housing complexes. I thought you were going to talk to him."

"I did. Do you know who is going to sell out?"

"Probably everybody." Adella shook her head. "If you spoke with him, how come you didn't know that?"

"We spoke, but we couldn't agree," BJ said, thinking that was certainly an understatement. Josh's new tactics frightened her. By buying out the homeowners, he cut the power of the residents. Less people meant less leverage.

"All you need to do is sweeten him up a bit," Adella said.

Adella was definitely off the mark if she believed that, BJ thought. Neither she nor Joshua were eager for any compromise. Nothing was going to come between Joshua and his business. And she wouldn't give up her principles, not even for love.

After she'd spoken to several other clients, she joined the people on the street. By now, the group had grown, and Mr. Green was there.

Joshua caught sight of her and approached. "Do you mind telling me just what you're doing here?"

"This is my area. I have every right to be present."

"You're here as a social worker, not to interfere."

"You can't tell me what I can do," BJ said.

"The VanderWeil Foundation has no fight with what I'm doing. You're the one interfering in things that have nothing to do with you," Joshua said.

Despite his words, BJ said, "I've heard you offered money to the owners. Just like you to be underhanded."

"There's nothing underhanded about it. It's good business practice. Besides, there are reasonable, rational people who want to move away from this hell hole."

"No matter what you do, it won't work. We're in the right, and we're going to save that block for the people."

"There you go, rattling all that insanity again. Why these people listen to you, I'll never understand. America was built on free enterprise, you know."

"America was also built on the robber barons stealing from the poor to line their own pockets."

Mr. Green saved her from saying more by coaxing her to leave with him. The rest of the crowd was enjoying the contretemps and hoping to see more. BJ followed the older man reluctantly.

"He's right about the Foundation," Mr. Green reminded her. "If you confront him like this, word will get back to them."

She took a deep breath and wanted to shake herself. It infuriated her to have Joshua get away with this. "You're right. I need more subterfuge," BJ admitted.

Later most of the tenants of Number Three Ashley Place met without the others on the block.

"If Joshua Hendricks is buying up the properties, we're not going to able to hold out alone," one man said.

"If we could get to the media, you might have a chance," BJ said, thinking out loud.

"The media," Mr. Green said, looking interested.

Adella perked up, too. "Honey, what do you mean? We're performers, and everybody knows performers are what media's all about."

It was as if a light dawned. "That's it!" BJ said, excitedly. "That's how we could get everyone's attention. You can approach one of the black radio stations as black theater people from the past."

"She's right. Most of us have even been interviewed at some point in the past, and this being March, there's still some interest in black history. We could play on that."

"We could dress up or something like that," Adella said. "And put on a play."

"I don't know about that—" one of the older men said.

"No," BJ cut in. "Adella's right, only if you don't want to put on a play, maybe you could exhibit some of the memorabilia that's in this house. Once we have everyone's ear, you can tell them of your plight."

"I like it. We could clean up the two apartments downstairs and have it right there," Mr. Green said.

Oh, oh, BJ thought, looking at the elderly people around her. Who was going to clean up? It would probably be her, she guessed. Well, she was committed, and she'd do what had to be done.

"Okay, this can be our contingency plan. Let's first wait till the meeting. Maybe none of this will be necessary," Mr. Green said.

"How am I going to attend after everyone's warned me off, including my boss?" BJ said. At that moment, an idea occurred. She looked at Adella and smiled. "Adella, you know that big hat you showed me with the veil? How about lending it to me so I can attend the meeting?"

Adella's eyes lit up. She glanced around at Mr. Green.

"Sounds good to me," he agreed.

"Girl, when I get finished dressing you, you'll be ready

for the performance of your life," Adella said and drew
BJ into the back room.

A week later, the meeting between the residents of Ashley Place and the Hendricks Corporation was called to
order in Charity Tabernacle Temple. There was a good
number of people from the neighborhood, including
many from Ashley Place and the surrounding area. Lucy
was there, sitting in the front near Joshua's people. Even
Darlene was there, sitting toward the back with husband,
Carlos, and Tiffany.

BJ dressed in the clothes that Adella had loaned her,
including the voluminous black veil that hid her face, and
sat midway on the far left. She was surrounded by the
people of Number Three. It was a wonderful disguise, for
she could watch and not be seen herself. The only problem
was that it was a bit outlandish and did attract attention.
*I won't worry about that. No one will guess in a million years
that it's me.*

Lucy stood up and walked to the podium. She spoke
briefly about their hopes and aspirations for the area. BJ
couldn't believe that her very own godmother was involved
with this horror. She was tempted to challenge Lucy right
then and there and start the sparks flying immediately.
However, Lucy soon introduced Joshua, and BJ noticed
that murmuring broke out among the people around her.

Joshua walked to the front to speak to the group. BJ
could barely contain herself from heckling.

Joshua looked around and spied the group of people
from Number Three Ashley Place. He searched for BJ, but
obviously she hadn't come. Darlene with husband, Carlos,
waved from the back. BJ's absence was definitely odd. It

disappointed him a bit before he realized that he should be glad.

"As you all know," Joshua started, "we've called this meeting to discuss the intention of Hendricks Development Corporation to develop Ashley Place."

"What do you mean by developing?" one older man, who'd been dozing, asked.

"We are going to put a complex of housing here," Joshua said, knowing this would start the fireworks early.

"What you going to do with the houses already there?" came another male voice.

"Most of the existing houses are in a state of total disrepair—which as a builder, I will say that while it is not irreversible, the expense makes it prohibitive."

"What about the expense of demolishing the block, carting the debris away, and then still having to rebuild? Why doesn't anyone compare that with the cost of renovating? What's wrong? Not enough profit for you?" came a tremulous woman's voice.

Joshua's glance searched the area to his far left, looking for the person who'd spoken. The questions had been fired by an older woman dressed all in black, with a large quirky black hat and veil. The woman's voice had had a peculiar effect on him. There was something not quite right, but he couldn't quite put a finger on it. For one thing, he couldn't figure out who she was. He believed that he'd met all the residents. *She must be from one of the other blocks.*

It was impossible to determine particular features of her face under the old-fashioned veil. The whole thing was rather dramatic, he thought. He couldn't shake the feeling that there was something off about it. It stuck in his mind until he realized what it reminded him of—a costume.

The woman was distracting, because although he didn't recognize her, he kept thinking that he'd seen her before.

His attention was drawn increasingly more to the woman, but he was also distracted by questions from the others.

One man stood and said, "I've spent a lot of energy and time on fixing up my house. It's been slow going because I can't get low-cost financing. I didn't buy my house to lose it to some big conglomerate."

"You'll be able to recognize a handsome profit," Joshua said.

"I don't want to sell. I want to raise my children there."

"Why should we be displaced just because some big company sees where it can make money?" said a woman from the back.

Joshua spent the next few minutes answering some tough questions. He'd been through this before and wasn't particularly upset by the residents' resistance. He believed he was doing the right thing for everyone, and it was his experience that they'd come to agree with him in time.

The thing that bothered him was his nagging feeling that he should recognize the woman in the black veil. He glanced frequently in that direction. The back of Joshua's neck tingled.

He had been at it with the residents for some time when he saw some movement among the people of Number Three. Several heads were together before one man stood to speak. "Don't you have to give adequate notification before a project such as this?"

"That we did," Joshua said.

"In the *Law Registry?*" The same older woman in black stood up, incensed.

"The *Law Registry* is a respectable paper that's well known for this type of notice," Joshua answered. He started moving slowly to his left toward the woman's seat.

"That can't be adequate notification to tear down lovely old homes and build boxes on top of each other. Why not publish in a local paper?"

Suddenly Joshua thought, *boxes! BJ in disguise?* But he pushed the insane idea away. *She wouldn't dare.*

Joshua started moving closer. All he wanted was a more careful look at this very angry female detractor. He saw the woman scrunch down in her seat, and the people around her seemed determined to block his view. The whole thing became increasingly more suspicious the longer it went on. Every time he tried to get a good look, one of the elderly tenants of Three Ashley Place would jump up, as if trying to foil him. An uncomfortable murmuring broke out as people wondered what was happening.

"Instead of putting people out of their homes, you should be repairing the houses that are there"—that from Adella, standing with arms akimbo.

"Would the lady who asked about publicizing in local papers, please identify herself," Joshua said, trying to see behind Adella.

Adella stood up and said, "My name is Adella St. John, and I am one of the oldest residents of this street. I can't believe a nice young man like you would let me die a homeless person."

Joshua cleared his throat before answering. "Now Mrs. St. John—Adella, there's no way that would happen."

"Then you'd better not tear down my home," Adella finished.

"Our plans will benefit all involved, Mrs. St. John," Josh said. "But I wanted to speak to the other lady." Joshua leaned so as to see behind Adella. "Would you identify yourself, Ms.—"

One of the older men stood up. "Many of the people of Ashley Place love their homes and want to stay right where they are. Why should they suffer just because others want to abandon the old neighborhood?"

"And who are you talking about abandoning the old

neighborhood?" one rather tough young woman said. "I'm tired of trying to keep my old house from falling down."

"I'm selling out because you fat cats always have the politicians in your pockets," someone said. "It's not worth fighting City Hall."

"Well, I for one am glad to sell out, and you old people ought to get with the program."

"While it's true that some want to sell, many want to stay and maintain the history of the areas," the woman in black said.

This time Josh had the distinct impression that she tried to hide behind one of the residents.

Linda spoke for the first time. The people's attention turned to the blond woman. "By history of the area, you must mean Saint Albans, but this place is no better than a South Jamaica block."

"You watch what you say." Another older woman jumped up to join the confrontation. "South Jamaica is as good as Saint Albans, any day. I lived there for many years. It don't take any big fancy homes to make a neighborhood memorable."

"No, but it sure do help." This was said by a younger woman clad in blue jeans.

"What you know 'bout it? You're just dying to get out." The older woman challenged the younger, jean-clad woman.

"I sure am." The second woman jumped up. "I agree with Mr. Hendricks. It needs to be pulled down and rebuilt."

"Ladies," Joshua intervened. "Let's stick to Ashley Place, block number one eleven," he read from the paper in his hand.

Linda said, "Why do you people even want to live there? It may have certain . . . ambience, but it's just a ghetto."

* * *

To this, BJ—who had been trying to keep out of any further notice—jumped up to confront Linda. "Excuse me. Saint Albans, which includes Ashley Place, is not a ghetto. Is that what you call your area, a ghetto? Ashley Place is a black *neighborhood*. The same as there are white neighborhoods, there are black ones, too. I am offended by the assumption that an area populated primarily by blacks is inferior."

Linda faced BJ to speak again. "Ma'am, these are—"

BJ thought even the title, Ma'am, sounded condescending. However, whatever the woman was going to say was cut off. Joshua stepped in before Linda could finish.

"We're certainly not trying to put people on the street, and of course the present tenants would get first choice in the new apartments. We are also aware that indeed Ashley Place is a part of an established black neighborhood, and it's for this reason that the city has agreed to the rebuilding."

When Joshua had walked to the left aisle, he could see that Linda wanted to stop him. But he was too fascinated to find the woman in black's identity to stop. Now he slowly made his way up the side aisle toward her.

"Many of the tenants will be displaced and may never get back in. For others, it won't matter whether they get first choice. They won't be able to afford the new rents," the woman said.

"By these tenants, are you including yourself? Are you a tenant, madam?" Joshua asked.

BJ suddenly realized how close Joshua was. She had been so busy butting heads with Linda that she'd forgotten he was advancing on her. People had become uneasy with Joshua's curiosity, thinking something was going on that they weren't privy to. Even Lucy was standing up, trying to see who she was.

BJ glanced around quickly, wondering how she would escape. They'd done a good job on her disguise, but it wouldn't fool anyone up close, and Joshua seemed quite determined to get close.

"She don't look like one of the tenants to me," one young woman said.

People were standing, trying to get a better look at her. The meeting was deteriorating quickly, and most of it was due to her and the efforts of the tenants of Number Three Ashley Place.

Several of her clients suddenly took to the aisles to surround Josh, and BJ could see possible escape. She moved across the people into the far aisle and headed for the door. It was difficult passing the people who stood at the back. They slowed her progress. Once, glancing back for Joshua, she realized that she didn't see him anywhere. She had almost made it when people stopped her to congratulate her for speaking up to Josh.

BJ was sneaking toward the door when someone slapped her on the back, saying, "Good for you, Grandma." She had almost forgotten to hunch over to disguise her height, and her back was killing her in that position. She was trying to rub her back as she hurried out the door and was still looking backward when she slammed into Joshua. He stood there with arms folded across his chest.

"You mind telling me what this farce is all about? And do you know there's a law against misleading people and inciting a riot? And weren't you the one who yelled conflict of interest?" he said sarcastically.

"*Me,* inciting a riot? What about *your* misleading people? Maybe that's what started the trouble." She parted the veil, exposing her face, to talk.

"Everything that I intend to do is in my original proposal," Joshua said.

"Sure—written in print so small no one could read it."

"I also posted in newspapers other than the *Law Registry.*

Everyone was duly notified. It's not my fault you couldn't lower yourself to pick up a newspaper.''

It was a low blow but true nevertheless. "You led me to mislead people, too.''

That seemed to stymie him but only for a moment.

"Is that so?'' he said. "Do you think that I should call your boss about your activities today and this getup you're wearing? What a shame to mislead him, too.''

"Do what you like,'' she bluffed.

Suddenly there was a click and both of them turned toward it. BJ had her heart in her mouth but was relieved to see it was only a young smiling girl with a Polaroid.

"Would you like to be interviewed?'' the girl said.

"Not today,'' Joshua answered.

This gave BJ the opportunity to escape, and she headed for her car. However, before driving off, she looked back. Joshua was now talking to people—and there, a short distance away, stood Linda. Linda was not talking to the group but was observing BJ in her very distinctive old car. It gave BJ a shudder, and she hastily drove away.

Three days later, BJ opened up one of the very same local papers that she'd told Joshua he should have made his notification in, and there was a picture of her and Joshua arguing outside Charity Tabernacle Temple. Fortunately her face was turned at an angle to the camera. *No one will recognize me.* But she crossed her fingers unconsciously.

Chapter Seventeen

A week later, BJ hadn't had chance to settle in at her desk when Cody came. "I'd like to see you in my office. Now," he said.

She had never heard him sound so demanding, but BJ knew that the old sympathetic Cody was gone. She followed him into his office, the only one that was closed off from the large area where the other workers sat.

He closed the door after her and pulled the blinds. This, BJ thought, did not bode well. Cody rarely closed the blinds.

"Sit down," he said.

After he'd rounded his desk and sat, he leaned back in his chair and looked at her for long moments. There was a new element in his attitude. Despite the wealth of his family, Cody usually appeared incredibly insecure. Today he looked more concerned than insecure.

She sat forward. "Okay, Cody, what's up?" she broke the silence.

He sat up and picked up a sheet of paper from his desk.

"There's a complaint here about you. Seems you attended a meeting at the,"—he paused to read—"Charity Tabernacle Temple Church, in which you were a disruptive element, causing a major incident."

"Major incident? Give me a break," she said.

BJ was shaken. True, she and Joshua had become real protagonists, she couldn't believe he'd actually sent a complaint to her job. And who else would have sent it if not Josh?

"That's what it says here," he said, then rifling through the papers in front of him he found a news clipping and handed it to her across the desk. As she'd known, it was the picture of her in the outlandish getup. "However, the real issue is your insubordination to the Foundation," Cody finished.

She took a deep breath and started to bluff. "Surely I can attend a meeting with my clients if they request it."

"You were ordered not to get involved," Cody reminded her.

"All right, Cody, what do you want to do?" BJ said, resigning herself. What could he do, she wondered, suspend me?

"It's been suggested that I terminate your employment."

"Terminate?" It came as a shock. She couldn't believe the Foundation would go that far. She felt as if someone had just poured cold water on her.

"Yes." He watched her closely.

"Just for attending a community meeting?"

"And causing a public disturbance," he added. "However, if you can promise me that you'll withdraw from this fracas, I know the board will back down from that position."

She wanted to exhale with relief, but her conscience wouldn't allow it. While she needed her job, she couldn't promise that she wouldn't help her clients, and she didn't want to lie. What could she do?

"Cody, I can't promise that," she said.

He looked sadly at her. BJ feared it was the end of something that she'd thoroughly enjoyed—her time at the VanderWeil Foundation.

That next weekend, BJ was first to arrive at the ground floor of Three Ashley Place. It was time for plan B. She had come prepared with cleaning rags, bucket, mop, and a scarf for her hair. For clothes, she had donned a pair of old shabby jeans and sweatshirt. The apartments were in a mess, and there was no sense using good clothes.

She opened the doors of the two empty apartments with the key that Mr. Green had provided. She glanced around, wondering where to start. The task was monumental. It was going to take a lot of work, she realized, to get the place into any sort of order. Deciding that the first job should be to remove the debris that crunched underfoot and prevented access to the rest of the room, she grabbed a shovel. Plaster dust filled the air, and she stopped to tie a clean rag over her nose and mouth.

She was hard at it, moving the rubbish into the middle of the floor for removal, when Adella entered. Adella was dragging a very reluctant and a very tall young man through the door.

"Grandma," the young man whined, "I've got important plans for today."

"I know all about your plans, and you can just forget them. Today you're going to do what I say."

BJ stopped and stood up, smiling at Adella's bullying. When the older woman loosened her grip on the man, he stood up. At that glance, BJ realized that although he was very tall, he was really quite young.

"BJ," Adella said proudly, "this is my grandson, Nathan."

Nathan? BJ was surprised. *Surely he's not the same one Adel-*

la's been trying to match up with me? He's just a kid! But BJ simply put her hand out to the young man, who she judged to be still in high school, saying, "Nice meeting you, Nathan."

When the youngster got a look at BJ, he stopped struggling. "Well, well," Nathan said, grinning appreciatively. "Good morning."

He straightened up and looked to be about six-foot-seven, BJ guessed. He stepped forward, and taking her hand, kissed her fingertips. BJ snatched her hand back and thought, oh, brother. Nathan's presence did not bode well.

BJ's fingers were crossed when she turned to Adella, saying, "Do you know how many people are coming today?"

"Didn't I tell you that I had everything fixed? Nathan is going to help." Adella beamed at her grandson.

Oh, no, BJ thought, how are we going to get any work done using one overly testosterone-producing adolescent?

Nathan, on hearing his grandmother's words about work, gazed unhappily around the apartment and frowned. This can't be happening to me, BJ thought.

But she straightened up and determined to see the job through, said, "We need more than two people if we're going to make a dent in this place today. Where's Mr. Green?"

"He's not feeling well enough to help today," Adella said.

Now young Nathan's eyes gleamed. "Two people sounds good enough to me," he said.

Adella looked crestfallen. "I couldn't find anyone else, and I asked everyone I could think of, including Joshua."

"Joshua?" BJ said.

"I was desperate," Adella said.

"Certainly not. We don't need *him!*" BJ responded.

"That's what I said," Nathan agreed and grinned. "Just

you and me, babe," he said to BJ. Adella chuckled, obviously thinking it the height of wit.

BJ sighed and with a glance at Adella, said, "Oh, well, here goes . . . whatever." She looked at Nathan and said, "I'll shovel, and you fill the garbage bags."

"No problem," he said and sort of slowly drifted to pick up a garbage bag.

He turned back to Adella and kissed her on the check. Adella looked inordinately pleased.

"You can go back upstairs and rest, Grandma," Nathan said. "I'll take over down here."

BJ rolled her eyes upward but didn't say anything. Nathan was actually doing them a favor.

Much to her surprise, Nathan turned out to be a better worker than she'd thought. He wasn't exactly a dynamo, but he did try. He also loved talking about himself. In a short time, BJ had learned that he was a young basketball hopeful, recently graduated. Nathan was taking remedial classes and waiting to get into college. True, he thought himself a divine gift for the coeds, but considering how much male egotism she'd seen in the past two months, Nathan in comparison was as sweet as a lamb.

He was young, strong, and willing to show off for her, which meant that he worked fairly steadily. He had no intentions of letting a woman best him, and an older woman at that.

Young Nathan had invited her to the movies later that night, but she had no difficulty begging off. Yet it had been fun, and she'd enjoyed his flirting. Coupled with the workload, it had kept her mind off Joshua—for long minutes at a time.

The day went on, and although Nathan took frequent breaks to talk about himself, they were doing well. Much of the debris in both apartments had been cleared away. When Nathan went to eat lunch, BJ stayed and attacked the spackling.

It was a difficult job, trying to cover the holes in the wall with plaster. Also, her work wouldn't win any awards for beauty. She did manage to close the holes, but it dried in rough uneven patches.

She had stood back to observe this when she heard a noise behind her. It was Joshua.

Suddenly her chest was tight, and she could barely breathe. Despite all their fights, despite the fact that she was now among the unemployed, she still wanted to run and hug him. She wanted to lie down right there on the floor and make love, too. Lord, what fool a woman in love can be.

Of course he was dressed to kill in a long black coat over a double-breasted glen plaid suit that shouted money. *For pete's sake, it's a Saturday afternoon. Doesn't he ever loosen up?*

Joshua stood there, also evaluating the spackling job she'd just done. He didn't look too impressed, either.

"Well, I'm not a plasterer," she said impulsively.

"Did I say anything?" Joshua responded, shrugging.

Then she realized that having spent the whole morning working, she had become incredibly grubby. She was suddenly very embarrassed in front of this handsome man. Even at her best she wouldn't win any prizes.

BJ was annoyed. After the last time Josh had complained about her clothes, she'd gone shopping. Now she figured that she'd put enough on her credit cards to keep her in debt for the rest of her life at 16 percent. And he'd come on *this* day when she was truly at her worst, trying to get the apartment ready for the display.

Her hair, which she had spent a great deal of time to arrange, had already turned fuzzy and unmanageable. Not that she cared, she reminded herself. She had reluctantly called quits to all her fantasies concerning him or of having wonderful little darlings with his honey brown eyes. What did she care how she looked?

"What are you doing here, anyway?" she demanded. "Wasn't it enough that you got me fired?"

"I did not get you fired, and I do have an interest in this site."

"You can't just walk in whenever you want."

He shrugged again and looked around at what had been done. "This is for your memorabilia exhibit?"

"Yes, it is," she snapped.

"Okay," he said. "I only asked."

Nathan came back with the snack that he'd gone to buy, and Joshua turned at the boy's entrance. It was rather peculiar, but BJ had the distinct impression that both males bristled on sight of each other.

BJ took the moment to introduce them, annoyed that she was being more polite than she wanted. "This is Nathan, Adella's grandson," BJ said.

"Another blind date?" Joshua asked nastily.

"What's it to you?" Nathan said, responding to Josh's statement with young male pride. Nathan was young and inclined to be hotheaded at any slight—real or imagined—but what was wrong with Joshua? "We were doing just fine with just the two of us," Nathan said.

"You wish," Josh retorted then turned, ignoring the younger man, and said to BJ, "He's too young for you."

"Yeah? Why don't you go away?" Nathan said before BJ could speak. "We were doing fine until you came."

"Why don't you just shut up?" Joshua said calmly.

Things deteriorated quickly when the young basketball hopeful made a few choice remarks about Josh's age. She never thought of Joshua as being old, but to Nathan he was positively elderly. It would have been funny if the two men hadn't looked like two dogs ready to have a go at each other.

And much as she hated to admit it, she was alarmed for Joshua. Besides being quite a few years younger, Nathan was also some inches taller. That didn't deter Joshua from giving back tit for tat in the mouth department.

"Would you act your age," BJ said to Josh as she stood in front of Nathan. "Do you want him to kill you?"

Her statement irritated Joshua more than she expected, for he said, "Me, let that twerp beat me—"

Because Josh had turned to argue with her, he hadn't seen the punch coming and took it square on the eye. Immediately his eye began to swell. He stumbled backward but didn't fall.

"Josh, omigod," BJ screamed. "Speak to me. Are you all right?"

Josh shook his head, trying to clear it. Slowly he circled away from BJ.

"How could you?" BJ yelled at the young basketball player. "You should respect your elders."

When Josh turned to face Nathan, he looked like a mighty warrior.

"Josh! No!" BJ screamed.

"Come on, old man," Nathan said and did some very fast footwork.

BJ tried to stand between them, but Josh put her aside and took a swing at Nathan, hitting the younger man in the stomach. Nathan sat down, winded.

Totally confused by this turn of events, BJ rushed to protect and sympathize with the young basketball player.

"Oh, no. What am I going to tell Adella? Are you all right?" she asked Nathan.

Josh pointed to his eye, saying, "What about me?"

"You should be ashamed of yourself. I'm supposed to be taking care of him," BJ said to Joshua.

"I think he broke my nose," Nathan said in a helpless voice. He leaned his head on her shoulder.

"Hey, you leave her alone," Josh said to this last move. "I didn't even touch your nose."

"Really, Josh. Grow up," BJ said. "He's just a kid."

"Kid? He's bigger than both of us!"

"Can you stand?" she asked Nathan.

"I'm not sure," Nathan answered.

"I didn't do anything to his legs, either," Josh insisted.

"Maybe I'm in shock," Nathan explained to BJ.

BJ frowned at Nathan, wondering if he was putting her on. "Let's see if you can. Lean on me."

"Okay," he said in a small voice.

"Don't you dare lean on her," Josh said. His face was a study in annoyance as he came to help.

"Leave him alone," BJ said to Josh.

"He's too big for you to carry," Josh insisted, taking Nathan's arm over his shoulder.

"I'll go easy on her," Nathan said.

"Over my dead body," Josh gritted out through clenched teeth.

"This is all your fault," BJ told Joshua.

"Yeah," Nathan agreed.

"You shut up," Josh said, staggering under Nathan's weight.

Fortunately the whole thing was stopped when Adella came and rescued Nathan. But that's not all the older woman did. She also told Joshua, "Since you've been so smart and put BJ's only helper out of commission, you'll just have to help out today."

"Adella," BJ said, "I do appreciate your efforts—however, I'm afraid that I simply can't—"

"We've got to have this finished if we're going to have that display, and don't either of you try to stop it," Adella snapped.

Joshua took off his coat and jacket, rolled up his sleeves, and picked up the spackling knife. He then dug out all the plaster BJ had applied and started replacing it, making perfectly planed surfaces. Soon Joshua's pants and shirt were spotted. BJ wisely decided not to say anything about this.

They toiled together long into the night. The next day, Joshua returned, ready for another day of labor on the apartment. Although they'd worked almost shoulder to shoulder the whole weekend, they'd barely exchanged a word other than to ask for a tool or some such except for once. This occurred during the Sunday night dinner break. Most of the hard work was done. In the two days, they'd discarded the debris, plugged up the holes, painted, scrubbed the floors, and installed vinyl floor coverings.

All that was left was to put out the memorabilia, placing the truly wonderful things on display stands that had been donated by a local neighborhood store. There were old newspaper clippings, wonderful photos, and more vintage clothes. BJ had gone to buy dinner, while Joshua remained to sort through the collectible pieces. When she returned, he was happily ensconced on the floor going through the contents of one of Adella's trunks.

She snuck a look at his eye, which had been swollen yesterday, and realized it hadn't fared as badly as she'd feared. That wonderful caramel-colored skin was obviously also durable and tough.

"Would you look at this." He held up a man's vintage straw hat.

"Aren't those things fantastic?" she said and went to sit beside him and laid out the food.

They spent the next few hours looking through the trunks and setting up the exhibit. Joshua showed more enthusiasm that she'd expected. He also looked pensive.

What's more, she knew that he was bending over backward to help them. The very nature of the display was to stop him in rebuilding here on the street.

She wondered if she'd been too hasty before. But considering that he was cooler to her now than he'd ever been before, she realized that it was too late for them. Aside from coming to accept this, those two days had been the happiest time she'd had in weeks.

By Monday morning, the apartments were ready. And there was no denying that much of it was due to Joshua's efforts.

Two months later, BJ sat at her desk, thinking back to the last day she'd spent with Joshua. A lot had happened since then. For one thing, the display on Ashley Place was a huge success. The exhibit did so well that the city was considering using it as a museum. The story wound up on the six o'clock news, where Mr. Green made an elegant spokesperson, and a local public access television station filmed an hour-long special.

Lucy announced that plans for the rebuilding of the street were changed. Razing the block was out. Everything would be renovated to preserve the historical integrity of the neighborhood. Lucy was very good with words. BJ shook her head. Somehow, without actually saying it, Lucy managed to make it look as if she were responsible for everything.

Joshua's company offered low-cost loans for those owners who wanted to remain, and for the homes that had already been purchased, he planned to renovate and sell.

And indeed, Adella had been right. There was a second company, but that was totally stymied when Three Ashley Place, through Joshua's efforts, went for landmark status. BJ had learned from Lucy that Linda Collins had been a spy in Joshua's office for the second company. Also BJ suspected that it was Linda who'd sent the letter to her job.

Speaking of her job, after all the good publicity, the VanderWeil Foundation had offered her her old job back on one condition—she would no longer work at Ashley Place. That assignment was given to another worker, who to all appearances, was a wunderkind.

Her pride almost made her throw it back in their face,

but unfortunately she couldn't afford such an act. At least not right away. She needed to work while she thought of what she'd do next.

But not working on Ashley Place depressed her. She felt left out now that she was no longer needed there. True, she was still involved with the exhibit and saw the tenants frequently, but it was different.

Both Darlene and Lucy had given up trying to find her a husband since she'd been instrumental in stopping the razing of Ashley Place. Now they considered her a woman who didn't need any help. She still either saw or talked with them almost daily, but there were no more offers of blind dates. Sometimes she missed their old manipulations.

What she longed for the most was Joshua. Mourning his loss left her apathetic and saddened. They had barely spoken in the last two months, although he was friendly with Darlene and Lucy and still frequently spoke with her parents. She missed him more than she would have believed possible. She even missed his tendency to make smug sexist pronouncements.

The telephone rang. "BJ?" Lucy's voice spoke. "Isn't it time for you and Joshua to make up? Hasn't this—whatever it is—gone on long enough?"

All apathy vanished as BJ hurriedly glanced around, feeling as if her godmother had read her mind. "Lucy, what are you talking about? Did Josh say that?"

"No. But you two were so obvious that we all figured it out long months ago."

"We?"

"Darlene, your parents, and me."

Figures, BJ thought. For a few moments, she longed for the days when Lucy could have set her up on a blind date with Joshua. Ah, well. "Well, forget it. That's all over."

"Never count your chickens before they hatch."

"What do you know about chickens?"

"Chickens? Who's talking about chickens?" the irrepressible Lucy answered.

"Never mind," BJ said, rolling her eyes heavenward. She sat back.

"I want to tell you that I've been thinking of running for an elected office this time."

"What office?" BJ sat up again.

"Maybe the mayoralty race."

"You're what?"

"Well, maybe I'll start with something smaller, but that's my goal. Anyway, what with the way you handled the Ashley Place thing, you'd be the perfect person to be on my campaign. What do you think?"

"Lucy . . ." BJ started but at that moment she looked up and saw an incredibly handsome man step out of the elevator. He was holding a beautiful bouquet of flowers. He headed straight toward her desk. If she didn't know better, she'd have thought it was Josh.

But that was impossible because this man wore jeans and a hard hat!

"Lucy, I can't talk anymore," and she hung up hastily.

She folded her hands on her desk and tried to look unconcerned, but with the way her heart was pumping, she feared the whole room could hear it. What she truly wanted to do was run and throw her arms around him, but chances were he was here for some official reason.

"What are *you* doing here?" she asked when Joshua came to stand at her desk. Her efforts to sound cool and disinterested probably failed when she sneaked a look around to see if anyone was watching.

He dumped the bouquet of flowers on her desk, stood with arms akimbo, and said, "BJ, will you marry me?"

"Huh?" she said stupidly. Then she tried to whisper, "Why are you asking me that now?"

"I asked you months ago, but you said my proposal was obscene."

"I mean we haven't seen each other in months! Why didn't you ask before?"

"I was working on something."

"What?"

"Eliminating all your complaints." He counted on his fingers. "First, you said I was after a permit, so now I already have a permit. Second, you said I'd have to exhibit compassion. So I've just invested a fortune in Ashley Place, and if that ain't compassion, I've never seen it. Finally"— he held his arms wide—"here I am, jeans and hard hat!" He placed both hands flat on her desk and leaned close to command, "BJ, marry me."

She gestured for him to lower his voice. The last thing she wanted was for her co-workers to hear this. She remembered only too well how the women had behaved on his last visit and didn't want to encourage that again. *"Why* are you proposing?" she persisted.

"Would you stop with all these whys? Why do men usually propose? I want you to be my wife," he said.

"That's not what you said before."

"All right. I said a lot of things before, which one are you referring to?"

"You said it was because I was pathetic and inept. And that I needed a keeper."

"Well, you have to admit that your taste in men leaves a lot to be desired," he said.

"That's no reason to propose," she said. "What about your plans to marry when you're forty-five?"

"Dumb plan," he answered.

"Don't be flip, this is important."

"Okay, so I've changed my mind," he said.

"We can't get married. We've known each other for only a short time." Even to her own ears, that sounded a bit contrary.

"Now suddenly when you're dating all those deadbeats,

looking for a sperm donor, you believe you have to know me longer?''

''Shhh,'' she said and looked around embarrassed. She suspected her efforts to keep this conversation private was failing. They were becoming the focus of several pairs of eyes. ''A husband is more than a sperm donor,'' she hissed.

''Don't tell me you've finally caught on to that?''

She knew that no matter who was listening, she had to stand her ground. She wasn't going to accept anything less than love from Joshua. She couldn't accept anything less. She would be too heavily invested in any relationship with him. She'd rather return to Columbia, where he wouldn't be around to tempt her, than take him on any terms other than total commitment.

''Marry me because I love you,'' he said softly.

By this time one of her co-workers, a grandmotherly type, had moved close and was obviously listening to everything they said. But BJ was so shocked by Joshua's last statement that she decided not to pay any attention to their audience.

''What did you say?'' BJ demanded of Josh.

''The same thing that I've been saying all the time. Will you marry me?''

''No, the other thing that you said.''

''I love you.''

''You never said that before.''

''Oh, for pete's sake. Marry me and save my life. Marry me and plant another garden on Ashley Place. Marry me and decorate my apartment. Will you marry me?''

There were several of the women listening now, who all sighed at Joshua's words.

''Tell me why you think you love me.''

''I don't just think it. And why do you need a reason aside from you play a great game of one-on-one?''

''I just do. I've read about your other dates, and they were nothing like me.''

"How about maybe it was your great-looking legs? No? Okay, how about when I first saw you, I recognized you?"

"Recognized me? We'd never met before. I'd have remembered if we did."

"I've seen you in my dreams, and I knew immediately—you were the woman who'd make my life complete. You make me want to be a better person. Does that make any sense?"

"Yes," she said, sounding breathless.

"You remember the first time I saw you?" he continued. When she nodded, he added, "There you were, dressed as if you were in an armored truck, with Lucy and Darlene standing guard over you. You looked like a princess in a tower. I wanted to rescue you. There's another reason, too." He looked at her out of the side of his eye.

"So tell me," she insisted.

"You make a cute little old lady. And now that I know what great legs you'll have in fifty years, I've decided not to let you get away."

"Yes!" and she grabbed him around his neck, pressing a big kiss on his mouth.

The whole office clapped, even Cody, who had come out to see what the commotion was. People gathered around to congratulate them. But after a few minutes, Joshua grabbed her hand and started urging her through the door. Before they got on the elevator, Cody came over to them.

Cody looked genuinely happy for them when he shook hands with Joshua, saying, "You're a lucky man." This time they didn't do the crushing male handshakes.

Once the elevator doors closed, Joshua took her in his arms and kissed her tenderly. When he held her away from him, she said, "Of course you knew I'd say yes."

"I did?"

"Someone had to save you from that empty, bleak apartment."

"What about my arrogance and my conceit?"

"I've decided to forgive you."

"What about my evil businessman's ways?"

"I'll reform you."

"Well," he said, and a big sexy grin lit up his face. "That's more like it." When his mouth came down on hers, she promised herself never to let him go.

"One thing more," she said.

"Yes?"

"I want children—and if that's a problem, then you'd better speak up right now," she said.

"Children?" He cocked his head as if thinking hard on that. Then he said, "Okay, but on one condition only."

"What condition?" BJ asked suspiciously.

"That we have a half dozen little girls with your looks and Tiffany's charm. Maybe we should start with twins."

Dear Readers,

It's been great receiving all those wonderful letters. It's been gratifying to hear how much you enjoyed reading *Sweet Promise, Home Fires,* and *Wind Across Kylarmi.* Please keep them coming!

I hope you also enjoy reading about BJ Jones and Joshua Hendricks in this, my latest book, *Something So Right,* as much as I did writing about them. My next book, a story about the enduring love between Geoffrey McMillan and Sara Turner, will be on the stands early next year. Until then let's keep romance in our sights.

You can still contact me: Layle Giusto, P.O. Box 120421, St. Albans, NY 11412-0421 or E-mail at <layleg@sprynet.com>

ABOUT THE AUTHOR

Layle Giusto danced professionally in Modern and African folk dance before she left the theater to marry and raise a family. She then got a degree in nursing and now works in a drug/alcohol rehabilitation center. She enjoys writing, sailing, swimming, and travel.

Look for these upcoming Arabesque titles:

April 1997
HIDDEN AGENDA by Rochelle Alers
CONSPIRACY by Margie Walker
SOUL MATES by Bridget Anderson

May 1997
SOUL DEEP by Monique Gilmore
INTIMATE BETRAYAL by Donna Hill
MAMA DEAR, A Mother's Day Collection

June 1997
RHAPSODY by Felicia Mason
ALL THE RIGHT REASONS by Janice Sims
STEP BY STEP by Marilyn Tyner

LOOK FOR THESE ARABESQUE ROMANCES

ENJOY THESE ARABESQUE FAVORITES!

FOREVER AFTER   (0-7860-0211-5, $4.99)
by Bette Ford

BODY AND SOUL   (0-7860-0160-7, $4.99)
by Felicia Mason

BETWEEN THE LINES   (0-7860-0267-0, $4.99)
by Angela Benson

ENJOY THESE SPECIAL
ARABESQUE HOLIDAY ROMANCES

HOLIDAY CHEER   (0-7860-0210-7, $4.99)
by Rochelle Alers, Angela Benson,
and Shirley Hailstock

A MOTHER'S LOVE   (0-7860-0269-7, $4.99)
by Francine Craft, Bette Ford,
and Mildred Riley

SPIRIT OF THE SEASON   (0-7860-0077-5, $4.99)
by Donna Hill, Francis Ray,
and Margie Walker

A VALENTINE KISS   (0-7860-0237-9, $4.99)
by Carla Fredd, Brenda Jackson,
and Felicia Mason